Blood Legacy

Marianne Morea

Coventry Press Ltd.

Coventry Press Ltd.
Somers, New York
http://www.coventrypressltd.com

ISBN-10: 0988439603

ISBN-13: 978-0-9884396-2-7
Second Edition: Coventry Press Ltd. 2012

Cover Artist: Fantasy Frog Designs with Marianne Morea
Editor: Jen Safrey

Printed in the USA

…For the Moms in my life…
Angela and Norine,
Without you, none of this would have happened.

Love is passion, obsession, someone you can't live without. If you don't start with that, what are you going to end up with? Fall head over heels. I say find someone you can love like crazy and who'll love you the same way back. And how do you find him? Forget your head and listen to your heart. I'm not hearing any heart. Run the risk. If you get hurt, you'll come back. Because the truth is there is no sense living your life without this. To make the journey and not fall deeply in love…well, you haven't lived a life at all. You have to try. Because if you haven't tried, you haven't lived.

William Parris
From the movie, *Meet Joe Black*

Chapter 1

Avalon
Condemned church-turned-nightclub
New York City, midnight

Carlos pulled onto the street and seamlessly slid his black Jaguar XLR to the curb across the street from the club. He heard its pulsating beat from almost a block away, and his blood answered in anticipation.

As he got out of the car, he noticed the ritual line-up of players and wannabes well under way behind the red velvet ropes. Most were teenagers out for an illicit night of fun, their excitement radiating from them like steam from a subway vent in winter. Carlos glided past and inhaled their mingled scent, savoring their collective flavor.

With barely a nod of acknowledgement, he breezed past the bouncers and up the stairs toward the main doors. Avalon was an anomaly not unlike himself, a blend of the contemporary and the old world, of the sacred and the profane. His hand trailed lightly over one of the brass handles as he passed, lingering for a moment on the embossed cross still intact on the door pull. He couldn't help but chuckle at the Hollywood irony.

He entered the main level of the club. The place was so dim he wondered how anyone was able to see—that is, anyone without the help of preternatural senses. Winding his way past the people at the main bar, he paused for a moment at the edge of the dance floor. It had once housed the main body of the church, and aside from the bodies in motion, one could still feel the lingering shadow of the old pulpit.

Carlos quickly scanned the upper galleries. He admired the gothic arches of the old steeple still intact, and the streamlined chrome and neon bar that now sat nestled in its arms, wondering for a moment what the owners had done with the organ that had originally occupied that space.

Casually climbing the stairs to the upper level, he settled into a quiet corner in the back. Plush low couches and small tables covered the entire area. The lighting was set low, like candlelight, still dim enough to be intimate, but light enough that you could actually see who you were talking to.

So far, no one had sparked his interest, though from this vantage point he could survey the entire club. By New York standards the night was just getting started. A small crowd had already gathered in the gallery lounge, and it would certainly get more crowded as the night progressed. However, by then too many would either be too drunk or too drugged for his liking.

No, he preferred the earlier crowd—the eager young ones who came looking for excitement, anticipating a taste of the forbidden. The youth of America went out every weekend looking for a thrill, and those who found Carlos usually got more than they bargained for.

He smoothed the front of his black silk shirt. Dressed in a pair of dark grey jeans that molded his body, Carlos looked like a he belonged on the cover of *GQ*. He was dark and gorgeous with just a hint of mystery and underlying danger. He wielded his presence like a finely honed sword. With just one look, he could leave women breathless and men questioning their own sexuality. It didn't take much to lure them in, but Carlos prided himself on being proper, always giving his chosen ones a choice.

His little family, as he liked to call it, hadn't had any "new blood" in quite a while. He grimaced. Just the thought of having to wade through the throngs made his head throb. There had to be a fire or spark of soul to the one he chose, something that left him wired with anticipation.

Unfortunately, it appeared his efforts tonight were going to be a waste of time. He wasn't just looking for another pretty face. If he were honest, he would have to admit he'd grown bored of the superficial, and jaded with the life he had built around himself. It had served its purpose, and for a while had filled a void. Lately he had been looking for more, craved it almost as much as he craved blood. Except now, even the blood couldn't fill what was missing in his life, in him. He was looking for something much more, only he didn't know what.

"Can I get you anything?"

Carlos looked up. The waitress stood over him, her pad and pencil leaning on a little round serving tray that had a few half-finished drinks on it. "Rum," he said. "A tumbler, no ice…and leave the bottle."

She started to tell him she wasn't permitted do so when he looked at her. He held her mesmerized for a moment, sliding a wad of cash onto her tray. "I think we understand each other. *Comprendes*…Susan?"

The waitress mumbled something and walked away confused, shaking her head as if trying to clear a fog. Carlos just smiled a little as he watched her head back toward the bar.

"Hi!" A pretty brunette chirped, walking up to where Carlos sat. "Mind if my friends and I share?"

"The more the merrier. *Por favor...*" Carlos flashed them a suggestive and slightly predatory grin. He saw the brunette shiver and smirked at how easy the reaction was to elicit.

"I, um, I…I'm Brandy," she stammered, obviously flustered. She cleared her throat. "Whoa, and I haven't even started drinking yet. Let's try this again…I'm Brandy, this is Sharla, and this is Gwen." They slid in one after the other, Brandy now flashing Carlos a brilliant smile. "Thanks for letting us join you."

He looked at each one of the girls. *"De nada,"* he replied, politely inclining his head with a just a hint of amusement crinkling the corner of his eyes. The girls were all fresh and beautiful. They couldn't be much over eighteen, and their eagerness made the air around them taste faintly of electricity and perfume.

The waitress walked over again. "Girls, I'm going to have to see some I.D."

As the girls fished nervously through their tiny purses, Carlos considered spelling the waitress again into letting them pass.

However, as he watched them fuss, he admitted none of them truly interested him, so he let it go.

"I don't seem to have mine with me," the blond one said innocently, giving the waitress a hopeful smile.

"Sorry, then I can't serve you," the waitress answered with an apologetic smile of her own. "I think maybe you girls should go back downstairs."

They got up with disappointed huffs, and the brunette whined so peevishly that Carlos couldn't help but chuckle. Jerking her head around, she shot him a look that had him laughing even louder, his hands up in mock defense.

They said their goodbyes and walked toward the staircase, giving Carlos one last glance before disappearing down the stairs.

The waitress stood there until she was sure they had gone. "I did you a favor, my friend. That was nothing more than disaster zipped into a miniskirt. Underage girls can get guys like you into a heap of trouble. I'll get you your drink." She nodded once and headed back toward the bar.

Carlos raised an eyebrow as she left. However well intentioned she might be, she was off by a mile. He was the dangerous one.

She brought his order over and winked at him as she set the tumbler and the bottle on the table. "Will there be anything else?" she asked, pouring his first glass.

"No…no, thank you, Susan."

She flashed him a warm smile that he had bothered to remember her name. "In that case, would you mind settling your tab at the bar? My shift's up and my tables need to be closed out before I can leave."

"No problem," he answered, handing her a credit card.

"Thanks. I'll be right back with your receipt." With a nod, she turned back toward the bar, but stopped. "And thanks for the extra cash tip, I really appreciate it." With a wink, she pivoted on her high heels and headed for the bar.

Carlos laughed. *Tip? Shrewd. Very shrewd.* He lifted the glass, and the dark liquid hit his tongue, familiar and satisfying. He closed his eyes and inhaled through his nose, savoring the underlying scent of molasses and sugar cane. The rum did nothing for him though, neither the alcohol nor the taste. He loved its warm, sweet aroma.

The scent brought back so many memories from his human life, memories he was glad weren't lost to him. He had read somewhere that a person's olfactory memories were the earliest and most poignant, the ones most likely to be preserved. He guessed that rule applied to his kind as well.

He picked up the bottle and turned it in his hand, absently running his thumb over the label. He found it funny that of the limited choice of human fare he was able to consume, the one he liked the best had a black bat for its logo. He chuckled at the classic Boris Karloff irony.

The club got crowded. The music pounded, and the bodies on the dance floor gyrated like so many disconnected arms and legs moving in time to the frenetic rhythm. Carlos took his glass and walked toward the railing that overlooked the downstairs.

Leaning his elbows on the polished chrome, he watched the human drama below unfold like an unscripted reality show. So many different scents swirled past him, each one a tiny glimpse into a host of human thought and emotion.

"What the hell?" he said to himself as he caught a slight variation in the air around him. His eyes narrowed and he pressed his lips together. "No way."

Closing his eyes, he lifted his head and inhaled. Reaching out with his senses, he scanned the club for its origin. His eyes snapped open and he growled low in his throat. It came from downstairs near the back bar across from the dance floor. "Young bloods. I don't believe it," he muttered under his breath.

Inhaling again, he caught the scent of fresh blood. "No fucking way!" Pushing himself away from the railing, Carlos moved with such speed he was within five feet of them in seconds. Somehow, they managed to lure a girl to the back of the club near an empty stairwell. She was clearly underage, even more so than the three girls he had encountered earlier, and she was drunk.

He saw them clearly. The two had constructed wards in a hasty attempt to obscure their activities from the humans, but they were clumsy and haphazard. Carlos clenched his fists. Had someone invited them? If so, who? Admittance to his territory was by invitation only. He wanted to shred their pathetic wards and tear them to pieces, but years of experience told him he needed to watch and wait.

Vampire politics was even more corrupt and fickle than anything the human world could imagine, and the consequences infinitely more brutal. He wanted to save the girl, and maybe even teach the two young ones a lesson they'd never forget, but he also didn't want to incur reprisal against his entire family by being rash.

The girl was on her knees. One of the boys had his fangs buried deep in her throat while the other had his cock buried deep between her legs.

As the first one drank, Carlos could hear the sloppy, sucking sounds coupled with the girl's moans. Blood dripped from the young one's chin to the floor, splattering the gray tiles with red. With her miniskirt shoved up to her waist, the girl arched her back as the other sank his fingers into her soft flesh, jerking her hips back with each thrust.

"Dude, don't be a pig about it. Leave some for me," the one nailing her from behind said as his hips slapped a rhythm against her bare ass.

Jerking his head up, the other pulled his fangs out of her throat with an audible pop. "What are you complaining about? She's not the only cock jockey out there willing to play. No one hunts here and no one patrols, so it's all good."

Grabbing the girl by the hair, the one at her throat lapped at the blood smeared across her neck and chest. He licked it clean, scraping his finger across his chin the way a human child would lick cake batter from a mixing bowl. "*Mmmmmm*, sweet!"

With a bloodstained grin, he picked up one of the girl's shoes from the side of the bench and threw it at his friend. "Hey, man, this ain't no porno film! Hurry up and shoot your load. My balls are turning blue just watching you. And don't get any ideas—I fuck the next one first."

Carlos's lip curled in disgust. For ages, he had tried to distance himself from just this kind of behavior, and now it was in his own backyard. He had seen enough. Without warning, he walked right through their wards, grabbed the closest one by the hair and yanked him backwards. The young vampire screeched, hissing that Carlos dragged him off the girl, his pants twisted around his ankles and his unspent member purple and bobbing up and down. With a flick of his wrist, Carlos sent him crashing into the wall, and he slumped to the ground in a cloud of concrete dust.

The other one quickly backed away, leaving the girl covered in blood and writhing on the bench as if high on ecstasy, her own hand shoved between her legs. His eyes darted back and forth while he crouched and hissed, baring his teeth like something out of a B-rated horror flick.

Carlos laughed scornfully. "That Hollywood vamp act isn't going to work on me, *amigo*. Tell me…didn't Sandro warn you about coming here? Or are you just playing hooky from daddy tonight? This entire area is mine and Sandro knows it."

The one who hit the wall got to his feet. He turned his head side to side, cracking his neck before wiping his hand across his mouth, smearing a small trickle of his own blood across his cheek. "What makes you think we care what arrangements you have with Sandro?" he scoffed, pulling up his pants.

Carlos just looked at them. They were typical. Unbelievably beautiful, but dumb as a box of rocks—definitely Sandro's type. Why should he be surprised? Sandro liked to surround himself with pretty boys, and couldn't care less whether or not they had any intelligence. In fact, he preferred them that way.

"Are you really both that dense? Did you honestly think I wouldn't smell Sandro on you? You both reek of him and his blood. He and I may not agree on many things, but the one thing we *do* agree upon is territory. As I said before, Avalon is mine, and I'm willing to bet daddy dearest has no clue you are here tonight…*no*? You two trespassers need to clean this mess up and leave or I will make you clean this up, then send you back to Sandro in pieces."

"Yeah, right. We know all about you, *amigo*," the one covered in concrete dust sneered, mimicking Carlos's accent. Taking a step forward, he spit, raising his chin in defiant arrogance.

Carlos growled in warning, but the young blood ignored him. "Yeah, Sandro says you're a pussy. That you used to be a real badass, but traded your fangs and your balls for a bunch of crybabies. Says you're all a bunch of whiners wishing you were still human. Hey, why don't you do all of us a favor and toast yourself, huh? Leave things for the real vamps."

With a low and feral snarl, Carlos let his fangs descend and his face and jaw distort completely. He threw his arms up, solidifying the tattered wards with one word. He took a step forward and let his eyes flash from black to red. He let the full impact of his intentions hit, and when the two younger vampires' eyes went wide, he sprang.

"Holy crap!" the one talking the most trash yelped as they both started to back away. In a flash, they tried to run, but Carlos moved like lightning. His bloodline was older and stronger, making the young bloods no match. He grabbed them each by the throat, raising them above his head and squeezing their necks until their eyes bulged before throwing them full force against the back wall. The sound as they hit was deafening, the crack causing the windows to shatter, splintering glass all around. Sheet rock and cinderblocks crumbled as sparks flew from snapped electrical wires.

The two vampires lay in a crumpled heap. Carlos squatted down in front of them, menace dripping from his voice. "If you ever trespass in my territory again, I will pull your fangs out with my bare hands, and they won't grow back. Do *not* disrespect me again." He took each of their arms and in one swift move, snapped them in two over his knee like so much dried wood. Unfortunately, they'd heal quickly enough, but not before they had to return to Sandro and explain what happened.

Carlos stood up, leaving the boys in a broken pile on the floor. Looking around, he snuffed out any potential fires, but decided to leave the mess as a message for anyone else who might be lurking in the shadows looking for a challenge. Turning, he spotted the now terrified girl cowering in the corner. The glamour they had spelled her with had worn off and her eyes were wild with fear. She screamed as he approached, scrambling even farther back against the wall.

Gently he held out his hand, spelling her so she would calm down enough for him to help her up. With his tongue, he cleaned her neck and shirt the best he could, healing her wounds completely. Straightening her skirt, he wiped her memory. "Find your friends. Tell them you feel ill and need to go home immediately. Under no circumstances are you to linger."

As he picked up her purse from the floor, he awakened her, handing it to her as if she had only just dropped it. With a subtle wave of his hand, he let her walk out ahead of him, confused but otherwise unharmed. He watched as she disappeared into the crowd.

"What a waste," Carlos sighed looking around at the mess.

The young ones stirred. They might have been stupid and arrogant, but the instinct for self- preservation was a vampire's greatest asset. He knew they'd skulk off into the night licking their wounds, talking trash as soon as they were at a safe distance. However, they were Sandro's problem, not his. He had other fish to fry, so for now he would leave the wards intact until he had time to deal with the situation.

With a last look of disgust, he brushed off his clothes. Minuscule shards cut his palms, healing instantly before they could even bleed. The music penetrated the wards, and behind the miasma, it was just another Friday night. Carlos intended to enjoy the rest of the evening regardless of Sandro's untrained fledglings.

Picking the last bits of concrete from his tie, he glanced up. A woman stood in the open doorway, staring at him. It was obvious she could see right through the wards, and by the look on her face, had been standing in shocked disbelief for quite some time. A round silver tray hung limply from her hand, and her pen and pad were on the floor by her stilettoed feet.

Carlos moved quickly, positioning himself to silence her if she started to scream. He needed this added complication like a stake through his heart. The woman didn't move or blink. In fact, if it weren't for her heartbeat he would swear she wasn't breathing. She stared at him with the greenest eyes he'd ever seen. He could smell the fear rolling off her skin, keeping her immobile, but there was something else riveting her as well. However, he couldn't place it.

Raising his fingers to her face, he expected her to flinch, but she didn't. Gently he brushed the side of her cheek, glamour radiating from him in waves. "The back stairwell is off limits. It's being renovated. You know this. You. Didn't. See. Anything."

She tilted her head, exhaling slowly, her breath sweet and full of life in his nostrils. As expected, he watched her eyes glaze over. She blinked a few times, but then remarkably met his gaze dead on. "Like. Hell. I. Didn't."

Carlos's eyes narrowed, but before he could question her, she was gone, disappearing into the throng on the dance floor. Stunned, he blurred after her, scanning the club as he ran. But the place was too crowded to decipher anything.

There was no sign of her. *But how?* How did she get away from him without warning? Furthermore, how was she able to see through his wards? Picking his way toward the bar, he searched the faces on the dance floor and the surrounding tables.

"Can I get you anything?" the bartender asked, putting two bottles of Heineken down on the bar next to Carlos.

"What? Yes. Bacardi 151, neat." Distracted, Carlos's mind raced through possibilities while the bartender filled his glass. Throwing a twenty on the bar, he picked up his drink, but stopped halfway to his mouth. *The girl had a tray in her hand.* He frowned. Talk about being slow on the uptake tonight. Catching the bartender's eye, he raised his hand calling him over. "There's a cocktail waitress…long, auburn hair, really green eyes. You know her?"

Putting a couple of glasses under the beer tap, he gave Carlos a quick once-over while working the levers. "Sure, I know her. What's it to you?"

"She's a very pretty girl. Just wondering what her name was, that's all."

Putting the two drafts on the bar, the bartender picked up a towel and wiped his hands. "Look, you're wasting your time. You'd do better with any one of the honeys hanging out by the dance floor. They're the ones on the prowl, not Trina. She's not the type."

Nodding, Carlos raised his glass to his lips. "Thanks for the tip." Turning around he leaned his back against the bar facing the dance floor. He inhaled, taking in all the heightened scents. "Trina," he whispered. The taste of her name lingered on his tongue, and for the first time in centuries, the dark alcohol burned as it slid down his throat.

Chapter 2

Trina was dreaming again. As always, she stood at the edge of a narrow path, the familiar echoes from a distant waterfall greeting her like an old friend. Turning her head to the south, she caught a whisper in the breeze, a gentle prompt beckoning her to follow. With her eyes closed, she moved nimbly along, savoring the call of the birds winging overhead and the feel of the cool, pine-scented air rippling along her skin. Everything was intensified. Everything she heard and smelled, and everything she felt. All of her senses heightened—save one.

She opened her eyes, but no light or shadows penetrated the darkness. The blindness didn't alarm her. She smiled instead. It meant only one thing…he would come.

Reaching her destination, she stood as before at the edge of a clear pool, the clean, loamy smell of fresh water strong in her nose. The atmosphere was tranquil. She heard the water lapping gently against the rocks and mud, while the sound of insects buzzing among the reeds filled her ears.

Trina knew she was dreaming, aware that this surreal setting was nothing more than a product of her own subconscious. What she didn't know was why this exact dream? For the past two weeks it didn't matter how or where she fell asleep, she always ended up here.

The woods behind her were a cacophony of sound, as if the same anticipation that coursed through her body also rippled through forest. Feeling around behind her, she quickly found the same smooth, rounded boulder that was always there. Lowering herself slowly, she sat down to wait. He would come. She knew it, felt it. He would come as he had before, or why else would she be here? Why else would she be without her sight?

The forest grew quiet. Even the buzz of the insects had muted. She smiled as the air around her changed subtly. She didn't turn around. She knew who it was, and held her breath.

He came up behind her and slid his hands onto her shoulders. Gently he brushed her hair to one side and kissed her neck. "I knew you'd be here," he whispered in her ear.

Trina closed her eyes and leaned back against him. His voice was so familiar, setting every nerve in her body tingling. "Yes," she murmured, tilting her head, allowing his lips to wander along the curve of her throat. "But why am I here?"

Nuzzling her neck, he feathered kisses along her jaw line. "You are here because it is what you want, yet what you fear. You search, but refuse to see."

Trina shivered, feeling his cool lips leave her skin. Trailing his fingers along her cheek, he stepped around and pulled her to standing, wrapping his arms around her waist.

Reaching up she traced the contours of his face, the curve of his jaw, his cheekbones and the feel of his lips beneath her fingers. "Then why are you here?"

She felt the corners of his mouth turn up in a smile, his breath whispering gently into a soft kiss. "I am here because your blood called me."

She didn't understand, but then again, when had dreams ever followed the path of logic? Breathing in his scent, all her questions ceased as her senses took over. Trailing her hands lightly over his chest, she pressed herself against him, locking her arms around his neck. Trina twined her fingers in his hair as his lips sought hers. There'd be no more talk.

He kissed her long and hard, leaving her breathless. When he finally broke their kiss, he lifted her in one swift motion, carrying her away from the water's edge. Trina held on to his neck, her own body humming with need as he laid her down on the soft grass, its sweet smell a perfect counterpoint to his clean, masculine scent.

Leaning over, his hands traveled the full length of her body, memorizing every curve. With her nightgown gathered around her hips, she pulled one leg in, resting her bent knee on the ground, her most private parts open to his touch. She trembled, not certain if it was the chilled night air or the touch of his fingers that left her quivering.

He worked his way back to her mouth, teasing her, grazing her bottom lip with his teeth, drawing blood. With a quick rasp of his tongue he lapped at the droplets, whispering the word "soon," into his kiss, tempting her until—

The phone rang.

Trina rolled over, its shrill tone pulling her back into reality. With one eye open, she groped around on her nightstand, knocking almost everything, including the phone to the floor. *Ugh.* A faint voice called her name repeatedly as she leaned over the edge of the bed for the handset. "Okay…okay," she grumbled, flopping back onto her pillow. "Hello?"

"Well, it's about time you picked up the damn phone! Girl, do you know what time it is?" Louie yelled over midday traffic.

Trina pulled the phone back from her ear. "And good morning to you too, Louie. What time is it? Why are you calling so early?"

"*Hmph*…it's not early. Not if you still want me and Susan to help you today. You'd better get that sweet ass of yours out of bed, because we're downstairs at the front door loitering like a couple of Jehovah's Witnesses!"

Trina grabbed the clock off her nightstand and stared at it in disbelief. "It's one o'clock? Oh, my God… Louie, I'm so sorry," she stuttered, stuffing her feet into her slippers. "I'll be right down."

She tossed the cordless phone onto her bed and threw a sweatshirt over her pajamas, yelling, "Coming…I'm coming," as she scrambled down the stairs.

Rumpled and still bleary, she hurried over and unlocked the front door. "I'm so sorry, guys! Thanks for waking me up. I can't *believe* I overslept."

Susan gave Trina a hug, then shrugged out of her jacket. "No problem, sweetie. We weren't waiting that long, but you know how impatient *Miss Congeniality* here can be."

Louie rolled his eyes. "I'm just going to ignore that." Looking at Trina, he frowned, his glance sweeping her face and the dark smudges beneath her eyes. "Honey, talk about a train wreck! You look terrible. Are you feeling okay?"

"Subtle as always, Louie. And before I've had a cup of coffee, no less," she teased, stifling a yawn. "I'm fine. I just haven't been sleeping too well, that's all."

"School?" he asked, draping his leather jacket over the banister.

She shook her head, closing the front door. "No, I wish it was that simple, at least then I'd know what to think." She hesitated, not sure what to say. "I never told you guys, but something weird happened at the club a couple of weeks ago. I still can't figure it out, and it's been haunting me every since."

Susan tossed her jacket alongside Louie's and dropped her purse on the floor next to the stairs. "Honey, you wouldn't believe some of the bizarre antics I come across during my shifts. What's to figure out?"

Trina shrugged. "That's just it, I can't remember. It's as if my memory is malfunctioning or something. I know in my gut something happened, something terrifying. But every time I try to piece it together, I get a dull headache. It's all fuzzy, like bits and pieces from a nightmare. And now I keep having these intense dreams."

"Oh, honey, that's horrible! With nightmares like that no wonder you're not sleeping."

Trina exhaled sharply, running a hand through her hair. "Except it's not fear keeping me on edge. My dreams are intense, but they're definitely not nightmares, more like hardcore porn," she admitted, heat flooding her cheeks.

Both of her friends just stared.

"Porn? You?" Louie smirked, one eyebrow arching almost to his hairline.

"It's always the quiet ones," Susan said with a sly, shit-eating grin. "Care to share?"

"Not a chance!" Trina chuckled, but still wasn't about to elaborate. How could she admit that every night she went to bed longing to have the same dream? That she was addicted to a lover who didn't exist and whose face she had never seen. It was just a dream, but the problem was it felt real. How could she explain without sounding pathetic? She'd known Susan most of her adult life, and Louie for the past year. There was no need to guess what they would think. She needed a man, a real one and quick.

Louie pursed his lips. "Well, that's promising," he teased, drifting casually into the parlor. "Because we all know you're not getting any while you're awake."

"Louie!"

"Don't waste your breath, Susan, I'm used to it. I think Louie must have a bet going or something, because nobody else is as preoccupied with getting me laid as he is…not even me!" she said following him through to the parlor.

Louie sniffed. "Well, you know what they say; the longer you wait, the harder it is to get back on the horse. And honey, you're getting to the point where we're going to have to use a crowbar to pry those legs apart just so you can mount up!"

"Ha! You're just lucky my great-grandmother isn't around to hear you talk to me like that!"

Susan held up a hand. "She's right, Louie. You're no match for that one. Walking stick and all, she'd come after you with a bar of soap!" she said, shooting Trina a wink. "How's she doing by the way?"

Trina sighed. "Nanita's good, I guess. I go see her everyday and she seems to have accepted the fact that she needs assisted living. She has aged so much just in the last year. I need her to be in a place where I know she's safe and there are people around if something should happen. I can't go through what I did the last time I came home from work and found her on the ground." Her voice cracked a bit at the memory.

"Does she seem happy? How is she being treated?"

"The people seem very nice and they tell me she's adjusting slowly. Her nurse, Jeannette, is a blessing, and doing everything possible to get her to interact with the other residents. I just have to keep reminding myself it's not a nursing home. Nanita has her own apartment and still does almost everything for herself. It's just that I have peace of mind knowing there's a full nursing staff right there twenty-four/seven if she needs it."

"It's all good then, so why do you sound so down about it?" Susan asked, concerned.

Trina lifted one shoulder and let it drop, yet despite herself, tears pricked the corners of her eyes. "I guess I can't help but feel guilty about being away from her, but with school and working nights, there was no way I could be around like I was before."

Susan gave Trina's shoulders a squeeze. "It's for the best, you'll see, and she's going to love it. You know how hard change can be for most people. Can you imagine at her age? How old is your great-grandmother now anyway?"

Trina wiped a stray tear away with her knuckle, and chuckled to herself. "I have no idea, if you can believe that! She won't tell me and I've even tried snooping in her papers, but everything she's got is locked up in a safe deposit box."

"No way!" Susan laughed.

"Yeah, go figure. She told me everything I ever wanted to know about her would be given to me when she passes."

Exhaling loudly, Louie turned around and clapped. "Okay…on that delightful note, let's get started, or did you forget that you asked us over for a reason?"

Like a five-star general in designer boots he turned on his heel and surveyed the entire room. In seconds, he had the place transformed into an interior design triage unit. He sent Trina to shower and dress, and Susan to make some coffee while he packed boxes.

"What time is the furniture being delivered?" he called up the stairs as he heard Trina come out of the bathroom.

"They said between three and five o'clock, but I managed to get them to put us last on their schedule so we could have more time to prepare," she yelled down, slipping into jeans and a T-shirt.

Trina had wanted to do this for as long as she could remember. She was proud of her Spanish heritage and had listened for years as her great-grandmother talked about her life in Spain with such nostalgia. Leaving wasn't her choice, but Trina's great-grandfather had made his life in England, and his wife had no alternative but to follow. Back then, she was only able to take a few of her favorite pieces with her, and as the years passed and they immigrated to the States, she had no choice but to leave even more behind.

It had taken a while, but Trina located some of her great-grandmother's lost things, and now they were in transit to arrive in New York today. Smiling to herself, she imagined the look on the old woman's face when she finally saw everything she believed lost to time and circumstance. Trina prayed the surprise didn't give the old woman heart failure.

They packed boxes and moved furniture all afternoon. Susan helped Trina press and hang the delicate lace sheers on the bay window in the parlor, while Louie fastened the heavy brackets needed to support the ornate curtain rod Trina had bought for the drapes.

"Where'd you find these? They're gorgeous! And so authentic looking," Susan said admiring one of the bronze rosettes Trina struggled with at the end of the heavy rod.

"That's because they are. I searched the Internet for weeks trying to find a pair that fit the description of the ones my great-grandmother had in her house in Spain."

"*Uhmm*, can you hurry it up over there? This rod weighs a ton, especially with these brocade monsters you call drapes hanging from it. When you asked me to help, you neglected to mention this redecoration project was going to be straight out of *Gone with the Wind*. I hope you don't expect me to make you a dress from this lot," Louie added dryly.

Trina rolled her eyes. "Keep your panties on, princess, I'm almost done."

Looking at the clock on the mantel, she frowned. "I wonder where that delivery truck can be." Climbing down, she dragged the stepladder to the other end of the window seat and took the rod from Louie, hoisting it into its bracket.

The doorbell rang.

"Finally!" Louie said, rolling his shoulders before sweeping out of the parlor to open the front door. He directed the deliverymen like Toscanini conducting a symphony. The art of Feng Shui at its worst, with each piece choreographed to the point of being painful.

When the guys were finished, Trina gave them each an apologetic look and twenty dollars. "Well, that was easier said than done," she muttered, closing the front door. She walked back across the tiled foyer into the parlor where Louie stood looking at the line of photographs, artfully displayed on the oak mantelpiece.

"Wow! And who is this hottie?" he asked, picking up an older photo that was propped against the wall.

"That's a photograph of my great-grandfather. I think it was taken sometime in the early 1920s."

"Kind of delicious in a Clark Gable sort of way, don't you think?" Putting the picture back, he sighed wistfully. "They just don't grow men like that anymore."

Susan rolled her eyes. "Okay, Betty Davis, back to work," she said, and hoisted the last of the boxes to be moved onto her hip. "Hey, Trin…speaking of delicious, you'll never guess who's been at the club almost every night." Not waiting for an answer, she leaned in, her eyes flashing with the juicy secret. "It was that guy, the sexy one who gave me that all that cash. He's definitely *not* one of the walking wounded, if you know what I mean. Plus, he isn't shy about spreading the wealth. He doesn't say much, but who cares when there's such a terrific view?"

Trina laughed as she picked up leftover bubble wrap from the floor. "Really? The walking wounded? I don't think Avalon quite cuts it as a hangout for urban intellectuals."

"That's because you've been stuck working the dance floor bar. After all the times you've covered for me up in the gallery, it's time you asked Rick for a couple of permanent shifts. Tips are better, and you can actually hear yourself think—not to mention a serious decrease in the weirdness factor. It's true. The closer the proximity to the dance floor, the more weirdos per square foot!"

Trina laughed. "*That* I believe!" she said shoving the bubble wrap into a garbage bag. "I'll ask Rick tonight and see what he thinks."

"Honey, for what it's worth, I think Susan's right. You deserve a bit of a break. And besides, what could be better than working with *moi*," Louie added cheekily.

"Not a thing," Trina said with a wink, and headed back toward the windows. With a few final tugs at the brocade, she turned and dusted off her hands. "*Voila*! I think we're done. How does it look?"

With his finger on his chin, Louie walked back and forth in front of the window. "Amazing. I thought for sure it would look out of date, a real dust fest. But, honey, it's just elegant. Very old world. Well done, girl!"

"He's right, sweetie, it's perfect," Susan said, holding the old photographs Trina had used as a decorating guide. "It looks as if you reached straight into the photos and took the whole room out of time and space."

Turning the yellowed and cracked images over in her hand, she whistled long and low, glancing at the faded dates written on the back. "Wow. Some of these are seriously old. I always knew your family had been in the States for a while, but based on these, it's even longer than I thought."

Trina grabbed a bottle of water from the coffee table and sat on the bottom rung on the ladder. She took a sip, toying with the bottle's plastic cap. "Well, I know most of my family is originally from Spain and England, but I'm not really sure how or when they immigrated to the States. It must have been a while ago because this house has been in the family for about one hundred years." She frowned, looking around. "Looks it too."

"No honey, it's vintage, and vintage is just fabulous!" Louie said with his usual *joie de vivre.* "Besides, do you expect to do everything yourself? You're finishing school, you work, and you take care of your great-grandmother—so unless you're hiding it in that closet of yours, I don't remember you having a red spandex outfit with the words *Super Girl* written across the chest!"

Susan's lips twitched. "No, sweetie, that's your department!"

Laughing, Trina sucked in a breath and nearly choked, spraying water everywhere. Coughing and sputtering, her eyes streamed as she wiped her hand across her mouth and chin, staring at Susan's matter-of-fact expression.

"Meow, meow, meow" Louie answered, wrinkling his nose.

"Come on. Let's clean up and go get a drink. We deserve it after a job well done." Susan said handing Trina a bunch of paper towels, and giving her back one last pat. "Whaddaya think? Martinis?"

"Amen to that, sister!" Louie snorted, sweeping past her toward the front door.

***

The three walked into Angelo & Maxie's on 19th Street and Park Avenue and sat down at the bar. "Order me a lemon drop martini with extra sugar on the rim. I'll be back in a sec," Trina said, grabbing her bag and heading toward the restroom.

Louie put his elbows on the counter and linked his fingers together. "So, when are you going to tell me why you so graciously offered to come help us today, *hmmm*?" Raising an eyebrow, he shot her a look. "Come on, Susan, I know you and you don't offer to do manual labor for nothing. Spill it."

"That obvious, huh? I need to ask Trina to cover for me at the club tonight," she admitted sheepishly. "Don't look at me like that. I know she's covered my ass a lot lately, but tonight is super important. My band is playing and there's supposed to be some record company scout or somebody going to be there. I can't miss it."

Louie swiveled his seat to face her. "You know she's going to say yes. She always says yes, that's half her problem. Except she never says yes when it counts, if you know what I mean. I swear, in her next life the woman's coming back as a pack mule. She's got to stop shouldering everything for everyone around her." He looked at Susan over the top of his square-rimmed glasses. "When's the last time Trina went out with a guy? Or went out at all, for that matter? It's not right. She's gorgeous and she's wasting it. I mean, just look at her. She's hot and everyone knows it but her."

Susan shrugged. "Maybe she just hasn't found the right guy, Louie, that's all."

"That's what?" Trina asked as she walked back to the bar.

Both Louie and Susan were too quiet and Trina's eyes narrowed a bit. She knew they had been talking about her, but she knew her friends well enough not to be annoyed. "Come on, guys, what gives?"

"Susan has something she wants to ask you. Don't you, Susan?" Louie said, deftly changing the subject.

Susan shot Louie a dirty look. "He's right," she said with a guilty smile. "I need a favor, but first you have to promise you won't get mad."

Trina just laughed as the bartender brought their drinks. "Susan, don't you think I knew the minute you volunteered to help that something was up? Just tell me what it is you want."

"Can you cover for me at the club tonight? My band has an important gig and I can't miss it. We're not on till the third set so I can work until about midnight, but then I'll have to run. Will you cover the rest of the night for me? That way if I punch in, Rick will think I'm somewhere else in the club and won't give me any crap. I'll be back by four a.m. I promise," she said, crossing her heart.

Trina sighed, shaking her head. "Yes, I'll cover for you…again. I'll meet you at the club at midnight and don't worry about rushing back. But you owe me. You have to take my shift tomorrow night as well as next Saturday or no deal."

Susan squealed. "Thank you!" she said, and jumped up giving Trina a squeeze. "And don't worry. I'll cover whatever shifts you want."

Trina laughed, pulling out a chair to sit down. "You'd better or I'm telling Rick."

Louie looked at Trina, impressed. "Wow, honey, I'm proud of you. You actually bargained for yourself this time and got two weekends off out of the deal. It's about time!"

Trina just shrugged. "It's no big. Who knows? Maybe I'll get lucky."

Louie laughed. "Oh, honey, that would be a dream come true!"

Trina closed her eyes as she took a sip of her drink. "You have no idea," she said under her breath.

Chapter 3

With an aggravated sigh, Carlos settled himself back against one of the plush couches. He never fashioned himself a barfly, but with as many times as he'd frequented Avalon in the past two weeks, he was starting to fit the bill. And for what? A human girl who had some sort of extrasensory perception. Still, he was intrigued. Humans with sensitivities to his kind weren't unheard of, but for her to have seen through *his* wards? Perhaps he was losing his touch after so many centuries.

He had already scanned the club, but sent his senses out again just to be sure. He half expected every young blood in Manhattan to show up and try their luck. It would be just like Sandro to stir up trouble for him as payment for what happened with his boys.

He and Sandro had a long, unpleasant history. They had once been friends and rivals, though Sandro was older. However, that was a long time ago, and though they maintained a gracious front toward one another in public, they would never see eye to eye. In fact, Sandro had never forgiven Carlos for opening his home to Eric after Sandro had cast him off. Carlos had offered Eric a home and a chance at reclaiming some of his humanity, something that Sandro disdained. Cruelty was the only thing he understood.

Sandro would retaliate; it was only a matter of time and place. He would consider Carlos's actions excessive, even though his boys were clearly in the wrong. He would regard coming to the aid of an unclaimed human proof of Carlos's weakness.

He sighed again. He was so tired of all the infighting, of the impolitic cruelty of his kind, and hoped this time Sandro would be reasonable.

He inhaled, and caught the scent of something new in the air. It wasn't another vampire. This scent was dizzying yet familiar. He didn't turn his head but he knew—it was her—and slowly slid his gaze around.

She was of average height, and had what looked in the dim light to be long, auburn hair, the same kind of soft, curling mass he loved to run his fingers through. Her body was curvy, healthy, and full, just the way he liked it, not the emaciated, heroin-addicted look that girls today preferred. And her eyes—greener than the deepest of Colombian emeralds. He had etched their memory in his mind, but even his heightened recollection hadn't done them justice.

His mouth watered and his incisors lengthened. She seemed familiar, yet not. The feeling was both elusive yet palpable, and went deeper than their fleeting moment in the stairwell. His body suffused with heat and his thirst hit him full on. He hadn't had a physical reaction to someone like this is ages, and willed himself to relax.

"Hi," she said with a smile. "Can I get you anything from the bar?" Pen in hand, she clicked the end of the ballpoint.

"Bacardi 151, no ice," he answered, his eyes never leaving hers.

Her lips curved again. "No ice. Got it," she repeated, and leaned forward to pick up a few empty glasses from the table. Giving it a quick wipe, she put a clean coaster down on the table and handed Carlos a napkin.

Her smile sent shivers down his spine, but when his fingers brushed hers the feel of her skin was almost too much for him to bear. Her touch made the shivers electric, like sparks running up and down his back and straight into his groin.

"I see by your name tag that you're Trina. What a beautiful name. Is it short for Katrina?"

"Nope. Alastrine. It's Celtic for defender of mankind." Trina shrugged. "My mother was fascinated with things of that nature, but thank you anyway."

"Both beautiful and unusual," he said, taking her hand without warning. "Well, it's a pleasure to meet you…Trina." His eyes locked on hers and held for a fraction longer than was polite.

The serving tray slid from her hand, and empty glasses and napkins fell to the carpet by her feet. Her hand flew to her stomach, and her fingers clutched the black satin of her low cut vest. She closed her eyes and inhaled, and as she filled her lungs, the increased volume pushed her full breasts tight against the shiny lapels.

"Um, how are you doing? Would you like me to bring you more ice?" she stammered, as color flooded her cheeks.

Carlos's lips twitched as he watched. She was both irritated and confused by her unexplained state, but of course, he knew the reason behind her loss of composure. His senses keyed, pulsating with her effort to maintain control. Her natural reaction to fight his glamour intrigued him. This was the second time she hadn't succumbed immediately, and it amazed him more now than when she witnessed the incident with the young bloods. She was an anomaly. He studied her, wondering what her genuine response would be to him as a just man.

As he released her, Trina relaxed, her breathing grew more even and her pulse beat in a steadier rhythm. He allowed her to pull her hand away from his, and smiled. "But my dear, you haven't brought me my drink yet, and I asked for it neat…no ice remember?"

Trina cleared her throat and shook her head slightly. "I'm so sorry, sir…" Flustered and embarrassed, she bent to pick up her tray and the spilled glasses. "I'm not really sure what just happened. You'll have to excuse me and please accept my apologies."

His eyes held hers, and for a moment time seemed to stop. "Don't worry," he assured with a wave of his hand. "It's nothing, and please, my name is Carlos."

Confused, Trina's brow furrowed. "Okay then," she mumbled, avoiding his eyes. "I'll just go get you your drink." Resting the tray on her hip, she turned, giving him a nervous glance as she headed back toward the bar.

***

The club was at full capacity, packed with people, and Trina worked up a sweat clearing her tables and carrying trays of drinks back and forth from the bar. She did her best, but by the look of things a half dozen servers wouldn't have been enough.

"Have you worked here for very long?" Carlos asked as she refreshed his drink.

"A few months. The hours fit my schedule right now and the money's decent. I'm still trying to finish school," she said with a shrug. "I'm going for a master's degree in psychology."

"Why do you sound so halfhearted? An education is a noble thing to want to attain."

"I know. It's just taking a lot longer than I expected, plus I'm already older than the average graduate student."

"Ahh, so it *was* your bones I heard creaking then, huh?" he added wryly, sliding his eyes to her as he took a sip of his drink.

Smirking, she laughed. "I'm twenty-six. That's old to still be in school, not old in general, smart aleck. Thankfully I'll be graduating soon, as long as this job doesn't cripple me first."

Bracing her tray against her hip, Trina sighed and rolled her shoulders. Her feet and her lower back ached from her spiked heels and her head throbbed from the music. "Thank God I'm off tomorrow. I don't think my back could take another night in these shoes."

"Then why don't you sit for a moment?" he suggested, patting the soft velvet next to him.

She smiled, but shook her head. "Thanks, but I can't. House rules."

With a dismissive wave, he pulled her down to sit beside him. "That's ridiculous."

"No!" she said, her voice low but sharp. "I don't know you and besides, you'll get me into trouble."

Her eyes flew open as he picked up her hand and kissed it. "Nonsense. You can take a moment to sit with me. Trust me, *señorita,* no one will even notice."

His touch was unbelievable and his eyes so compelling, it made the simple gesture seem erotic. It was nothing more than a mere whisper of a kiss, yet it was so sensual. Trina swallowed, her heart skittering a few beats.

Butterflies exploded in her stomach. She let the air out of her lungs slowly, conscious of the fact she was front and center with her nerves and her libido surging irrationally. She pulled her hand from his, willing herself not to yank it from his grip. It felt tingly, like she had held one of those handheld personal massagers for too long. Forcing herself to focus, she stared at the floor.

With her hands locked in her lap, Trina sucked in a breath and looked up. "Carlos, I'm here to do a job, and while I don't mind the small talk, I'm not here for anyone's personal entertainment. I have to stay mindful of anything that could be misconstrued. In this kind of work, you have to draw the line somewhere, or the lines get blurred. I hope you understand. I get a little touchy when things get, well…touchy."

Carlos just raised one eyebrow in surprise. With even less of a suggestion, any other woman would be giving him a lap dance by now.

"You seem like a nice enough guy, and while I appreciate the gesture, I think it would be better all the way around if we kept things professional, okay?"

She waited for him to say something, anything, but Carlos didn't say a word. Uneasy, she pushed herself up from the couch and stood with her tray on her hip. She sighed, with just a hint of regret lacing her tone and tucked her hair behind her ear. "Well, I'd better get back to work." Looking around at her other tables, she hesitated. "Again, I'm sorry. I'll check in to see how you're doing with your drink a little later.

***

As the night progressed, Carlos couldn't tear his eyes from Trina. Three times, she had fought his glamour, each time regaining her composure more quickly than the time before. He searched his memory and his senses for an explanation, but couldn't find one that sufficed, and his interest moved beyond mere curiosity.

Her presence played on every predatory instinct he possessed. He watched her as she moved from table to table, and it was all he could do not to spell her into leaving with him immediately—not that it would work. He focused his senses and tried to read her but couldn't. Instead, all he could hear were his own racing thoughts.

The way his body had reacted, coupled with her resistance, had left him struggling with himself. He fought an almost overwhelming urge to dominate, to make her his, to have her body and soul. In the back of his mind, a warning voice urged him to leave before he did something he'd regret. But he couldn't. He was obsessed. Again, he would watch and wait.

On the far side of the bar, he watched her take another order from the bartender. She headed over to a group of guys who sat not far from him and she gave him a quick smile as she passed, her tray filled with bottles of Corona.

The youths had caught his attention earlier. They had been drinking for a while, and with each round had gotten louder and more vocal with the women that passed their table. Their thoughts broadcast their intentions loud and clear, but after dealing with the two young bloods, Carlos was in no mood for more disrespect in his territory—vampire or human. He'd turn the tables on them before he'd allow that to happen, and save some unlucky girl a regrettable mistake in the process.

From their accent, it was obvious they were from out of town. Carlos watched as Trina put their drinks down, her body graceful and sexy with each subtle movement. He caught an unspoken exchange between two of the young men and tensed, his body coiled in anticipation.

"Hey baby, why don't you let us buy you a drink?" One of the guys drawled as Trina handed him a beer, his eyes traveling the length of her body.

Trina just smiled professionally. "Sorry guys, can't," she answered politely only to have one of his friends put his leg up on the chair behind her, in effect blocking her exit.

Carlos watched as she closed her eyes and exhaled in annoyance. He was sure she'd dealt with drunks before and could probably deal with this, but tonight he was on a hair trigger, with absolutely no patience for bullshit.

"Come on baby, wanna have some fun? How 'bout you show us a good time. We'll make it worth your while, sugar, what do you say?" another said while his friends laughed, egging him on.

Trina's eyes narrowed and her smile fled. "Let me pass." Her voice was low but severe.

The first guy got up and took hold of Trina's arm. "Don't be that way, sweet thing, we ain't gonna bite," he said, running his hand suggestively up her arm and grazing her breast with his thumb.

Carlos felt a snarl rumble low in the back of his throat. His eyes flashed red and he was about to strike, when without missing a beat, Trina reached over and grabbed the guy's wrist. She spun him around so fast that his arm was completely twisted and yanked backwards.

Pushing on the guy's elbow, she forced his arm even further up his back. "Ow! You're breakin' my arm, bitch!" he yelled as Trina shoved him up against one of the mirrored walls, his cheek pressed hard into the glass.

Trina got right up behind his ear and shouted, "Is that the way your mama taught you to treat a lady?" she mimicked, pushing painfully on his elbow. He yelped even louder. Lowering her voice, she added, "If you or any of your friends ever put your hands on me again it'll be the last thing you ever touch. Got it?" Her voice was no more than a whisper, but her meaning was loud and clear.

At this point the boy just whimpered, all his previous bravado gone. His friends scrambled to get their jackets as Trina's boss and a couple of very large bouncers approached to escort them from the premises.

Carlos's body was still tense and poised to attack, but as he watched the events unfold, he was curiously proud of the way Trina handled herself.

He inhaled deeply. Her heart raced with adrenaline as underlying anger and fear poured into her blood stream, scenting it with a metallic tang. Bouncers escorted the boys from the premises, and Carlos had to stifle the urge to follow and rip their throats out. He clenched his fists against a sudden wave of possessiveness, hardening himself as it crashed over and then receded.

After that, Trina was gone for a while, and he found himself growing edgier by the minute waiting for her to return. When she finally came out on the floor, he called her over. "Are you all right?" he asked, allowing only a hint of concern into his voice.

Trina shrugged. "Yeah, I'm fine. I've had to deal with situations like that plenty of times, but it never gets any easier. Alcohol just brings out the worst in some people, I guess."

Carlos knew the threat was much more real than she let on, and he knew that deep down Trina knew it too. "Please, sit down," he insisted. "I think you need a moment just to breathe. Besides, we never got to finish our conversation, and I think after what you've just been through you deserve a little break, *no?*"

Trina sat down without hesitation this time, and he handed her his glass. "To steady your nerves."

She smiled and took the glass from him. "Thanks," she said, and glanced down at the dark liquid. Raising the tumbler, she murmured, *"Salud,"* and took a sip. Swallowing hard, she coughed as she put the glass down on the paper coaster.

"Would you like something else instead?" Carlos asked. "I can get you something from the bar, a soft drink, perhaps?"

Trina put her hand on his. "No, I'm fine, thanks. I like rum. It's just I haven't really eaten anything tonight and drinking it straight like that probably isn't such a good idea. I still have to work, you know. My shift isn't over."

She looked down at both their hands. "I guess I didn't give you a fair chance before, Carlos. I'm sorry. I was just trying to be professional. I'm usually a pretty good judge of character," she added, a little embarrassed. "I'm just not myself tonight. I guess I need to work on my people skills."

He picked up her hand and kissed it again, holding it while his other hand trailed lightly over her forearm. "Oh, it looks to me like your people skills are pretty well honed. I'm impressed. Where did you learn to move like that?"

Trina blushed. "Martial arts. I hold a second-degree black belt in traditional Japanese karate with a strong emphasis on self-defense and jiu-jitsu."

Carlos was pensive for a moment. He thought about the girl Sandro's boys had lured to the back and wondered how she would have fared if she'd had the same training and presence of mind. "I think that's commendable. Most women would have found themselves at a loss and probably would have panicked."

Trina shrugged. "Maybe. Adrenaline plays a big part in it too."

They were quiet for a moment. Trina picked up Carlos's glass and took another sip.

"What are you doing tomorrow night? I thought since you said you weren't going to be working that maybe you'd like to spend it together."

Trina choked a bit, but not from the rum. "I'm sorry?"

Carlos smiled. "I asked if you'd like to get together tomorrow evening."

She looked at Carlos for a moment, and a little smile spread across her mouth. "I'd love to. I'm ashamed to admit the thought crossed my mind too, regardless of my little speech earlier."

"Ahh," Carlos said, running his finger along the side of her cheek and down toward her neck. He felt her shiver slightly and the corner of his mouth twitched. This was an entirely new experience for him. Very human. Leaning over, he kissed her softly.

He heard her breath catch in her throat, but she put her hands on his chest and gently pushed him back. "Carlos, please don't. You'll get me fired. I shouldn't even be sitting with you. It's against the rules of the club to fraternize with the patrons."

He took in her profile and the soft curve of her face and neck as she spoke. Her slight agitation had caused her color to rise, and his hands itched to feel the satin of her skin and the thrum of her pulse under his fingers. "I told you no one will bother us, trust me." Trailing kisses along her shoulder to the spot where her pulse beat beneath her skin, he let the tips of his fangs elongate and gently grazed her neck. Not enough to break the skin, but enough to make his mouth water with expectation.

He cupped her face and kissed her lips again, savoring her sweet taste as he teased her mouth with his tongue. Trina kissed him back tentatively, as his hands caressed her shoulders and back while his lips captured every part of her mouth. She sighed and opened to him, kissing him back without reservation.

Carlos wrapped his arm around her waist and pulled her against him, his hand sliding over the curve of her hip to cup the weight of her full breast. As his thumb grazed the sensitive edge of her nipple, it hardened in response beneath the thin satin of her vest. Trina threw her head back, arching into his hand, her hair falling like a curtain of silk behind her, exposing her throat.

Carlos pulled back, his fangs descending fully. Her kiss was heady and his body was hard with need. He growled low and caressed the tender skin beneath her jaw line with his lips, his breath ragged against her skin. Her pulse beat erratically and its pull pushed him to the edge. He slid his razor-sharp fangs into the blue vein that throbbed deliciously beneath them.

Her blood filled his mouth, and the moment its taste hit his tongue he knew. Stunned, his head shot up in disbelief and he looked at her. "*Isabel,*" he whispered.

He could hardly breathe—not that he actually needed air or that his lung functions were anything more than rote muscle memory, but his breath literally caught in his throat.

He sat speechless for a moment and licked her blood from his lips. Its taste was incomprehensible, steeped with Isabel's essence. This felt like a dream, or maybe some kind of nightmare. Even if she had lived to a ripe old age, his Isabel had died over two centuries before. But this girl, this woman—there had to be a connection, but he couldn't see how. Souls, even reincarnated ones, didn't carry the same blood signature from one lifetime to another.

A small trail of blood trickled its way down between Trina's breasts. With a groan, Carlos licked it clean, and then sank his teeth once more into the existing wound. He groaned again as the taste of her filled him, flooding his senses with images from the past as well as the present.

He took more, pulling deeply at her vein and trying to find an answer in the hot, coppery liquid. Trina gasped and arched her body even further. Electricity tingled beneath his hands as if her skin coursed with lightning.

She shivered in his arms, the heat from her arousal sizzling against his lips. With his hands, he followed its warmth down across her breasts and past her belly until her wet climax exploded against his palm.

Carlos's mind reeled. Her blood was potent and exhilarating and he moaned with the visceral pleasure of it. Her climax startled him with its force and his body urged him to take more. He hadn't fed in weeks and knew if he didn't stop now he'd end up taking her life.

He withdrew from her, and clenching his jaw, willed his need to subside. He had almost lost control, something he hadn't done in nearly two hundred years and he refused to do so now.

With a quick swipe of his tongue he sealed the marks on her neck, watching them heal instantly. Kissing her deeply once again, he gently released her.

Trina sat back. She was breathless, flushed and clearly a little embarrassed. "I'm sorry. I…I don't usually..." she stammered, folding her hands in her lap and looking down at them. She took a deep breath to steady herself, and then looked up, meeting his eyes. "This isn't like me," she whispered.

"Shhh…There is nothing for you to be ashamed of," Carlos murmured, taking her face in his hands and kissing her gently. His want still throbbed in his head as well as in his groin, and the pull of her blood was strong, almost beyond reason.

Trina blanched. It was obvious she hadn't a clue he had sampled her blood, yet her eyes read both pleasure and pain, registering the danger and ecstasy inherent in a vampire's kiss. She put her hands on his shoulders and gently eased herself back, "I'm sorry, but I think it's best if I get back to work." As if heeding some internal warning bell, she took an uneven breath and pushed herself up from the couch, her hands shaking a bit. "Thanks for the drink."

Carlos watched her smooth her skirt before walking back toward the bar. "Same here," he murmured, and poured himself another shot. Trina wasn't the only one shaken by the encounter.

Chapter 4

*T*rina slid behind the bar and grabbed a towel. Glancing over to where Rick counted out part of the night's receipts, she mumbled an apology for being gone from the floor for so long. Truth was she didn't know how long she'd sat with Carlos, and Rick's grunt didn't offer much of an answer either. It seemed like only minutes, but who connects on that kind of level in just minutes?

None of it made any sense. Not her behavior, and certainly not the way her body reacted. Impulsive and rash weren't part of her vocabulary, so what had made her act so out of character?

Disgusted, she threw the towel over her shoulder and occupied herself with stacking rinsed bar glasses. *Minutes.* All the time she'd spent talking with Carlos tonight, still only added up to just minutes.

She'd couldn't believe she'd let him kiss her. And judging by the wetness in her panties, that was the least of it. Her body still hummed with arousal, and as the tingle spread, she touched her face, mortified at the heat beneath her fingertips. How could she have allowed herself to lose complete control in an utter stranger's arms? But if he was an utter stranger, then why did he seem so familiar? She couldn't shake the tiny nagging feeling of *déjà vu* that tugged at her regardless of her embarrassment.

His words sounded like music and felt like chocolate melting in her mouth. Something about him made her head buzz, she had felt it before, but for the life of her, she didn't understand it. In addition, she certainly didn't understand why this time she chose not to fight the deluge of sensation.

She knew this feeling. For the past two weeks, she'd woken up every morning in the same warm afterglow. *This is no dream. This is the way I'm supposed to feel.* Her mind revolted. *It's not the same!* This was simply the result of a reckless act, a momentary lapse in judgment. The other was just a side effect of her subconscious fantasies.

Then why did it feel so personal, so intimate? The feel of his hands, the taste of him—it was as if her body acknowledged what her practical mind refused to believe. It was then the words from her dream came back to haunt her. *You are here because it is what you want, yet what you fear. You search, but refuse to see.*

Could it be possible? Could this be the reason she'd been having the same dream repeatedly for weeks? *Impossible,* she thought. But it was the only answer that reconciled what her body knew to be true. It was him. He had come—only this time he was real.

Her mind raced. She was too pragmatic for this—she wasn't the type to lose herself in either a relationship or even a one-night stand. Maybe she was reaching, trying to make something out of nothing because she wanted it to be true. For the first time in her life, her great-grandmother's belief in all things mystical seemed like a legitimate possibility. How else could she explain what she was feeling? The only other explanation was that she had finally lost it, that years of shouldering responsibility and living like a nun had finally pushed her over the edge.

She finished stacking the glasses and picked up her tray. Agitated or not, she had a job to do, and though most of her tables had cleared out, there were a few stragglers still hanging around looking for a last-minute hookup. At this time of night, most couples were busy grinding it out on the dance floor. Musical foreplay. Heat rose in her cheeks again at the images those words conjured, and she stole a quick sideways glance at Carlos, still sitting on the couch in the corner nursing his rum.

The last call for alcohol had come and gone, and the bouncers herded anyone remaining toward the main exit. At this point, she didn't have much of a choice except to clear Carlos's table and let him settle his tab. She was so attracted to him it unnerved her, and as embarrassed as she was for acting like a poster girl for Sluts 'R' Us, just approaching his table sent her body into overdrive.

"Um…it was nice to meet you, Carlos," she said, not quite making eye contact as she picked up his empty glass and the almost empty bottle of rum. "Maybe I'll see you here again sometime."

He reached out and ran his knuckles over her forearm. "The pleasure was all mine, but don't tell me you've changed your mind about tomorrow night."

His fingertips sent little electric sparks across her exposed skin and she nearly dropped her tray. "No, I haven't changed my mind..." She trailed off, not trusting her voice not to crack.

"Good. I can think of nothing that would give me more pleasure than spending time with you. In fact, I'd like to see you home if you'll permit me."

Trina's cheeks burned at his words, but shook her head. "I appreciate the offer, but I'm going to be here a while longer. I have to help clean up this mess." Shrugging one shoulder, she looked around the club in dismay.

"Wait here just a moment," Carlos said with a deliberate smile, and walked off toward the bar.

Trina's expression was one of complete curiosity as he walked back from the bar, a satisfied grin on his face. "All settled. We can leave," he told her.

"Wow, you must have given Rick a hefty tip. He never lets anyone leave early."

"Something like that, but I have my ways," Carlos said, slyly tapping the side of his temple with his index finger.

Shaking her head again, she just laughed. "I'd better get my things before he changes his mind." Walking toward the door marked, "staff only", she grabbed her coat and bag. As she passed the bar, her boss gave her a nod as he stacked dirty glasses. "Have a good night, Trina," he called after her.

"You too, Rick." Hooking her bag over her shoulder, she hurried back toward Carlos, still wondering what he could possibly have said or done to get Rick to let her leave so early.

Carlos was waiting for her by the stairs. "Ready?"

Trina nodded and took his hand. "Just for the record, what *did* you say to Rick when you went over to talk to him?" She looked sideways at him, holding the railing while carefully navigating the steps in her heels.

Carlos gave her an innocent shrug. "I merely told him that your feet hurt, and that an older woman such as yourself should be allowed to go home to your footbath and Epsom salts."

She stopped in mid-step and just looked at him, but burst out laughing at the wicked smile twitching at the corner of his mouth.

***

The temperature had dropped overnight, and the wind whistled as it whipped down the street. The calendar may have said spring, but the lion hadn't quite yet turned into a lamb, and Trina's thin coat wasn't much help against the March chill.

Carlos put his arm around her as they made their way out. At the bottom of the steps, they stood on the sidewalk in awkward silence. "I said I'd see you home, so why don't you let me give you a lift? You look like you're freezing, and my car's right across the street," he said, indicating the Jag parked at the curb.

"I usually take the subway, but considering how cold it is tonight, a ride would be nice for a change." Cupping her hands, she blew on them for warmth.

"Then allow me," he smiled, offering her his elbow.

"Such a gentleman." Trina chuckled and linked her arm with his.

Carlos didn't respond, but the words *not even close* echoed through his head as he watched her climb into his car. He slid effortlessly into the driver seat and started the engine. "Where to?" he asked pulling out onto the deserted street.

"East 19th Street, between 3rd and Irving."

"Gramercy Park?"

Trina nodded. "My family has owned a home there since the early 1900s. It's been passed down over the years, and now I live there with my great-grandmother. She'll be one hundred and four on her next birthday—at least I think that's how old she'll be."

"Nice," he said, then after a moment looked at her, a little puzzled.

"I know what you're thinking. Then why a barmaid, right?"

"Considering what New York City real estate is worth, basically, yes."

"It's complicated," Trina said, running her hand through her hair.

He caught her agitated gesture and his curiosity piqued. From his peripheral vision he could see her eyebrows had furrowed slightly and she looked preoccupied.

"What's so complicated? Tell me."

"It's nothing, forget it. Just family drama and I wouldn't want to bore you," she added quickly.

Carlos watched Trina catch herself before she nervously ran her hand through her hair again. She was uneasy, but what interested him was that she was obviously policing herself. Trina smiled nervously, and folded her hands in her lap. "Tell me more about you. You said your home is upstate somewhere. Is it far?"

"Without traffic, it's about two hours from the city. But I have a place on the Upper East Side that I use when I'm in town."

Impressed, Trina nodded and they fell into an awkward silence.

"I'm a pretty good listener, you know. Every family has its own brand of drama. In fact, I think it's a prerequisite. At times my own could earn nominations for the Tony Awards," he offered, pressing a bit.

Trina looked at him wryly. "I'll bet. But my family..." She hesitated, chewing on her lower lip. "Do you remember the line from that old movie *Arsenic and Old Lace?* The one where Cary Grant says, 'Insanity runs in the family, but in ours it practically gallops'? Well, in my family that just about covers it."

Carlos laughed aloud. "Come on, after something like that you've got to tell me now."

"Nope."

"*Hmmm*. What if I guess?"

She grinned. "Not a chance. Let's change the subject. What kind of books do you like to read?"

Carlos raised an eyebrow. "Books?"

"Yeah, books. You know those things with all the words in them that come in paperback or hardcover. Some even have leather bindings."

Carlos smirked at her. "Very funny. Smart aleck…wasn't that your word? Okay…books. I like all kinds of books, both fiction and non-fiction, but I enjoy history and biographies most. What about you?"

She hesitated for a moment. "Romances. All kinds of romances."

"Really?"

She raised an eyebrow as if she had expected this reaction. "And what's wrong with romance novels? I want to spend what little free time I have reading stories that spark my imagination rather than something dull or depressing. Isn't real life mundane enough? The required reading for my degree is so dry it practically puts me to sleep. I like romantic suspense. It's an escape from my everyday life and I love it. In fact, I just finished one about a girl and her vampire lover and it was terrific."

"Really. That good, huh?" Carlos slid his eyes sideways and held her gaze. In seconds, Trina began to shift uncomfortably in her seat. A fine sheen of sweat broke out on her face, and he could smell the arousal pheromones coming off her in waves. When he gave her a seductive half smile she literally gasped, and he had to chuckle to himself. He broke eye contact with her, but wasn't sorry at all. He couldn't resist giving her a little taste of the real thing.

"Interesting," he murmured, as he pulled onto her street. Parking in front of her house, he cocked his head to look out the car's window. An attractive, ivy-covered brownstone sat exactly park side on what New Yorkers call "the block beautiful."

"So, are you ever going to tell me what makes your family so…special?"

He could tell she was still a little flustered, but she met his gaze head on, regardless. With a mischievous look, she opened the door. "Maybe," she said and blew him a kiss as she got out of the car. "See you tomorrow."

He laughed aloud again, a huge grin spreading across his face. "Maybe, indeed."

***

Freezing on the top step of the brownstone, Trina dug for her keys at the bottom of her purse. Normally she would've already had them in her hand before getting out of the car. Silly as it was, she knew Carlos would wait, watching until she was safely inside the house. It was juvenile and she knew it, but she wanted his eyes on her for as long as possible.

Finding them, she ceremoniously unlocked the door and stepped halfway into the vestibule. With her heart thudding in her ears, she turned and waved, giving him one last smile before stepping inside.

The door barely clicked shut behind her before she raced like a boy-crazy teenager toward the bay window in the parlor. She knelt on the window seat, peeling off her thin, leather gloves and peeking surreptitiously through the curtain lace.

She could see him clearly, as the car sat idling in front of the house. Just then he turned, looking straight at the darkened window were she sat as if he knew she was there. Her breath caught in her throat. Putting his car in gear, Carlos drove off, and Trina knelt staring at the empty street.

"What a night!" she murmured, sliding down onto the cushioned seat. Nervous butterflies winged their way around her stomach and it gurgled. Looking around the empty room, Trina sighed, wondering what her great-grandmother would think about tonight's escapade. She missed her and their midnight talks. The old woman wasn't much for sleep, and the two often giggled like schoolgirls over a late night cup of tea.

Too tired to do anything but shower, Trina pushed herself up from the window seat and headed upstairs. Letting the water run until the bathroom was filled with steam, she stood in the spray, the warmth seeping into her muscles easing her sore back and feet. Closing her eyes, she relaxed, letting her mind wander. *Carlos.*

Squeezing the washcloth at her chest, she sent frothy, whipped cream bubbles and warm water cascading over her breasts. Her nipples tingled at the feel and she shivered. "Get a grip, Trina…he's just a guy," she mumbled, shaking herself out of her reverie. Somehow, she knew he was much more than that.

Pulling back the shower curtain, she stepped out of the tub and onto the cold tile. "Shit!" she cursed catching herself as she slid forward. She glanced at the floor and at the vanity. No bathmat and no towel. *No brains either*, she thought chastising herself. *Great. The one time in your life you go gaga over a guy, and you turn into a complete idiot.*

Trina dripped her way over to the closet. Rubbing her arms, she wrapped a thick cotton towel around her shoulders and dropped a mat to the floor. She wiggled her way back toward the shower, mopping up the wet mess as she went along.

After drying off, she slipped on a pair of fleece pajamas, and quickly ran a comb through her hair before climbing into bed. She burrowed deep under the covers, bringing her knees into her chest. Exhaustion clouded her thoughts, edging its way in until she felt herself go weightless. Carlos's image played across her mind as she let herself drift. She remembered the feel of his arms, how wonderful he smelled, and the memory of his kiss was her last conscious thought before sliding into her dreams.

***

Carlos made his way up First Avenue. With the exception of a few cabs trolling for after-hours strays, the streets were deserted. Even the traffic lights were cooperating and he flew up the east side of Manhattan with ease. He loved speed and the feel of the road falling away behind him. It centered him, centered his thoughts. After tonight, his thoughts were on one thing. *Trina*. In no time, he found himself in front of his own townhouse on E. 67th Street.

He parked the car and let himself in, throwing his keys on the hall credenza. He hung up his jacket and poured himself a drink, sitting in the dark to mull over the night's events. It took two weeks for their paths to cross again. A search for another pet had instead yielded possibilities. Possibilities he'd thought long dead. Who would have guessed?

Upstairs, some of the staff already stirred. He knew it was getting close to dawn, and they would be up and about soon, running errands and taking care of the things he needed accomplished during the day.

Half the household staff was on for day and the other half for night. Carlos had planned it that way so there was always someone around. It was the same way at the main house upstate, and it wasn't just so the family had people to service them. It provided another level of protection and a way to maintain the illusion of normalcy.

They weren't expecting him, but then again they had learned over the years to expect the unexpected when it came to him and his family.

Carlos frowned. His family. It was a given they were all going to be curious about Trina, especially since they all knew his history. However, it was too soon to think about that, and he would never bring an addition into their lives unless he was sure it was a perfect fit. It was too risky.

As for his not finding any new blood? Well, they all knew how particular he could be and besides, there were already enough pets to keep them happy and sated. Too many if you asked him, and Trina was someone he couldn't pass by. There was something more to her than just attraction. She could change everything for him. Again, *perhaps.*

The light snapped on in the living room followed by a startled "Oh!"

"Good morning, Rosa," Carlos said quietly.

"*Señor* Salazar! I'm sorry…I didn't know…I mean I didn't expect…" his housekeeper said, both embarrassed and a little flustered. After all this time, he knew she hated that the family could still catch her unawares. Like a bunch of mischievous kids, they loved to startle her.

Carlos smiled. He loved the old woman, but couldn't help laughing at her same reaction. "*Càlmase,* Rosa, it's okay. I was in the city late and didn't feel like driving back to the main house. Everything all right here?"

"Yes, sir. Mr. Julian is here as well. He went up to his room just a little while ago."

"Did he? Is he alone?"

Rosa pressed her lips together. "No. Melissa is with him. He told me not to make up a separate room for her, that she'd be spending the night…I mean, day…with him."

Carlos chuckled at Rosa's sniff of disapproval. She was very protective of them all, but for some reason Julian especially. He always suspected he reminded her in some way of the son she had lost many years ago, and Carlos gathered from her reaction that she didn't think very much of tonight's choice of companion.

"That's fine Rosa, *gracias*…and how was Julian tonight?" He couldn't help but bait her a little. He still loved to watch Rosa bluster and fuss over those she referred to as her boys.

Rosa took a small white cloth out of her apron pocket and began to clean the nonexistent dust from the sideboard. Carlos knew that was something she did when she had something on her mind. "He seemed fine, but you know him…like a child with a shiny new toy."

Carlos chuckled. "Okay, Little Mother, there's no need for that. Melissa is actually a very sweet girl, and Julian likes her very much. She's part of our family now, same as you…" He hesitated for a moment, not wanting to sound reproachful, but he knew he had to set things straight or Rosa would make Melissa's life miserable. "I hope she will be treated with the same respect you have always shown members of our household and that you and everyone else will do what you can to make her feel welcome. *Comprendes*?"

"Yes, sir, I'll make sure of it," she said with a nod, but the set of her mouth told him she wasn't happy about it.

"What's bothering you so much about this, Rosa? Is there something else?"

She hesitated a moment. "I…I don't want to make trouble, *Señor* Salazar, but I have to tell you I saw this same Melissa with Mr. Eric a few weeks ago, and now she's with Mr. Julian. I had never seen her before, and I thought it was nice that Mr. Eric finally found...someone," she hesitated again. "I don't want any fighting between my boys, *señor*, and nothing starts trouble between brothers like a woman."

A smile twitched at the corner of Carlos's mouth. "Ahh. I see," he said, trying to keep a straight face, not wanting to insult her. "Melissa only joined our family a short while ago and she has been staying at the country house. Eric was simply showing her the house here in town. I agree he should have introduced her to you properly, but you know Eric and how complicated he can be. I assure you she's not playing one brother against the other, so don't worry. She only has eyes for Julian, on that you have my word."

Rosa opened and closed her mouth a few times before she sniffed again, stuffing the cloth back in her pocket. "I understand and I'm sorry if I overstepped my boundaries, but you know how I feel about all of you," she said, making her way back to the door. Her eyes had been downcast and when she looked up they were wet.

Carlos felt his heart clench. In her own meddlesome way, she truly loved them all. "Not at all, Rosa, and you know how I appreciate the way you worry over us."

She straightened her shoulders and nodded, pulling herself up to her full height—all four feet, ten inches. "You are my family," she whispered. "I'll be in the kitchen if you need anything."

He chuckled quietly to himself as she left, closing the door behind her. Carlos knew the older woman was just following her maternal instincts, but he had to laugh. Who in their right mind felt maternal to a bunch of vampires? Rosa was one of a kind and they loved her for it.

He sighed and finished his drink before heading upstairs. It would be a while before he sought sleep.

Carlos walked into his room, and even without the noise from the staff's morning routine, he knew the sun had risen. Rosa had drawn the heavy blackout curtains in his bedroom closed.

Carlos stripped and walked into his bathroom and turned on the shower. He stood under the spray, letting the hot water cascade over his body. He closed his eyes and let the warmth soak through and tried to relax. But his mind kept wandering back to Trina.

Everything about her down to the sound of her voice drifted through his head—her scent, the way she laughed, and the fire that flashed at times in her eyes. The water from the shower flowed over his body as images of her flowed through his mind.

Memories of her lush curves taunted him—how her soft skin felt under his fingers, and the taste of her mouth. His body jerked in response and he felt himself grow hard.

He could still feel her body, how his hands had roamed over her hips and waist to her soft, full breast. He could still feel how it swelled and peaked under his caress.

He groaned and wrapped his hand around his shaft. Electric currents began to shiver down his spine and into his groin once again and he moved his hand in time with their pulse.

He leaned his forehead against the tile, the water pounding on his back as he jerked and exploded in his own hand. He turned and leaned his back against the wall, the water hitting his hard stomach and his sated but still sensitive member.

He stood there for a while, his head pounding even as his blood cooled. How long had it been since he had needed to self-satisfy? *Centuries*. So why now? He had any number of willing partners at his fingertips, eager ones who would be at his door in a matter of moments so he could satisfy both his body and his thirst. So what was wrong with him?

Isabel…Trina. There had to be a connection, or perhaps it was simply an eerie coincidence? Carlos shook his head. He didn't believe in coincidence. Things happened for a reason.

He finished rinsing off and got out of the shower. He put on a soft terry robe and towel dried his hair while his mind turned over possibilities. He propped pillows up against his headboard and sat down with the remote, hoping a bit of mindless channel surfing would lull his mind and relax him.

He turned on the television and started flipping through channels. He flipped to *A&E* only to find Cary Grant starring in *Arsenic and Old*

Lace. "Great," he muttered as he turned it off, tossing the remote to the side.

He put his hands behind his head and leaned back against the polished wood. *Isabel.* It had been nearly a century since he had given her more than a passing thought. Irritated, he took a deep breath and exhaled. Memories of Isabel were painful, conjuring images best left forgotten—images of home and family and of how it all ended. He leaned over and pulled opened the drawer to his nightstand. Inside he took out a black velvet box and ran his fingers over the soft fabric, lifting the lid. Inside was piece of yellowed lace. Unwrapping it gently, he stared at the tiny image preserved within, and bid the memories come.

Chapter 5

Valencia, Spain
November, 1737

The fire in the hearth burned low, its embers a flickering glow against the advancing dark. Esteban Salazar bent to stoke the flame, adding more logs and kindling until a new blaze sparked, filling the room with warmth and light. He stood up and turned toward his son as he brushed his hands against his soft black britches, the lines in his face etched deep with worry.

"This time it's too dangerous, Carlos," he warned. "I forbid you to go."

Carlos glanced up at his father. "I'm sorry you feel that way, but I'm going nonetheless," he answered as he continued to pack.

"If you won't think of your own safety, then by God, think of the rest of us. You must know of the sanctions against us because of your affiliations. Your mother and sister are no longer received, and now merchants whisper behind our backs. Our own servants are only too eager to stir the gossip."

Carlos just looked at his father as he crossed the room gathering his simple belongings. There would be no trappings of wealth on this journey.

"Pedro De la Cruz has rescinded his offer of marriage to your sister."

Carlos stopped. "Why? Surely it can't be because of me?" he asked incredulously.

"His reasons are innocuous, but we can't help but wonder. Your mother has taken to her bed, sickened over all of this," Esteban said, catching his son's eyes. "Carlos," he continued hesitantly, "you do realize you are already under suspicion, and that this time there is far more risk than ever before. For Christ's sake, boy, the whole family is being watched."

Carlos sighed. "Father, the whole of Europe sees us as intolerant barbarians. Surely, you must know that. The king's ministers may try to paint a rosy picture, but you know as well as I that their secret tribunals carry out the Inquisitor's work much in the same manner as they did more than two hundred years ago. Even the Holy See of Rome has abandoned us. It's wrong. It's become a witch-hunt."

"I agree with you, but it's become too dangerous to even think about openly voicing any opposition," Esteban said.

Carlos gestured his arms in vain. "I never meant for this to hurt you or our family. Nevertheless, what would you have me do? In the past, I've risked my life to help complete strangers, but now that it's someone I care about, you ask me not to? Antonio da Silva has been my friend since we were boys, since we met at school when he first came from Brazil. How can I in all good conscience not help him escape? Would you rather I leave him to the Inquisitor's guards?"

"Of course I don't want that, my son, but there has to be some other way."

"What you really mean is some other person."

"That accusation is not fair. Others of your group do not have as much to lose, or family that can be caught in the crossfire—and what of Isabel? Do you suppose she's happy that you care nothing about the risks you take, that you chance throwing your life away so easily? Her life? Do you suppose her family is happy with your actions? Your betrothal contract is precarious right now, Carlos, or don't you care?"

"Isabel understands, Father. I only wish you could as well."

Esteban shook his head. This was a difficult situation. He was proud of his son, of his bravery and righteous fire, but this was tantamount to suicide. The Inquisitor General and his minions showed no quarter in their tribunals, and God help anyone, Jew or Catholic, consigned to an auto de fe. It was a death sentence.

"Why couldn't Antonio leave well enough alone? He's a lawyer, and a good one. Did he have to add satirist to his name as well? His comedies aren't so funny now that a warrant has been posted for his arrest," Esteban added sadly. "Was being lauded at the *Carnivale de Cadiz* worth the price? He threw away his immunity as a member of the *Conversos* the minute he put pen to paper."

"I can't answer for him, Father. All I can do is try and help."

His father sighed and turned away. He stood looking at the fire, his shoulders hunched as if they carried the weight of the world.

Carlos laid a hand on his father's shoulder. "Do you honestly think I made this decision on a whim, that I could be so cavalier? I know the risks involved, but it was you who taught me to stand up for what is right so I could respect myself as a man. It's true it would be easier for me to stay, to just look the other way. But then how could I look at myself in the mirror every day?"

"I understand, I do, and I respect your decision. However, I am the head of this house and responsible for everyone in it. I must warn you, Carlos, as God as my witness, if this plan fails I will not let you ruin this family. I will disown you."

His father's voice cracked as he spoke, but Carlos could see the determination in his father's eyes. As much as it would pain him to do so, his words were no idle threat.

Their eyes met, but his steely reserve couldn't disguise the hurt behind them. He knew from this moment there was no turning back. He was at a crossroads and had to make a choice.

***

Carlos rode for a little more than a week. The journey was long and hard and the roads dangerous, testing his mettle at every turn. The constant threat of highwaymen and thieves made sleep somewhat easier said than done, and the heavy November rain made the roads nearly impassable. By the week's end, every step jarred his insides, his thighs burning with the effort of gripping the horse's flanks. It was as if nature itself was telling him to turn back. He stopped whenever exhaustion threatened, but otherwise kept moving.

The monotonous sound of the horse's pace and the loneliness of the road soon set his mind to wandering. The faces of his loved ones haunted him. The grim set of his father's mouth and his mother's tears were the last images he held of his family. His sister hadn't even come down to say goodbye, and the note his younger brother Pedro had sent from the university didn't exactly wish him Godspeed.

With a heavy heart, he made his goodbyes. For the first time doubt shadowed his mind with a sense of foreboding that it would be for the last time. But with each passing mile, it was Isabel's face that haunted him most.

"May God keep you safe and guide you back to my arms," she choked through her tears.

When he gently pulled away to take his leave, her hand caught his, and with sad eyes, she pressed her lace handkerchief into his palm. "So you won't forget what awaits your return."

Inside the finely starched linen was a tiny portrait. Carlos remembered the feel of the tiny brushstrokes beneath his fingers. The artist had captured Isabel's likeness perfectly, down to the soft dimples in her cheeks.

Moved by the simple gesture, Carlos kissed her deeply, surprised at how fervently she responded. Isabel was usually a shy slip of a girl. "I will keep it always," he murmured.

When he finally mounted his horse, their eyes met one last time. Isabel kissed her fingertips then touched the locket that lay at her breast. Inside were two other miniatures—one mirroring the image she had just given him, and the other his own likeness—two lovers forever joined in gold filigree. "As will I," she whispered, watching him ride away.

He rode now, his brow furrowed with memories. "My father is right," he mumbled to his horse as much as to himself. "I must be insane." The memory of Isabel's lips and the taste of her kiss left his groin thickening and he groaned, spurring his horse into a gallop. He rode stiffly for a while, trying to keep his thoughts on the task at hand. The Spanish port of Cadiz and his purpose for this journey were not far off.

***

Cadiz was renowned, known as the *Costa de la Luz*, the coast of light. The peninsula it rested on was beautiful, with sandy, sun-drenched beaches and swaying palms. It was an ancient city, comprised of narrow, winding alleys connecting a network of small plazas. Its busy harbor was a place where anything and anyone could be had—for a price.

It neared sunset as Carlos guided his horse through the dirty streets that lined the docks. Here the air was rank, despite the salt breeze off the water. It reeked of vice and menace. Finding the tavern where he was to make his inquiries, he liveried his horse and made his way there, determined now to be done with his mission and return home.

The tavern was dark. It stank of old wine and excrement and Carlos had to press Isabel's scented handkerchief to his nose like a pomander to keep from gagging. He found a table close to a meager fire in the back where the smell was not so bad, and sat down. He ordered a tankard of ale and some food and settled in, observing the comings and goings of the patrons while he ate.

As the evening wore on, the atmosphere of the inn shifted. Lively tempos poured from fiddlers and mandolin players and the tavern grew crowded with nighttime revelers. Prostitutes began their nightly circuit while dockworkers and seamen settled in to drink.

A small group of gypsies arrived and immediately set in circling the tables, dancing and selling fortunes for whatever coins the men threw. Their men folk settled themselves against the wall, while their children scurried around picking pockets and begging for food.

From the side of the room, a young dancer spied Carlos sitting alone, an easy target. She made her way to his table, her hips swaying and undulating in ways that held every man's attention. Her eyes were like jet, and her hair curled to her waist in the same shade of night. She laughed as she danced, her fingertips playing suggestively in the deep cleft between her breasts.

Carlos licked his lips, a familiar heaviness settling in his groin. He had been too long without a woman, and the memory of Isabel's kisses coupled with the gypsy's clear invitation left him aching with need.

A subtle nod was all it took to win her affections for the night, and uttering a silent act of contrition, Carlos reached into his pocket, the coins to seal the deal warm against his palm. Without warning, someone hoisted her onto another table, a pouch full of silver emptied at her feet. In a fit of giggles, she threw her arms around Carlos's rival, bending and preening as she gathered her treasure.

Carlos's chair scraped against the rough floor in noisy protest, but he was too late. The other man's face already reveled in her ample bosom. Irked, he sat down and drained his cup while bawdy laughter rang past him.

An older gypsy rounded the corner of his table with a small child in tow. Warming their hands at the fire, the little one peeked out to peer at him, her dirty face half hidden in the voluminous folds of the old woman's dress.

He smiled, offering her some of his bread and cheese. The child looked up, and at the old woman's nod, took the proffered food and ate greedily.

Pity pricked at his heart replacing his lust as he took in their forlorn state. Beckoning the old woman, he held out his hand. "Take this for yourself and the child," he said, handing her the coins in his pocket. "To buy food and whatever else you might need."

In the exchange his fingers brushed her palm and a sudden jolt surged through both their hands. Carlos jerked his hand away; his fingers burning as if he'd touched hot iron. But the old woman clutched at his hand, her bony fingers digging into his with a vise grip. "You must leave this place. Cursed evil waits, lurking not in the shadows, but in plain sight. It looks for blood, and yours is what it will want if you stay."

Her face was a mask of fear and her eyes held a terror he had never seen before. Shaken, he pushed her away. "Be gone! I don't believe in such superstitions."

The old woman gathered the child to her, her face stricken. Afraid, she turned to leave, but glanced back over her shoulder, her eyes pleading silently for him to do the same.

Carlos let out a breath and poured himself another drink. He didn't know how she did it, but the old woman unnerved him. However, he had no time to worry over superstitious notions. He had a task to complete.

By midnight, the tenor of the place had deteriorated, with as much blood spilled as wine. He was about to give up for the night, when those for whom he had waited finally arrived.

They were unmistakable. Most definitely seamen, but with a different air—not the seadogs and riffraff normally associated with life on the docks. Carlos knew them at a glance, with the captain fitting the description, down to his style of hat.

As the men took their seats, Carlos pushed himself up from his chair and made his way toward their table. The seaman to the left of the captain took out his pistol. Cocking it, he laid it on the table close to his hand, never taking his eyes off Carlos as he approached.

"May I buy you gentlemen each a draft?"

The captain nodded, a polite smile breaking his lips framing a set of stained if not intact teeth. "Well, my friend, I don't know about the gentlemen part, but you are certainly welcome to buy us a drink if you're so inclined."

With a nod, Carlos ordered a round for the table and sat down. No one said a word, as silent assessments were tallied on either side.

Drink in hand, the captain leaned forward, his eyes sharp. "So what brings you to Cadiz? It's obvious you're not a local lad. So my guess is that you want something."

Carlos did a quick scan of the tavern before leaning forward himself. In a low voice he explained what he looked to procure.

The captain leaned back in his chair, his eyes narrowing shrewdly. Under cautious scrutiny, Carlos met the man's gaze head on. "I know

I seem young, but I assure you this is not the first time I have arranged such matters. I am well aware of the risks not only to myself, but to you and your crew as well. I am more than willing to make it worth your while."

The captain took a deep breath. Lifting his tankard, he tilted it in Carlos's direction. "You can spare me the posturing, lad. I understand what you're asking. What I want to know is why—and don't try to tell me that it's for the greater good 'cause I'm not buying it. I didn't get where I am in this world by misjudging what's behind a man's eyes. I can see there's more to your story than you're willing to tell. Give me a better reason why I should risk my ship and my crew."

Carlos looked pointedly at the man, and with newfound respect began telling this stranger his story. The captain listened without interruption, and much to Carlos's surprise, it seemed in this instance honesty was the best policy. Loyalty, as it turned out, was valued more in the eyes of the captain when it came to a person's worth than all the money they could secure. The voyage to safety for Antonio and his family was set to sail from their home port of Valencia in less than a fortnight.

"If I may ask, where are you lodging tonight?" the captain asked, cutting a wedge of cheese.

"I planned to head back to the stables for a few hours' sleep before I ride. I want to return to Valencia as soon as possible. I leave at first light."

The captain chewed slowly as if considering his words. Knife in hand, he pointed it casually at Carlos. "I know this may sound presumptuous, but why don't you stay aboard with us? An extra set of strong shoulders is always welcome and as we're already headed your way…" The captain chuckled, driving the blade point down into his hunk of cheese. "Hell, I'll even let you stow your horse since it's only for a short time."

"I don't know. I've never worked a ship before."

"Nonsense. I wouldn't have agreed if we weren't set to make port in Valencia next week. Why travel overland when you can sail? And I promise we won't work you too hard. You'll have to share a bunk with one of my men, though, as we do have a passenger sailing with us. An Englishman, quiet bloke, keeps to himself."

"An Englishman? Isn't that a little odd, if not out and out dangerous, considering the political climate brewing these days? Many people feel another war with England is imminent. Our king is not well received in the courts of Europe, especially in regard to the topic of our recent conversation."

The captain shook his head. "No, he's a decent enough fellow from what I gather. Came with enough coin, that's for sure. He's been no bother, and from the look of things he seems to be tying up loose ends to some sort of landed property purchase along the sun coast. But enough about him. We set sail day after tomorrow. What do you say?"

***

Carlos walked along the deck as the sun hung low in the sky. The *Soledad* was a large galleon, with three decks and a substantial crew. They had made sail just as the captain promised, continuing in their journey from the Portuguese port town of Porto, named for its famous wine.

Commerce was the *Soledad's* main commission, and they were to transport barrels of Port wine to the French port of Marseilles for distribution throughout France before heading to Turkey. Valencia was to be a quick stop in between, where Carlos's journey would end and Antonio's would begin.

The gulls were keening loudly as the *Soledad* sailed quietly up the coast. Galleons were notoriously slow, the behemoths of the sea, but as the weather was fine no one seemed to mind the leisurely pace.

"Enjoying the air?" a strange voice asked from behind.

Carlos turned abruptly, a little startled. "Yes. I've been watching the gulls dive for their supper. It looks as though they've found a school of fish and have been feasting on it."

"You must be Carlos Salazar. I've heard the crew mention you were joining us for a short ride."

"Yes, and you must be the captain's English passenger."

The gentleman chuckled. "Robert Mayfield, at your service," he said with a flourish.

Both men shook hands and went back to watching the sunset on the horizon.

"Will you be joining us for dinner tonight?"

"No, unfortunately. Sea voyages leave my stomach rather temperamental, if you know what I mean, but I will gladly meet you for a drink in the salon afterward. It'll be nice to have someone new to chat with."

Carlos nodded. "I'd love to."

"Good. I look forward to it. Are you anxious to be home? I understand Valencia is your home port."

Carlos exhaled, leaning against the railing. "Yes. I have been away just a short time but it feels like forever."

"I gather you have family waiting for your return and by the look on your face, someone special as well, *hmmm*?" The stranger chuckled.

"That obvious?" Carlos laughed himself. "Yes, her name is Isabel."

"Ahh…."

"You don't look to be that much older than I. What, no special someone in your life?"

"Not for a very long time, my friend. In my world, companions are hard to…acquire," he replied.

Carlos nodded absently, puzzled by the man's odd choice of words. He took his leave, promising to meet him for a drink, but walking away he couldn't help but feel the man's eyes watching him.

He walked through the low-ceilinged corridor toward his room, passing the various mates as they went about the business of the ship. Passing the galley, he saw his bunkmate just about to leave. "On your way out?" Carlos asked, stepping aside to let the man pass.

"Yes, sir. I'm on duty in a little while. And just what mischief have you got to?"

Carlos chuckled. "I've been on deck. I just met the English gentleman. He seems a nice enough fellow."

"Maybe, but I don't know as he gives me the willies. I can't put my finger on it, but he does nonetheless."

Carlos just laughed as the mate shivered theatrically before making his way toward the upper deck.

***

Dinner had been pleasant, but as a storm brewed on the horizon, the captain called it an early night. He joked the sea was as fickle as a spoiled mistress, and he would need all hands at the ready if she decided to unleash her fury on them. The *Soledad* had made port that day, taking on more of its commissioned cargo, and no one was willing to leave it to chance.

The salon was dim as Carlos ducked to enter through the narrow doorway. Cigar smoke hung in the air like a thin fog. All manner of nautical devices and maps decorated the room. A few leather chairs surrounded a gaming table and a smaller one of mahogany housed a mother-of-pearl chess set.

"Do you play?" a voice asked from behind one of the high-backed chairs. Robert Mayfield stood in one smooth, fluid movement, a cloud of cigar smoke ringing his head. Tall and handsome, the man was dressed in a formal cutaway and silk waistcoat. He looked like royalty, and Carlos self-consciously fingered the frayed edge of his own travel worn frockcoat.

Dismissing the foolish feeling, Carlos replied. "Not very well, I'm sorry."

"Not to worry. How about a drink?"

"Thanks. Brandy, if you don't mind."

Carlos accepted the drink and sat down in the chair opposite Robert. "So you never said where you were sailing to. Are you going as far as Turkey with the good captain?"

"I don't actually have a destination in mind. I travel merely because it is something to do."

Carlos raised an eyebrow at his comment. "Something to do? I'm surprised. You don't strike me as someone who is idle. You have no affiliations that require your presence? No work or family responsibilities?"

"None to speak of..."

Carlos looked at the man over the rim of his glass as he sipped his drink. "That's unfortunate. You must live a very lonely existence if you have no attachments. I don't think I could ever be that alone."

"Oh, you'd be surprised at how easy it is."

"Easy, or just something you've become accustomed to?"

"*Hmmm.* That's a fair question. I never actually considered that possibility. Why don't you enlighten me? Give me the benefit of your life's story—tell me more about your affiliations and what motivates you to feel so 'attached', to use your term."

They spoke for a while and Carlos found himself telling the stranger all about Valencia and his life—about Isabel, and how his family disapproved of his self-imposed obligations. He spoke of feeling compelled to do so, as if it was fate.

"Yes, I know quite well what it feels like to be compelled. Like your very nature requires what it is you must do." He sounded weary, as if he carried a heavy burden with the way he spoke, and Carlos found himself wondering what kind of man the gentleman was.

"But, my boy, I find it makes life easier to just accept what fate has dealt us and acknowledge, even embrace our own nature. If you are compelled to do the things you do, no one should stop you. It's who you are."

Carlos shrugged. "Sometimes we must put aside our own desires and think of what is best for all involved, don't you agree?"

"No, unfortunately I don't. I, for one, don't see the wrong in seeking out that which you want and taking it. It's how I live my life."

"I'm sorry for you, then, but it explains why you are alone. One would need such a solitary existence in order to satisfy every whim without compromise, every desire."

"Yes...*hmmm.* It really comes down to just that, doesn't it? Desire..." Robert trailed off, but his eyes never left Carlos. His gaze grew in intensity and it seemed as if his eyes changed color, deepened as he continued to stare.

Carlos broke out in a sweat and his pulse began to race. His vision swam a bit and he stood up, gripping the chair for support. He couldn't fathom why he felt so frantic, why his heart pumped like he had been giving chase.

He looked up at Robert and saw the man's smirk, his nostrils flaring slightly like he could smell the tang of adrenaline coming off his body. The man got up from his seat in one swift motion and glided over to where Carlos stood frozen in place. He moved so fluidly that he almost seemed to float.

"Are you quite all right, my boy? You seem…flustered."

"I don't understand why, but I feel as if my blood is racing through my body."

Robert took a deep breath. "*Mmm,* it certainly is," he replied a little strangely.

"I'm sorry, but I think I need to lie down. If you will excuse me, I'm going to head back to my room."

"Of course. Would you like me to escort you?"

"No, thank you, I think I'll be fine once I get a bit of fresh air."

Carlos made his way to the door of the salon. As he stepped through, he glanced back over his shoulder to bid the man goodnight, only to find he had gone. Too lightheaded at that point to wonder how or why, he just stumbled across the deck toward the crew stairs, trying desperately not to fall overboard.

The room was empty when he finally got there. All regular crew were on duty because of the impending storm. Carlos unbuttoned his coat and shirt and threw them over the small cane chair in the corner of the tiny room. He splashed cold water on his face from the basin on the little wash table and stripped out of his remaining clothes and into a borrowed nightshirt.

He collapsed on his bunk and threw his arm over his head, not bothering with the bedclothes. His skin was clammy and he prayed he hadn't become ill. He lay there as the ship rocked gently, eventually lulling him into a dreamless sleep.

Carlos awoke with a start. Sitting bolt up in bed, he whirled his head around, disoriented, until he saw Robert sitting calmly in the cane chair staring at him again.

"Robert? What are you doing here? Has the storm hit?" Carlos asked his voice still a little sleep-muddled.

In the dim light, Robert's eyes seemed even darker, appearing distant, detached. He inhaled deeply. "You have no idea how your smell affects me."

Carlos's mouth fell open. "I insist you tell me what this is about! It's extremely ill-mannered, sir, and I demand an explanation!"

Robert approached the bed slowly, moving with a sinuous, predatory gait. He was in a state of semi-undress, with his ruffled dinner shirt unbuttoned to his waist. The hard muscled planes of his chest were smooth and his torso completely devoid of hair, at least until it met the undone buttons of his breeches sitting low on his hips. He licked his lips as he got closer, making Carlos acutely aware of his own vulnerability.

With a rush of anxiety coursing keenly through his body, Carlos moved quickly, clamoring out of the bunk into a defensive crouch, his nightshirt billowing out past his knees. All remnants of sleep had fled, and the menace he felt surrounding him was no leftover dream.

"Robert, I have no idea what you are about, but whatever your inclinations I assure you they are neither welcome nor reciprocated. You need to leave…now!" Carlos's eyes never left Robert. If the man didn't leave, he was ready to fight, and if necessary, to kill.

Suddenly Robert's face contorted. He lunged at Carlos, pinning him to the bunk. He became like some kind of animal, his jaws and teeth elongating and snarling, tearing at Carlos's nightshirt.

He reared up, his fangs sharp and glistening with blood as they tore into Carlos's throat. He tried to scream, but the only sound he could utter was the gurgling hiss of blood and air as it escaped through his ravaged flesh.

Carlos could hear the crunch of his bones and cartilage as Robert's teeth ripped through his neck. He could feel the blood pumping out of his veins, the warm, wet feel of it as it ran down his chest, coating his skin and the bed sheets as Robert gorged himself.

A blissful blackness settled on him and Carlos lost consciousness. The last thing he remembered was Robert telling him how this was only the beginning.

***

Carlos opened his eyes. He tried to move, but found he was too weak. He looked around disoriented, as panic welled up. Most of his memory was cloudy and vague except for one—the memory of teeth tearing into his flesh.

He was in a large bedroom, with carved stone walls hung with rich tapestries reminiscent of previous centuries. Heavy oak furniture surrounded a stone fireplace where a small fire burned low. Candles of different shapes and sizes adorned the heavy mantel, as well as the night table next to the large canopied bed where he lay, naked except for a sheet. The room looked as if readied in a hurry, and Carlos wondered where the hell he was.

There was a knock at the door, and without waiting for a response, a servant entered carrying a tray of food. He didn't say a word, just left the tray on the low table in front of the fire and left the room. Carlos tried to sit up, but fell back against the pillows. He had no idea how he came to be here or for how long.

"Hello? I need assistance! Anyone there?" he called out in a weak voice.

The door opened again and the same servant who had brought the food entered, followed by Robert Mayfield. The man was dressed unusually, in silken pants, loose fitting with a string waist, the kind Carlos had seen in books describing sultans of the east. Its matching robe fell in soft folds to his knees, and was completely open to the front. "I see you are finally awake. Are you hungry?" he asked nonchalantly, as if the scenario were perfectly normal.

"You! Where am I? How did I get here? I demand to know what you have done to me!"

"So many questions, and asked so rudely. I'm surprised at you, Carlos, and I thought you such a well-brought-up young man," Robert *tsked*, plucking a bunch of grapes from the tray.

"Robert, I warn you, I will kill you if you do not tell me what is happening here. I demand to know. I demand to be released."

"I'm afraid that I can't allow. Do you remember our brief conversation aboard the *Soledad*? The one regarding a solitary lifestyle? Well, you see, dear boy, I thought about all you said, about how lonely my existence must be, and I found I had to concede. So I've decided to make you my companion."

"You have no right to keep me here against my will!"

"Oh, well, there's the rub, my friend. That is where my concession to your way of thinking ends. I still very much live for my own wants, and what I want now is you."

"It's unnatural. I won't allow it!"

"Oh, my boy, haven't you figured it out yet? There is *nothing* about me that is *natural*," Robert sneered. His face contorted and he lunged for Carlos, pinning him down against the feather mattress. He sank his teeth into his throat, reopening his existing wounds.

"I have brought you home, Carlos. We are on the outskirts of Valencia," he said, sitting up and wiping his bloody mouth on his sleeve, laughing. "Aren't you grateful?"

Horrified, Carlos blanched struggling to sit up. "What are you?" he choked, but was too weak to do anything but gape.

"I am death…I am life," he said with a flourish. "As soon you will be also."

"I'll die first," Carlos answered, spitting in the man's face.

Robert just laughed, wiping the spittle from his cheek. "Oh yes…you'll die first all right, and it will be exquisite. Then you will be reborn to the same life I lead. We shall then see how well you can still exist with your…attachments, *hmmm*?" he taunted, fingering the tiny portrait of Isabel he drew from the pocket of his robe.

"No! You touch her and I'll kill you with my bare hands!"

Robert pursed his lips. "A possibility, if not an improbability. As that remains to be seen, it will be interesting to see just who kills whom, won't it?" he whispered, leaning over Carlos in a sick mockery of a lover's caress. He squinted, and an evil light filled his eyes

His tongue darted over the raw wounds puckering Carlos's bare chest, his hand plunging roughly between Carlos's legs. The young man cried out against his will, but Robert's voice held his body in thrall, a puppeteer jerking his manhood to attention, forcing his body to respond to his harsh ministration.

The tenor and timbre of his voice wielded some kind of power as he taunted, his fist wrapped tightly around Carlos's reluctant organ. "Full and thick, just the way I thought you would be." Shedding his clothes, Robert flipped Carlos onto his stomach, running the flat of his hand up the young man's back, pinning his shoulders to the bed. Forcing his hips up and back, he mercilessly drove his cold, hard member into Carlos's body, tearing at the man's core just as his teeth tore again at his throat.

Thrust after pitiless thrust, the vampire grunted and moaned while Carlos's mind screamed for the release of death. However, the young man's unwilling heart continued to pump precious blood into Robert's savage mouth. Powerless in body as well as in spirit, his life slipped soundlessly away while Robert stripped whatever remained of his soul.

Blackness poured into Carlos's sight and all was silent. Suddenly he was weightless, floating like vapor. He rose, watching with clarity as his body fell away beneath him, yet everything in the room remained as it was. Looking down, he could see himself still on the bed, immobilized as Robert continued to ravage his body.

Blood coated everything, every surface—Carlos's chest and back, his thighs and buttocks, and all the bedding. Robert's movements quickened, aided by the slick, crimson fluid until he shuddered, collapsing against Carlos's silent back.

Detached, Carlos watched Robert rest his cheek against his motionless shoulders in some sick parody of a lover's cuddle. He could hear the vampire murmur, curling his fingers through Carlos's limp and bloodied hair, but the words sounded muffled, as if heard at a distance.

Incredulous, Robert's face turned purple with rage. Sitting up, he grabbed Carlos's shoulders and flipped him onto his back, the blood-soaked bed protesting in a splatter of crimson. Cursing, the vampire shook Carlos's body, his eyes searching for some semblance of life. Carlos's head lolled to one side and Robert slapped the lifeless face, infuriated. With a snarl he tore into his own wrist, force-feeding his own blood past the silent body's pallid lips.

With a fierce jerk Carlos found himself falling. His eyes flew open and pain ripped through his body. Robert hissed in triumph, slashing at his own throat and forcing Carlos's face to the wound—urging him to drink, forcing him to swallow his blood.

Carlos struggled, twisting his face away until Robert's blood covered them both. He begged to die, for the solace it would bring, but Robert forced his face further into the hot liquid.

Choking, Carlos finally drank. The blood was like liquid fire, scoring his throat as he swallowed. He drank until he collapsed into unconsciousness.

***

Carlos heard voices as he drifted in murky confusion. He would wake shortly to a burning fever and each time given blood. He didn't know from whom or from where, but he gulped at it greedily before sinking back into oblivion.

He had no concept of time, only of the blood until he woke fully one evening to Robert sitting across from him as he had that night on the *Soledad*.

"Welcome back," he murmured, lips curving smugly in triumph. "And how do you feel?"

Carlos sat up. He looked around, taking in the room as if seeing it for the first time. He could see and hear everything with such clarity. A tiny brown spider sat in the corner of the window, and he listened to the whisper of its silk as it rushed from its body, watching its tiny mandibles move with such precision, weaving its web. He could hear the smoke from the fire as it wisped through the air, and the thoughts of the servants as they went about their duties in the house.

Carlos covered his ears, trying to muffle the sounds, as Robert laughed. "You'll get used to the noise. You'll learn how to separate the sounds and use them to your advantage when hunting."

"Thirsty." It was all Carlos could rasp in response.

"Of course, how thoughtless of me… I have brought you a present. Think of it as a sort of commencement gift to start your new life. You are now a dangerous predator, Carlos…in truth, the world's foremost. Moreover, my blood has made you strong. Oh, the adventures we will have!" he said, clapping his hands together. "Soon you will realize the world is full of prey just ready for the taking. You have no *attachments* any longer, save me as your maker. When I call you, you will come. When I want you, you will serve." His eyes blazed as he spoke.

Carlos growled, his eyes flashing. "If you have made me such a predator, what will stop me from making you my prey?"

"The laws of our kind forbid it, and the punishment for killing one's maker is death. That aside, my bloodline ascends from the oldest of our kind, each passing century adding to its strength. Unlike humans we do not grow feeble with age. We only grow stronger." He looked pointedly at Carlos. "I know what you are thinking, but I wouldn't bother if I were you. I am immortal and your sire."

Carlos scoffed. "Didn't you say we shall see who kills whom?"

"As a matter of fact I did," he said, his eyes narrowing. Robert glided across the room and pulled a thick silken cord next to the fireplace.

"Jeffrey!" he bellowed.

Almost immediately the chamber door opened. "You called, sir?" A timid man dressed in butler's attire answered. His eyes were downcast and it was obvious he was terrified.

"Bring my son his gift," Robert said imperiously, ignoring Carlos's raised eyebrow at the use of the term "son."

Carlos got up from the bed and began pacing, ignoring the sensual feel of his clothes against his sensitive skin. His new strength radiated from him and he ached with a maddening thirst. Pouring himself a snifter of brandy, he guzzled it down only to choke, sputtering like a child.

"Patience, my boy. You have to accept that you are no longer bound by human standards. Their paltry fare will no longer satisfy you, nor are you held to their perception of right and wrong."

Carlos sniffed the air. His eyes flashed as he turned toward the door. Robert chuckled from his perch across the room, his own eyes blazing with expectant lust, and he licked his lips in anticipation.

"Carlos? Carlos, where are you?" A female voice called from the hall. "You said he was here, you said he was ill. Which room is he in? I demand you show me!"

Jeffrey opened the door to the bedroom slowly, a young woman in tow. He turned quickly to her, hissing under his breath, "Run! If you value your life, *señorita,* run!"

"Jeffrey!" Robert snarled. "Bring her in or you die in her place!"

She ignored his warnings and pushed her way forward. "Where is he? Let me pass! I have no fear of illness..." The young woman's words stopped short in her throat.

"Carlos!" she croaked, her hand trembling at her mouth. With tears in her eyes she ran to him, only to stop short in terror as he turned.

Eyes blazing red, he inhaled, the scent of her blood and her fear driving him to near frenzy. She screamed and tried to run. He grabbed her by her hair and she fell against him crying, begging him to see her, to know her. But he was beyond comprehension, beyond caring.

A sound feral and untamed rumbled at the back of his gullet. He yanked her head sideways and licked her throat, savoring the feel of her pulse beneath his tongue. She struggled, screaming his name, fueling his frenzy till he savagely sank his fangs into her neck.

Her blood on his tongue pushed him over a precipice, beyond consciousness. He was primal, driven by pure instinct. The coppery liquid flowed down his throat like honeyed wine, quenching his burning thirst. It flooded his body and surged through sinew and bone, infusing him with strength and raw power. He wanted more, gorging himself till he heard her heart stutter.

When he finished, her limp body slid from his arms and slumped to the floor. Robert clapped in delight, his eyes gleaming. "A natural talent! Well done! Ha! You have proven my point without even knowing it—our kind has no need of attachments!"

Carlos was still leaning over the woman's lifeless form when he turned toward Robert. His mouth and chin dripped with red as the last of his bloodlust raced through his body. Cognizance slowly returned and he growled, "What are you prattling on about?"

"Attachments, my boy, or have you no recollection?"

Carlos continued to look at Robert, his eyes blazing even in his bewilderment as the man started to laugh. "You haven't a clue, do you? Look to the floor and see what I mean. I guess we know now who killed whom!" He threw his head back, laughing.

Carlos jerked his head around. He leaned over and quickly rolled the prone body onto its back. He smoothed the blood-spattered hair away from her face. *Isabel*! He stared in horror as her once beautiful eyes stared back at him lifeless and accusing. He had murdered her—had lusted for her blood, for her death—and took it without hesitation, without remorse.

He sank to his knees as memories of her flooded his mind, the sudden realization of what he had become too much for him to bear.

"She is of no consequence, my boy, a fleeting moment from your transitory human existence. You are an immortal, and she and all her kind are nothing more than sustenance. Remember that!" Robert's voice dripped with disdain as he watched Carlos's regret.

Carlos turned his head slowly. A black hatred filled his eyes. He had already murdered what he loved. Now there was nothing to stop him from murdering what he loathed.

Muscle and sinew tightened, vibrating beneath his skin, his fingernails pushing forward like sharpened claws. A grief-stricken roar broke from his throat, and in that moment Carlos understood what Robert meant when he said, "I am death."

His fangs slid down, their razor's edge slicing through still tender gums, and the taste of his own blood fed his rage. Numbness spread along his jaw and cheekbones as they contorted, reshaping his face to match his strange, new nature. He was predator and he had marked his prey. A hiss escaped his throat at the feral sensation, and his body tensed in anticipation. He lunged for Robert's throat, teeth bared and his hands like scythes.

Raising an eyebrow, the older vampire simply blurred to the side, effortlessly avoiding the assault. Carlos's head whipped around at the imperceptible movement. *How?* In the midst of his fury his mind churned and he skidded to a stop, colliding with the bookcase adjacent to the hearth.

Nostrils flaring, Carlos's chest heaved with the overwhelming scent of blood and sweat, a kaleidoscope of color and movement saturating his vision. In a tumble of wood and broken glass, he stood bracing himself against the soot stained bricks, a wave of vertigo setting his head to spinning. In his heightened state he gagged, bloody vomit rising into his throat.

Robert lounged unperturbed against a chair a few feet away, casually flicking splinters from his waistcoat. "Really, Carlos, anger is such a juvenile emotion, its impetus a feeding ground for a clumsy means of attack." Straightening his vest, he rose to standing, his movements like quicksilver, graceful yet cold.

"What's wrong, my boy? You don't look so well. Your new state of being giving you a bit of trouble? Well, I do suppose it could take a bit of getting used to. Perhaps you should give this plan of yours another think, eh? At least, until your senses stop reeling." His eyes narrowed, watching Carlos's hate flash white-hot. "No? More is the pity, then." Inclining his head, Robert stepped his foot back and bowed mockingly, his arms spread in invitation.

Gritting his teeth against the dizziness, Carlos wheeled around, but a swift backhand sent him crashing against the high four-poster bed, destroying the headboard and supporting posts.

"Can't you see your efforts are wasted? Accept what you are. I've made you a prince. Why do you insist on fighting me?" Kicking pillows and broken wood out of the way, Robert frowned at Carlos's inert form sprawled across the ruined bed, blood dripping from his ears from the impact.

Sidestepping the debris, the older vampire squatted at the foot of the broken bed beside Isabel's crumpled body to wait. Head cocked, he glanced sideways as the young vampire stirred, already healing from the blow.

"In time you'll learn to harness your power and anticipate an opponent's attack." Leaning forward, he ran his fingers along Isabel's pale cheek, dipping them into the blood pooled beneath her throat. "You'll also learn to be less hasty when you feed. Waste not, want not. Isn't that the saying?" he added, rubbing his fingertips together slowly.

Carlos half growled, half moaned his response, the ringing in his ears beginning to recede.

"Tell me you didn't relish the taste of her, the silky feel of her blood on your tongue, that you didn't crave more," Robert demanded, passing his fingers beneath his nose. The older vampire inhaled, his expression rapt as if savoring the bouquet of a fine wine. "So fresh, so young. Even cooled on the floor the scent makes me hunger."

Robert stood, his body uncoiling like a viper ready to strike. "You belong to me, Carlos. Your blood is mine," he said, licking Isabel's blood from his hand in a slow taunt. Wiping his fingers on his shirt, he stared pointedly at his progeny. "Concede, Carlos. You cannot kill me, so I suggest you end this silly game because I grow bored of it."

"Never!" Carlos snapped, exploding to his feet. The truth of his surreal reality bloomed cold and rigid in his mind. The life he knew was over. Stolen. But he'd be damned before handing over whatever life he had left. He charged Robert again, a piece of jagged wood clutched in his hand aiming straight for the vampire's heart.

A disgusted sound let loose from Robert's mouth. Launching himself at Carlos, he seized the younger vampire by the shoulders and threw him against the wall. Carlos crashed into what remained of the headboard, splitting it further down the middle.

"Such a disappointment," Robert uttered his tone both sulky and accusing. Grabbing Carlos by the hair, he dragged him away from the wall.

Listing to the side, Carlos's arms swung wildly, slashing at Robert's chest, but the older vampire simply spun him around, wrenching the makeshift stake from his hand. Air rushed from Carlos's lungs as his back hit Robert's chest like a stone wall, his spine and ribs reverberating with the impact.

Robert didn't flinch. In seconds he had Carlos in a headlock, his forearm crushing his throat like a walnut. With his free hand he pressed the jagged edge of the makeshift stake into the younger vampire's chest, piercing the flesh above his heart. "Lesson one. To dispatch a vampire, you must cut out its heart. Staking merely slows us down," Robert hissed.

Eyes bulging, Carlos's hands searched frantically to the front and sides for something to use, but found nothing. He gurgled as air escaped through crushed cartilage.

Dropping the stake, Robert continued pitilessly. "Lesson two. Decapitation. The head must also be completely severed." The older vampire squeezed tighter, this time fisting Carlos's hair, twisting his neck to almost breaking. Adding insult to injury, he whispered intimately, feathering kisses along Carlos's corded neck. "Otherwise, lover, we rise again."

With another bone-crunching squeeze Carlos's neck popped audibly. The realization he no longer required air hadn't yet dawned, and panic raced through his body as he tried in vain to draw breath. Forcing himself to relax he let go, concentrating instead on his new senses. Delving into his own mind he targeted speed and strength until they were all that encompassed him.

With Robert's arms still around his neck, Carlos reached up and over, grabbing him by the back of his collar. From the corner of his eye he saw the fractured edge of the bedpost, and centering all his strength and speed he dropped to one knee, flipping the older vampire onto the post's sharp, uneven tip.

In seconds, the serrated wood shredded Robert's torso, its bloody edge nailing him to the broken bed frame. Carlos's fingers pierced flesh and bone, his hands breaking open the older vampire's chest, exposing his cold, dead heart. Ripping it from its cavity he held it, bloody and black, dripping from one hand.

Stunned, Robert's eyes bulged in disbelief. But even as their light dimmed, they narrowed shrewdly, and a last evil smile spread across his lips. "I'll see you in hell, my boy."

Robert's head fell forward, but Carlos knew it wasn't finished. With a roar he pulled his hand back, and with a single strike ripped Robert's head from his shoulders.

What was left of him turned to ash, coating the room in a dirty, grey veneer. Isabel's portrait clattered to the floor from Robert's waistcoat, still hanging bloody and limp from the jagged post. Carlos's shoulders slumped in exhaustion as he bent to reclaim it. His body ached and his brain was numb, but his relief was short lived. Falling to his knees his mind chased the same thought. *Christ in heaven, what have I become?*

Blood and gore spattered every surface in the room. Desolate, he picked up Isabel's limp body and placed her gently on the broken bed. He wept as he tried to close the wound at her throat, falling to his knees again. He tried to pray for forgiveness, but was no longer sure God would hear his prayers.

He lay with his head on Isabel's cold hand, not sure what to do. The only other of his kind he knew lay dead by his hand. He calmed himself enough that he could once again distinguish the sounds coming from the house, and heard a distinct heartbeat loitering just outside the room. Jeffrey.

Carlos stood and turned toward the sound. "Jeffrey!" he yelled.

The manservant opened the door tentatively and choked at the horror in front of him. He cleared his throat, and in a strangled voice replied, "Yes, sir?"

"I need you to tell me everything you know about Robert, how he lived, and if there are any more of…of…his kind…around."

Jeffrey just nodded, seemingly afraid to open his mouth for fear of inciting whatever wrath had caused all this mayhem.

"Tell me, did Robert tell you of his plans?" Carlos swept his hand around the room. "Did you know that *Isa*—" His words cut off. He couldn't bring himself to say her name. "That the woman was attached to me?" he finished, his face heartbroken as he looked down at her.

Jeffrey shook his head quickly. "No, sir. I only surmised it when the lady was so concerned about finding you, about your welfare. It was then I guessed what Sir Robert had planned. He knew you wouldn't be able to control yourself."

"Thank you, Jeffrey," Carlos said softly as he knelt once again at the side of the bed. He wrapped his hand around Isabel's lifeless one and kissed it.

Stunned, Jeffrey stared at Carlos, watching him in his grief. In all the years Robert had been his master, he had never once seen him show any depth of emotion, only cruelty and self-indulgence. "Sir? There still may be a way to save your lady."

Carlos's head whipped around. "What do you mean?" he asked suspiciously.

Jeffrey shuffled back a little toward the door, his eyes widening in fear. "Forgive me, sir, but you would have to give her your blood," he said, wringing his hands.

Carlos pulled his lips back over his teeth and hissed. "What, and damn her to this same monstrous existence? She's better off dead," he snarled.

The poor man put his hands up in front of him and spoke swiftly. "That's not what I mean, sir. If she takes some of your blood, it might be enough to heal her."

Carlos climbed to his feet and took a few steps toward the man. "What do you mean *might* heal her?"

Jeffrey answered slowly, calmly, not wanting to give Carlos any reason to attack. He knew the man's humanity hung by a thread and didn't want to do or say anything to cause it to snap. "Please, sir. You asked me to tell you what I know and I know this—if there's even a spark of life within her, and she takes your blood, it will heal her enough that she might be able to survive on her own."

Carlos took a deep breath, not only to check his control, but to further evaluate the man's statement. He tasted the man's fear in the air and knew he spoke the truth. "Explain. How do you know all this?"

"Sir Robert," Jeffrey replied quietly, his eyes downcast. "I was a manservant in his father's house. Upon his death, everything, including the staff, transferred to Sir Robert. He had been gone for years, and when he returned to claim his inheritance we found him…much altered." Jeffrey hesitated, his face pallid as he spoke. "Of course no one knew for sure what had happened to Sir Robert, and though his proclivities were hushed, they were widely known amongst the staff. We lived in fear of him. One night his attentions turned toward me. I tried to run but…" Jeffrey's words froze, not sure whether to continue.

"Go on, Jeffrey, please. I will not harm you," Carlos encouraged.

Jeffrey cleared his throat, and when he spoke again his words were a mere whisper. "As punishment for refusing him, he nearly drained me, and when I was near death he forced me to take his blood. Only a few drops, not enough to cause a conversion. It took a while, but his blood allowed me to heal over time. I've been bound to him and to secrecy ever since. Until now."

Carlos looked at the man and felt pity. How many other lives had Robert ruined? How many others like himself had he made into living monsters?

"How long ago was this, Jeffrey?"

The poor man's hands shook as he wiped his brow. "The year of our Lord 1667. I was seventeen years old."

Carlos's face was blank for a moment as he took in the basic statement. The man in front of him seemed no older than Carlos's own father, but in fact was closer to ninety! If what he claimed was true, then not only could he save Isabel, but also give her the chance for a full life. *Perhaps God would hear him after all*. He prayed silently.

Carlos bent over Isabel and tenderly kissed her cold lips. He offered up another silent prayer that there was some spark of life left within her. He listened with his new hearing, trying to decipher any hint of a heartbeat, praying that God would grant him the strength to do what had to be done.

He slid his arms behind her neck and shoulders and lifted her slightly off the pillow. Her head fell back, plainly exposing her ravaged neck, and he swore.

Trying to move her as little as possible, he rested her head on his forearm and bit down lightly on his wrist. Jeffrey had warned him only a small amount of blood was required, and that too much would cause her conversion. He raised his hand above her mouth, and as the blood welled, it trickled into her mouth a little at a time.

Moments passed like hours and Carlos looked toward Jeffrey in frustration. "Be patient, sir. Her injuries are grave," the man answered nervously.

The vampire snarled at him in response, and the poor man backed himself against the wall.

The slow trickle ran over Isabel's chin and down toward her throat, mingling with what was left of her own blood. Carlos slid his finger over the tiny rivulet, and then brought it to his mouth, licking it clean. He jerked his head to the side, ashamed that even now, while trying to save what was left of Isabel's life—if there was anything left *to* save—the call of the blood was almost irresistible.

He turned to Jeffrey, who still cowered in the corner of the room. "Talk to me. Tell me what else you know about the life I now lead. Am I as alone as I feel?"

They talked as the minutes passed, each man glancing furtively to where Isabel lay motionless as stone while they spoke. Jeffrey told him all he knew about Robert and the life he led, but admitted his knowledge was limited to only what he had witnessed and overheard.

"Are there more like me?" Carlos asked, his voice a mere whisper.

"All I know is that Sir Robert did associate from time to time with others of his kind. He would throw amazing galas, dinner parties and invite all manner of guests. The next morning the staff would find…well, you can imagine what we found," he said, glancing around the room.

Carlos inhaled deeply and closed his eyes. "Then it's true—he made me into an inhuman monster," he murmured sadly.

They sat there in silence, the only sound the slow drip, drip of blood into Isabel's mouth. Suddenly Carlos's eyes snapped open. "Jeffrey, if this is successful, I will need you to bring Mistress Isabel home immediately. I cannot trust myself to be around her—or you, for that matter. When you leave here with her you must not return."

Jeffrey nodded. "Will you take my blood before I go?"

"Why in heaven's name would I do that?"

"So that if you ever need me you can find me. It will be the same with your lady. From now on you will always know where she is."

"Jeffrey, I have no idea what kind of monster I am. Terrible rage tears at my mind, while a gluttonous craving gnaws at my insides. The only thing keeping me from the blood in your veins is the woman in my arms, and my need to save her. You will leave, or you will die. It's as simple as that."

Carlos closed his eyes as he felt the thirst begin to rise. He gritted his teeth, concentrating instead on Isabel's pale face and blood-matted hair. Without realizing it he squeezed his fist, forcing more of his blood to flow into her mouth. As it gushed forward, Isabel's hands sprang up, clutching his wrist.

She fastened her mouth over the wound and sucked. She took long, deep pulls and Carlos could feel his blood rush from him. He growled low in his throat and felt his groin thicken. His sex grew more engorged with every drop she took.

He snatched back his wrist, sealing the wound with a swipe of his tongue as Isabel sagged against the pillow. Holding his wrist to his chest, he breathed raggedly, trying to regain his control. His body felt as if it were about to burst. He backed away from the bed and turned toward the windows. The realization this was the same kind of frenzy Robert had wrought on him left Carlos gulping for air. His chest constricted and his mind raced. This was to be what encompassed his new life: blood and sex, together with violence. He wanted to die.

Carlos swung his gaze back toward Isabel. He forced a deep breath and willed himself into control. At least some good would come of this horror. Isabel would live. She was weak, but she was alive. Her cheeks were still chalky, but they had lost the gray tinge of death, and the raw edges around the wound on her neck had somehow mended together.

Though far from healed, the scent of death no longer clung to her. Carlos instructed Jeffrey to fetch clean blankets from another room and to ready Robert's carriage for the ride into Valencia.

Isabel's eyes were closed, but Carlos knew she didn't sleep. He ran his fingers down her ashen cheek and her eyes fluttered open at their touch. "Carlos," she croaked her voice a weak whisper. "I thought I dreamed you…that I was dead."

"Shhh, Isabel, close your eyes. You need to rest," Carlos said, turning from her. He didn't trust himself to speak.

She looked at him, and even in her weakened state she knew he wasn't the same. "Are you an angel or a demon?"

"I don't know what I am anymore, but I know this—you are going to live and for that I will be forever grateful."

"Will I ever see you again?"

"No."

Isabel struggled to sit up. She reached for Carlos, pulling him down to her. "No, Carlos? Why? I don't understand!" She sobbed against him, her tears dripping to her breast as her blood had done earlier.

"Isabel, please. I can't tell you more because I don't even know myself. I will always love you, but my life as I knew it is over. What should have been between us is gone and can never be again."

She clutched him tighter to her breast. The scent of her this close and the thrum of her heart, even weak as it was, had his body trembling with thirst. Carlos had to turn his head as his incisors lengthened. Pressing his lips together, he fought the urge to tear into her flesh. His teeth pricked his bottom lip and the taste of his own blood was once again sharp on his tongue.

He breathed slowly, registering each breath as he clamped an iron fist around his control. When he felt sure, lifted her hand to his lips, kissing it before finishing what he had to say.

"This I vow: I will hear you if you call and I will come no matter where I am. With your last breath, I will kiss you and taste the true joys of your life. I will know then my own life had meaning in that I gave you the chance to live—even if I could not." With steely reserve he brushed her lips with his, sealing his promise.

The door to the bedroom opened and Jeffrey came in with blankets and a small bundle of clean clothes and some food. Gently he helped Isabel ready herself for her journey as Carlos stood at the window.

From the corner of his eye, he saw a faint glimmer of gold at the edge of the bed. He frowned as he bent to retrieve it. It was Isabel's locket. The once delicate ribbon used to fasten it around her neck was now torn and bloodstained. Scowling, he swiftly discarded the remnant, pulling a thick, silken cord from the tattered curtain and threading it through the delicate gold in its stead.

"We're ready to leave, sir," Jeffrey said, with Isabel safely ensconced in her blankets. "Will there be anything else before we leave?"

"Just this," he replied, fastening the locket around Isabel's neck where it belonged.

She reached up and touched it as she did just two weeks before. Two weeks. That was all it had been, and now it would be an eternity.

Jeffrey carried Isabel out. She turned and looked at Carlos one last time, her hand still on the locket. "I will keep it always," she whispered as they disappeared around the corner.

Carlos reached into his bloodstained shirt and held the tiny portrait against his chest, "As will I."

Chapter 6

Trina rolled over, her arm flung carelessly across her eyes as she breathed a contented sigh into the stillness of her room. Behind her eyes a familiar and longed-for scenario took shape once again. Even in her sleep she smiled as she took her first steps along the known narrow path, her eyes closed in anticipation. Somewhere in the back of her mind she had been afraid her dreams would cease now that she had met Carlos. But here she was again, as always, and her pulse raced as she moved quickly toward her spot by the water.

When she got to the pool she sat down on the same boulder and breathed in the fresh, clean air. She opened her eyes, expecting to find nothing but darkness, but instead had to shield her eyes from the blinding sun glittering off the water.

She blinked a few times as her eyes refocused. She could see! Everything was so beautiful, so vivid! She reached down to touch the soft down of the willow as it dipped into the water. It reminded her of a young girl's hair cascading into a soft pool. Smiling, she turned to take in her first view of the woods, trying to match the images with the familiar sounds that had surrounded her in the blackness.

Suddenly she was nervous. Would he still come? If she could see, did that mean things had changed? Trina couldn't help but wonder if meeting Carlos was the reason why tonight's dream was different.

Without warning she was on the other side of the pond, yet could still see herself sitting on the boulder, waiting. It was as if subliminal roles had changed and now she was outside herself, a spectator in her own dream.

She watched herself turn, startled by a noise from the forest, following as she saw herself stand and walk toward the trees. She smiled to herself, expecting to see Carlos step out of the darkness with his arms outstretched.

Suddenly the dream shifted and Trina was back in her body, but there was still someone watching her from across the pond. Shielding her eyes, Trina squinted. She could see the familiar woman standing there across the water, watching her as she had just done. Everything across the pond seemed a mirror image of where Trina stood, but something was wrong.

It was then she realized the woman across the water was her great-grandmother. For a moment Trina froze, stunned. Instead of an old woman, her great-grandmother was youthful and vibrant as she was in the pictures Trina had seen as a child.

Her great-grandmother laughed and held out her hand, but when Trina tried to move, she couldn't. She was frozen in place. From across the water she yelled to her for help, but her great-grandmother just shook her head and smiled. Turning toward the trees she laughed again, and the sound was like the tinkling of bells, flirtatious and playful, and it seemed a strange sound out of place and time.

A man stepped out from behind the trees, and his face was one Trina would recognize anywhere. *Carlos*. He walked with a seductive grace towards her great-grandmother, pulling her into a lover's embrace, stroking her hair and whispering to her.

Her great-grandmother whispered back, placing her hand lovingly on his cheek. From her distance in the dream Trina strained to hear, but couldn't.

She called to them but they seemed not to listen. Carlos slowly slid his hand around to cradle the back of her great-grandmother's head, gently running his fingers through her hair. He leaned down, and when he kissed her mouth she went limp in his arms.

Trina watched as he gently laid her on the ground. Her great-grandmother's face had changed. She was no longer the youthful beauty she had once been, but instead the old woman she was now—and she was dead.

Trina screamed and Carlos whirled to see her standing on the other side. He reached out his hand beckoning. He smiled calling to her, but just as she took a step toward the water's edge his face distorted, morphing into the face of a stranger. His smile was hard and cruel and she suddenly felt cold, tiny fingers of fear brushing across her skin. She turned and ran, tripping over roots and fallen branches, running in terror as if something followed close behind.

Trina woke in a sweat with her head pounding. Stumbling from her bed into the bathroom, she groped for the tap and splashed water on her face. Panting, she stood in the dark with her hands on the edge of the vanity. "What the hell was that?" she whispered, trying to catch her breath.

She stood there for a moment trying to shake herself back into reality. After drying her face, she opened the medicine cabinet and took two aspirin before she walked back to bed.

"Freaky, weird-ass dream." she said, and climbed back under her covers, mumbling about late nights and fried chicken. Tossing back and forth, she rearranged her pillows a few times, but knew there was no getting back to sleep.

Leaning over, Trina looked at the clock. Nine thirty a.m. She'd gotten only four hours of sleep. Flopping back onto her pillows, she stared at the ceiling. *Four hours.* If she didn't take a nap at some point this afternoon she would look like the bride of Frankenstein when Carlos came to pick her up this evening.

Carlos. She chewed on her bottom lip, and wondered what he'd think if she told him about her dream. *As if her life wasn't strange and tragic enough!* From the time she was very small she'd heard warnings of how their family was under some kind of curse. Her great-grandmother swore it was true, and even her great-grandfather, of whom she had only vague memories, had believed it too.

Trina's grandmother had lived with Nanita's crazy notions all her life, even after she married. When Trina's mother was born, the family had more or less broken all ties with the house in Gramercy Park. Trina could only remember seeing her great-grandparents a handful of times…until her great-grandfather's funeral. That was when everything changed.

She lay there and remembered how they all had flown in for the memorial service; her mother and grandmother barely speaking to her great-grandmother, and the hushed arguments that ensued over the next few days.

Trina could still remember peeking around the corner into the dining room, hearing her grandmother tell Nanita never to call or speak to them again. The woman stormed out of the room, leaving Nanita in tears. As far as Trina's family was concerned, that was the end of it, and they wasted no time leaving that very evening for the airport.

Trina closed her eyes remembering the sounds and smells of the accident. She remembered the screaming and the smell of burning fuel, and the horrible crushing sound of metal against metal—then nothing until she woke up in the hospital.

She was the only one who had survived the crash. Her great-grandmother came to collect her after that, and Trina had been with her ever since. She owed Nanita for everything. For her very life.

Trina squeezed her eyes shut squelching the queasy feeling that always accompanied her unpleasant memories. *Sleep. She needed sleep, not a memory lane minefield.* Sighing, she rolled over one last time and tried to coax whatever rest she could.

***

Trina yawned as she walked into the kitchen, the midmorning sun streaming through the windows making her squint. Dirty dishes and other remnants from yesterday's project, including the power drill, were still evident on the table and in the sink. Trina's shoulders slumped. *God what a mess.*

Eyes barely open, she pulled out the strongest Colombian blend she could find and filled the coffee pot. While it brewed, she cleared the table and emptied the sink, stacking everything into the dishwasher. The first few delicious wisps from the coffeepot tickled her nose, and she felt better immediately. She closed the door to the dishwasher, and with a half smile picked up the phone and dialed.

"Hello?"

"Good morning, Nanita. Did you have a good night?" Trina asked brightly, pouring herself a cup of coffee.

"Fine…and what about you? I didn't expect to hear from you this early. Didn't you work last night?"

"*Mmmhmm*. I worked a double shift."

"Covering for Susan, no doubt. You do realize she's taking advantage of you. I know she's your friend and all, but it's much too much." Nanita said with a bit of a sniff.

"No, Nani, she's not…not really. Besides, it's extra money and it's not like I had plans or anything."

"As usual," her great-grandmother pointed out. "I'm worried for you, Trina. You are too young to be alone so much."

"And *you* shouldn't worry so much. I'm fine." Trina could hear the familiar sounds of the old woman puttering around in her kitchen. "What are you doing? It's a little early in the day for you to be cooking. Besides, can't Jeannette help you with that?"

"Jeanette does enough. How was work last night? I hope you didn't get home too late."

"Work was…fine," Trina hedged, taking a sip of her coffee. "Nanita…I met someone last night."

"Oh, that's wonderful, *mi niña*!" she replied, a smile in her voice. "It's about time! Is he nice? I'm sure he's good-looking because I could practically hear you blush through the phone."

"Nani! Yes, he's nice as well as handsome, and I'm seeing him again tonight. He's picking me up around seven thirty," she said, wiping down the table. A million things buzzed through Trina's head that needed to get done before then, but talking with her great-grandmother made none of it seem important.

"Hey, why don't we do something together today?" she asked, flipping the dishtowel over her shoulder. "How about going to the salon like we used to? You know, hair… nails…the works?"

The old lady just chuckled. "Trina, my days of pampered beauty are long gone, but you go ahead. You're the one with the big date."

"Come on, please? It'll be fun just the two of us. Between my school and work we haven't had a lot of time together lately," she coaxed, trying not to let the guilt she felt about her moving her to assisted living bleed over into her voice.

Nanita laughed. "Oh, *mi niña,* you keep me young! Okay, but nothing too fancy."

"Great! I'll call for an appointment and pick you up in a little while," Trina said, pouring more coffee into her cup, actually looking forward to a day off for once.

***

Trina held the front door open for her great-grandmother, laughing as she brought in the shopping bags. "Nani, you should be ashamed of yourself. That poor hairdresser had no idea what to make of you!"

"Trina, I may be old, but I'm not dead. Besides, he knew I was just kidding."

"By the look on his face, I wouldn't be so sure about that. Thank God he didn't have a pair of scissors in his hand at the time! And just where did you learn that move anyway? What movies are they showing in the dayroom here…porn? The way he jumped when you slid your hand around his thigh, I thought he'd hit the ceiling!" Trina laughed so hard she had to wipe tears from her eyes.

"What? Do you really think your generation invented sex? I've been around a long time and your great-grandfather, God rest his soul—"

"Oh, no! Nanita…stop," Trina said, waving her hands in front of her. "Let's not go there, okay? I can't. My ears will start to bleed."

Striking a pose, Nanita put her hands on her hips. "Well, if you ever want to know, you know who to ask," she said with a snap of her fingers before sauntering down the hall toward her apartment.

After she left, Trina laughed, thinking that maybe she should take her great-grandmother out more often. They'd hit Macy's and about ten other stores until she found the perfect dress for tonight. Nanita had more energy than she did this afternoon, practically racing from rack to rack and store to store until they found the perfect outfit.

No one had taste like her Nanita. She always knew exactly what worked and what didn't. Trina took the beautiful copper dress out of the bag and held it up in front of her. It was perfect. The color showed off the honey highlights in both her hair and her skin and skimmed her every curve. The shoes she found to match were slinky, with spiked heels and little amber stones on the straps.

She laid the dress carefully on the bed and prepared to get in the shower. She'd have to hurry if she was to going to be ready in time. The phone rang, and for a moment she panicked that it was Carlos calling to cancel, but caller I.D. said it was the club. "Hello?" she answered brightly.

"Trina. Good, I'm glad I caught you. Can you come in tonight for a little while? Susan can't get here till later and I need someone to help me set up for the night. It won't take that long, I promise," her boss Rick said in a cajoling tone.

"I can't, Rick. I have a date. He's picking me up at seven thirty. Can't you get anyone else to help?"

"I guess I could try to see if Louie could come in till Susan gets here, but I still need you to stop by. I need your keys to the wine cellar. Mine have gone missing again and you're the only one with another set. Can you drop them by?"

Chewing on her lip, Trina mentally figured time. If she went in now, she could give Rick a hand so she wouldn't owe him for cutting out early the night before. But she'd have to get in touch with Carlos and tell him to pick her up there instead of here at the house.

"Tell you what. I was just jumping in the shower, but I'll bring you the keys and give you a hand for a bit. I can bring my clothes with me and change there for my date. That's if I can get in touch with Carlos and tell him there's been a change of plan. Can I call you back?"

"That would be great, because I know Louie can't get here till around nine. If you can give me a hand till, say, eight, I can handle the rest on my own till he gets in. You have no idea how big a solid this is, and trust me, I won't forget."

She hung up the phone and stood there for a moment. "You are nothing more than giant marshmallow, Trina Markham. A total pushover," she said aloud. Shaking her head, she dialed Carlos's cell number.

Chapter 7

Carlos hadn't gotten to bed until almost noon. Even then he tossed and turned, with images from his past drifting in and out of his consciousness, filling his dreams with unrest.

It wasn't until late in the afternoon that he finally fell into an exhausted slumber. He managed about two hours of real sleep before the noise from Julian's adjoining bedroom woke him completely.

Carlos cocked his head, watching his solid, oak armoire shake in time with the rhythmic pounding coming from the wall directly behind it. *Julian could use a few lessons in propriety and discretion,* he thought wearily. No doubt, the whole house was now privy to the many interesting, if not slightly pornographic sound effects, courtesy of his brother's sunset romp.

Carlos sat up and slid his legs over the edge of the bed. Even from behind closed doors he could smell the residual scent of Melissa's blood coming from Julian's room, and his teeth tingled. He had gotten so caught up with Trina the night before that he hadn't thought to hunt. At his age he could literally go for weeks without feeding, but for some reason Trina had stirred his instincts.

He stood up and stretched. Walking over to the blackout curtains, he pushed them aside, gazing out at the red haze of the setting sun still visible on the horizon. It would soon be twilight. The evening star glowed, the sky turning shades of crimson on its way across the spectrum of light toward indigo, and the inevitable blackness of night.

He loved this time of day almost as much as he loved the dawn with its streaks of pink and gold. In these two moments everyday, he held his breath at the profound nature of the universe, when the entire world could actually see time advancing in a blaze of color. It was in these moments that he felt sure there was some reason for his existence, some purpose to the course of his life. At other times, not so much.

Carlos took a deep breath. The house was quiet, with one very irreverent exception, and Carlos chuckled to himself as he picked up one of his shoes and threw at the far wall. He could hear Julian's booming laughter in response to its indignant thud, but just the same the noise quieted soon afterward.

In the meantime, the rest of the house would soon be waking for the night. He slipped on a pair of jeans and a T-shirt and went into the bathroom to brush his teeth and wash his face before making his way downstairs. He couldn't help but chuckle at what Hollywood would make out of vampires practicing oral hygiene.

The grandfather clock chimed as Carlos stepped onto the landing. Three bells—three-quarters past the hour. It was five forty-five, sunset exactly. The day shift ended at six o'clock and the staff would most likely be finishing up with dinner.

Barefoot, he hurried the rest of the way down the stairs to catch them while they were still in the kitchen. He liked to sit with them and hear the events of their day, mediating any issues that arose while he slept. Rosa usually handled it all for him with the precision of a five-star general, and he chuckled at the thought of his little *Patrona*. But he liked for his staff to know he was available to them as well.

As he approached, Carlos paused for a moment in the hall just outside the kitchen. He loved the sound of their camaraderie and he waited, drinking in the pleasant hum from behind the closed door.

"Did you hear the noises coming from Mr. Julian's room? *Madonna!* That boy either broke the bed this time or broke that poor girl's back!" their chauffeur, Jack, said laughing as he slapped the table.

Michael, the day valet, chuckled. "I know! I was preparing Mr. Trevor's and Miss Margot's room for this evening when I heard the commotion. They're coming in to see a show, but if you ask me they might want to stick around for the fireworks when *el Jefe* gets a hold of Mr. Julian! The whole house was a rockin' and a rollin', if you know what I mean. If it wasn't for Miss Melissa's laughter I would have thought—"

"That's enough!" Rosa yelled, cutting Michael off mid-sentence. "Mr. Julian may be capable of many things but he'd no sooner harm a hair on Miss Melissa's head then he would on any of you. He's much taken with her, if you must know," she sniffed.

Carlos had to stifle a laugh. Rosa might be one to complain to him about Julian, or any of them for that matter, but she certainly kept the others in line when it came to household gossip.

Without preamble he walked straight into the kitchen and both men nearly choked on their laughter as he stepped up to Rosa and gave her a peck on the cheek. *"Buenas noches, Patronita,"* Carlos said with a smile as he ran one finger down her plump cheek. "And how was your day?"

Rosa actually giggled. "Fine, Señor Salazar. I'm sorry for all the noise this evening," she trailed off, blushing beet red to her ears.

"Don't worry, Rosa. I heard them clearly myself and I agree they should be a little less obvious, no? I will speak to both Julian and Melissa when they come downstairs."

"That's if they can still walk." Jack snickered under his breath.

"Jack!" Rosa gasped at his impertinence.

Carlos just laughed. "That remains to be seen, my friend," he said with one eyebrow raised as he clapped the man on his shoulder. "So," he said, turning toward Michael, *"el Jefe,* huh?"

The man spewed his coffee across the table and down his shirt, coughing and sputtering as he tried to breathe. Jack just burst out laughing as he got up to help his coworker, but he couldn't help his guilty expression when he turned toward Carlos. "We meant it with all due respect, Señor Salazar," he said sheepishly as he continued to pound on his friend's back.

Carlos just winked at the two men, then turned toward Rosa who scowled at the miscreants. "Coffee ready?" he asked lightly.

"I just made a fresh pot. Sit and I'll get you a cup," she clucked and shooed him into a chair at the table before turning to glare at the other two still collecting themselves.

"Don't you two have something else you need to do before you leave for the day?" she asked with her arms crossed in front of her chest. Scrambling out of their chairs, they both mumbled affirmatively and quickly made their goodbyes.

Rosa just *hmmphed*, her mouth pressed together in a thin line as she poured Carlos his coffee. "Idiots," she muttered under her breath.

Carlos had to press his own lips together to stop himself from laughing as she handed him a mug. "Here you go. Just the way you like it, black and scalding hot," she said with a nod.

He blew across the rim, sending the steam curling outward over his hands. He glanced at the clock on the stove. It was getting late. "Rosa, did anyone else come into town with Julian, or was he alone with Melissa?" Since he hadn't fed, the thought of being in close proximity with Trina later on made him a little edgy. He'd have to hurry if he needed to hunt before leaving to pick her up.

"Yes, sir. Amanda and Tommy came in with him, but they're still asleep. Do you want me to wake them?"

"Not just yet, but yes. Give them another half hour and then send Amanda up to my room."

Rosa nodded as she turned back toward the counter to finish cleaning up. She dug in her apron for a handkerchief and wiped her mouth in agitation. Though they were clear as day, there was no need for Carlos to read her thoughts to know her misgivings. She was well aware of what went on with her boys and she loved them all regardless, but she'd never get used to the idea no matter how long she was with them.

At least they're kind, she thought, shivering involuntarily at what she knew they could be, and silently thanked God they chose to be otherwise.

Carlos's hand slid onto her shoulder. "You know that you and anyone who serves this house will never have to worry…ever. In this family, loyalty is always repaid with loyalty."

Rosa nodded silently and looked at him over her shoulder. She never spoke of it—had never even hinted about the nocturnal nature of the house—but her one look told him she felt compelled to now.

"Señor, I don't pretend to know what reasons God had in bestowing such a fate on you," she whispered, covering his hand with her own. "But I know in my heart it must of been part of his plan, and that it was because of how good a man you must have been all those years ago. But know this, you are *still* a good man, Carlos, and God has not forsaken you. Be happy in your life."

She'd never called him by his Christian name before, and he had to close his eyes against the blood tears that threatened. He cleared his throat and squeezed her shoulder gently. "How can I be otherwise when you're around, *Patronita*?" he said, and he smacked her bottom. He then quickly picked up his coffee and headed back to his room.

Carlos was just coming out of the shower when he heard a soft knock on his door. He shook his hair, sending droplets everywhere and wrapped a towel around his waist. "It's unlocked," he called as he ran his fingers through his wet hair.

He stepped out of the bathroom to see Amanda standing by the door, looking a little awkward. In the past Carlos had never sent for her, or anyone else for that matter, as he preferred the anonymity of the hunt.

She stood there in a plain cotton T-shirt and jeans, playing with the colored beads she had braided into her long hair, and her fidgeting reminded Carlos of just how young she was.

Both Amanda and Tommy were just barely eighteen and had been with the family for a little more than a year. Carlos remembered how he had found them huddled together under one of the Westside overpasses. Gang members had forced Tommy to his knees, making him watch as they raped and beat Amanda, leaving her for dead. Taunted and beaten himself, the thugs forced him to beg for his life before they finally slit his throat. He left a trail of blood from where he had fallen, to where he dragged himself to lay by Amanda's side.

They were both runaways, kids that somehow bonded together as they each tried to survive the cruelties of New York's underbelly.

They had clung to each other as they scraped to get by, and would have clung to each other in death if it weren't for Carlos.

He found them lying there as he hunted among the dregs, and his heightened senses told him they were still alive, if just barely. Giving them just enough of his blood to heal them sufficiently to move, he brought them to his home, where Rosa took over. She nursed them until they were both healthy and thriving.

It was then Carlos had given them a choice. They could both stay with him and be part of his family or they could leave.

Neither had a home to return to, and neither wanted to go back to the streets. After falling prey to the real monsters of this world they were more than happy to accept Carlos's offer. Understanding exactly what he required of them, they both swore blood oaths to keep the family's secrets and moved in permanently.

Carlos locked eyes with Amanda and beckoned her. She approached him, tentatively at first, but when he flashed a beguiling smile, she relaxed. She went to him, immediately wrapping her long, thin arms around his neck. Lifting onto her tiptoes, she ran her tongue over Carlos's bottom lip and pressed herself against him.

Reaching up he lightly took hold of her wrists and brought them down, holding them gently in front of him. "No, *mija,* that won't be required of you tonight. I need you to satisfy a different craving," he said, his gaze intensifying.

Amanda's pupils dilated at once as Carlos cradled the back of her neck. Gently he tilted her head to one side, his fingers a feather's touch against her skin. He could feel the throb of her pulse as he brushed her soft hair away from her throat, feeling its pace quicken beneath his hand.

His head pounded in time with her skittering pulse and his vision turned red. His fangs descended and with a hoarse moan, he pierced the delicate flesh of her throat without pause. He had waited too long to feed and knew he was being less than gentle.

Amanda cried out as his fangs slid beneath her skin into her vein, and he immediately waved his hand across her line of sight. She slumped in his arms, spelled and supple.

He took long pulls from her neck, breathing in the warm scent from her skin. He could taste her emotions in the back of his throat as the hot, coppery liquid flooded his mouth. Her contentment gave her blood a special sweetness, and for that, Carlos was grateful.

Too many times when hunting the emotions he tasted were so saturated with vice that he felt it would poison what was left of his soul. The fact that Amanda's emotions showed her to be happy was a miracle indeed, and he felt his spirits lighten even as he took her blood.

Carlos felt Amanda shiver as he withdrew his fangs. A tiny drop of blood trickled slowly toward her collarbone. He caught it with the tip of his tongue, rasping upward toward the bite marks to cleanse and stop the bleeding.

She was still in thrall, so he picked her up and laid her gently on his bed. She looked so small on its expanse. He gently ran his finger over her soft cheek, remembering how at first, neither she nor Tommy had any memory of him or how they had gotten to the house. Memories of their ordeal were sketchy at best, as happens with victims of trauma, but their nightmares were very real. It had taken more than just Carlos's gifts to dull their memories effectively enough to give them some peace. It had been a collective family effort.

With his fingernail he pricked his wrist and bid her take a few drops to help heal and replenish her. He watched as the marks on her throat closed, healing instantly.

Carlos gently straightened her clothes before waking her from her trance. Her eyes fluttered open and she sat up. "Carlos?" she asked, a little puzzled.

Carlos brushed the hair out of her eyes and kissed her forehead. "You can go back downstairs, *mija.* Tell Rosa I said for her to make you something to eat. She'll know what to give you to keep up your strength," he said, and took her hand to help her off the bed.

She was a little wobbly on her feet, but had no memory of what had just passed between them. Carlos nodded to her as she left before he turned to look at the clock on his nightstand. Seven p.m.—exactly a half hour till he'd see Trina.

Perhaps it was the fresh blood coursing through his body, but an image of her in full arousal, with her head back and her lips wet and swollen passed through his mind. His cock hardened as he remembered the silk of her skin and the feel of her pulse beneath his fingers.

An unusual pressure built behind his ribs, and the sensation was so alien he pressed his palm to his chest. Vampires didn't suffer cardiac episodes, but his blood pumped through his veins like a fever, and the burn was exquisite.

***

Carlos pulled out onto the street. His Jag purred like a well-fed cat as he made his way over to Park Avenue. He loved the feel of the car's horsepower, and he revved the engine at the light before merging into the southbound lane. He had expected some residual rush-hour traffic, but the roads were uncommonly clear for this time of day. It was as if the night was already setting itself up to fall exactly where he wanted it.

His thoughts centered on Trina. He gripped the steering wheel and licked his lips. If he had a pulse it would be ratcheting up at this point, and he ran his tongue over the edge of his teeth. They tingled in response, and he chuckled. A vampire's equivalent to an adrenaline rush.

He couldn't explain why, but Trina tripped every predatory instinct he had. Well sated, Carlos was confident his instincts would stay muted tonight. At least he hoped.

Impatient for this evening since he had dropped Trina off right before dawn, he let his thoughts drift. She had called earlier and the sound of her voice only increased his anticipation.

"Carlos? It's Trina. I hope I'm not catching you too late but there's been a change of plan," she said quickly.

Carlos frowned. "What kind of change? Are you all right?"

"I'm fine. It's just I need you to pick me up at the club instead of at my house. Rick needs me to give him a hand for a little while. He couldn't get anyone else on such short notice, and since I felt a bit guilty about skipping out early last night, I couldn't say no. I'm bringing a change of clothes with me so I'll be ready to go when you get there. I just wanted to call to make sure it was fine with you."

Carlos laughed. Trina hadn't stopped for breath once in her nervous explanation. "Of course I can meet you there. Would you rather I wait in the car until you're finished or should I come in?"

Trina laughed in relief. "Either. I'll see you a little later, then," she said happily and hung up.

The mere sound of her voice sent a jolt straight into his groin, and the reaction amazed him. At first he attributed it to his long-overdue thirst, but he had just fed, satiating himself to the point of sloshing. Yet his craving for her hadn't subsided.

He pulled up in front of Avalon and cut the engine. He sent his senses out, listening to the sounds of the different heartbeats inside and knew hers instinctively. He got out of the car and took the front steps of the club two at a time.

He knew exactly where she was inside, and headed straight for the stairs marked "private" when suddenly he stopped. He couldn't just charge down the stairs after her, even though that's what his body urged him to do. If he did, he'd be hard pressed to explain. So instead, he took a deep breath and sat down at one of the tables near the entrance to wait.

Someone had turned on the music, and even with its volume he could hear Trina coming up the stairs. He turned toward the door just as she pushed it open. She had two bottles in her hand and a big smile on her face at seeing him waiting for her.

"Carlos!" she said, as she hurried over to where he sat. "No one told me you were here. Have you been waiting long?" She gave him a hug as he stood to greet her.

He inhaled, discreetly taking in her scent. Her skin smelled of honeysuckle and vanilla, and her own natural musk beneath it made it a heady perfume. He closed his eyes for a moment and let it linger on the back of his tongue. "Not to worry, I just got here," he said lightly, hiding the effect she had on him.

She smiled, lifting the bottles. "For later," Trina said with a wink. "Rick felt guilty about making me come in tonight so he gave us these." She put the bottles on the table and ran a hand through her hair.

His gaze drifted past her right shoulder as Rick and Louie came up from the basement carrying cases of beer. She followed his gaze, then looked back at him. "I'll only be a minute. I just need to let them know you're here and change out of these grubby clothes so we can get going," she said, leaning in to kiss his cheek. His hand brushed her lower back, and though his touch was light, his fingers circled her skin with the promise of more.

She turned, and with the way she moved in her jeans, it was as if they had been made for her, hugging her rounded bottom and highlighting her narrow waist.

If that's grubby, then I'm in trouble, he mused as he watched her walk away.

Carlos picked up one of the bottles she had left on the table. Conundrum. It was a pretty good California white, and considering the name, it was both apropos and ironic.

Trina emerged about ten minutes later. Carlos looked up from his BlackBerry and froze. She was breathtaking. Her dress flowed around her body just skimming the surface of her skin. It shimmered in different tones of copper; catching the light and making her skin shimmer as it floated about her. Every smooth, full curve was accentuated, sensual yet graceful, as if held in a silken dance.

"Trina, you are beautiful," he said as he got up and crossed the floor. He took her hand and turned it over, kissing her palm. It was an old world gesture, courtly, yet he felt her shiver, and the flush of immediate arousal stained her cheeks.

A beautiful, dusky rose spread across her skin. "Thank you," she said, a little embarrassed.

Carlos helped her on with her coat and then took her arm. They walked toward the front entrance. "Night, Louie. Night, Rick," she said, as they passed the two men stocking the side bar.

"So, where are we going?" she asked, tilting her head to look at Carlos. Her eyes swept the stairs to the club and then back again, and her lips curled in a secret smile.

Carlos caught her look of *déjà vu*. "I know. It seems like we were just here, doesn't it?" he teased.

"That's because we were," she said, her smile widening. "It's funny. I've known you less than seventy-two hours but I feel like I've known you forever."

Carlos didn't answer, but just looked at her meaningfully. *Forever,* he thought. *You have no idea.*

He unlocked the car doors and they both got in. Fastening her seatbelt, Trina glanced over at Carlos. "Are you hungry?"

He raised an eyebrow and gave her a seductive half smile. "Depends," he said. "What did you have in mind?"

Trina blushed again. "I meant dinner, funny guy. I thought you might not have eaten since our plans had changed," she shot back, palm up in mock defense.

Carlos laughed. "I'm sorry, I'm just teasing. But you walked right into that one and I couldn't resist. No, I'm not hungry right now, but thanks for asking. You?"

"I'm fine right now, too. Rick takes good care of me. He made sure to order in sushi for me since he knows I love it. He comes off like a jerk sometimes, but he can be very considerate—especially when he wants something." Trina added, folding her arms.

Carlos frowned a bit, wondering what else Rick could want from her. "Has he been your boss for very long?

"Since I started at the club. In fact, he was the one who hired me. At the beginning, he wanted something other than friendship, but I let him know that was out of the question. Besides the fact that he's my boss, I just never felt that kind of vibe with him. He's cool with it, though."

Carlos wasn't so sure, and made a mental note to keep an eye on her supposed good friend.

"So you haven't told me where we're going yet," Trina said, unfolding her arms and putting her hands in her lap.

Her scent told him her nerves were on overdrive, and her fidgeting made it even more obvious. Carlos reached over and took one of her hands in his. "We are headed to the Metropolitan Museum of Art. They are having a special exhibit of Spanish art that spans from around the time of the renaissance up to modern day. I thought you'd enjoy it. There's a cocktail party as well. Perhaps after that, we could head north to a favorite restaurant of mine. It's just a hole in the wall, but the food is superb."

"Sounds great. I've always enjoyed the Met. I actually worked as an assistant in the Restoration Department while I was an undergrad. I even entertained the idea of becoming an art anthropologist at one point. I thought it would let me combine my two great loves, art and science."

"So what changed your mind?"

"My great-grandmother. Remember I told you my family was crazy?" Trina looked at him for a moment and when he nodded, she continued. "Over the years her obsessions have driven my family apart. Don't get me wrong, I love my great-grandmother to distraction, and it's my love for her that made me want to study the human mind and what ails it. You see, I believe she has suffered from delusions her whole life, and my great-grandfather—God rest his soul—loved her too much to do anything but coddle her, forever denying anything was wrong."

"What kind of delusions? Has she a doctor? What do the professionals think?"

Trina sighed. "She has seen many different doctors over the years, but it all boils down to one thing. She believes absolutely, that preternatural beings reside in this world. That they surround us, coexisting with the human race, some even feeding on us."

Carlos was speechless for a moment. The old woman must have had an encounter at some point in her life, and not had her memory completely wiped. He hesitated, then spoke slowly.

"Trina, there are people in this world who are more sensitive to things one might call otherworldly. Haven't you ever heard of the psychics that help police departments? And what about the stories of people in need helped by angels? Surely you're not so cynical that you believe all these accounts to be hysterical?"

"No, of course not. I believe in the supernatural. I always have. But where my Nanita takes things, I just can't go. She believes in magic, in vampires and shape shifters and such," Trina said, shaking her head.

"And you don't, obviously," he said, watching her reaction from the corner of his eye.

"Do you know anyone who does? I mean, outside of the downtown freaks that walk around like it's Halloween every day of the year?"

"As a matter of fact, I do. The legends come from somewhere, even if Hollywood has rewritten most of them. Science can only go so far and sometimes it becomes a matter of faith."

"I've heard this argument before. That may have been true centuries ago, but modern science and psychology have proved most of the myths to be false. I believe what I can see, for the most part, and leave faith up to the church."

"Maybe one day you'll see something that will change your mind," he said softly. "Perhaps restore your faith in legends and mythology."

Trina laughed. "Maybe. For now, I just worry about my great-grandmother. I'm the only one she has left."

***

Carlos pulled in front of the museum and handed the keys to the valet. Trina looked up at the building's imposing facade and couldn't help but be impressed. Draped with enormous banners highlighting the event, the museum looked even more majestic as they billowed like a silken waterfall in the wind.

Photographers meandered around, grabbing photo ops of New York society as they went up the red carpet. It was a veritable mix of socialites and social climbers, philanthropists and the bored elite, all hobnobbing in the marbled lobby.

"My, my, you must have some pretty important connections to score an invitation to this kind of an event," Trina said as she took Carlos's arm.

"They have to let me in. Most of the art shown in the exhibit is on loan to the museum from my private collection," he said as he took her coat and handed it to the coat check.

Trina was about to laugh when a tuxedoed gentleman came bounding over to shake Carlos's hand. The man pumped Carlos's arm like he was trying to draw water. "Oh, Señor Salazar, I am so honored that you decided to attend. The exhibit is a huge success. How can we ever thank you?"

Carlos flashed a gracious smile, and smoothly extricated his hand from the gentleman's grip. "*De nada,* Mr. Pierce, it is my pleasure to do this for the museum. Let me introduce you to my lady. This is Ms. Trina Markham. Trina, this is Graham Pierce, head curator for the Met."

Trina's mouth fell open for a moment. She quickly snapped it shut and tried to regain her composure. Carlos hadn't been kidding. "It's a pleasure to meet you," she said, quickly extending her hand and hoping she didn't appear to be too much of an idiot.

Pierce took her hand and bowed his head over it. "The honor is all mine. Any friend of Carlos Salazar's is a friend of ours."

The corridors overflowed with guests. People milled around, looking at the various artifacts and paintings, obviously enjoying themselves. Occasionally Trina would catch people whispering as they passed, and it was obvious everyone knew who the show's benefactor was. She even caught a couple of women giving Carlos the eye, blatantly flirting with him regardless of having their own escorts. Instinctively Trina tightened her grip on his arm and he chuckled.

"You have nothing to worry about, *querida*. Why would I be interested in paste when I have a true gem on my arm?" he asked, gesturing with his hand.

Trina's heart warmed at the compliment and he smiled, running his finger along the side of her cheek. "I know I told you before," he said, "but you truly take my breath away with how beautiful you are tonight."

Tears pricked at the corners of her eyes, but she blinked them back. She'd be damned before she let her mascara run and her nose get red after he paid her such a huge compliment.

They walked around admiring his artwork, and Carlos gave her the story behind each piece that caught her eye. But when they stopped at a particular oil painting depicting an *auto de fe* from the Spanish Inquisition and a woodcut of *Tomas de Torquemada*, he grew quiet and a little distracted.

"Carlos, you okay?" she asked, a little puzzled by his change of demeanor.

He gave her half a smile. "I'm sorry. I'm fine, really. It's just this time period always saddens me. So many people died needlessly from hatred born of ignorance and fear. Every time I'm reminded of this time in my country's history, it's a little sobering."

"Still brooding, Carlos? Why am I not surprised? So sad, really, how you still refuse to live for the day and the pleasures it can bring."

At the sound of the deep, baritone voice behind them, both Trina and Carlos turned. Stifling a gasp, Trina could only stare. The gentleman was imposing, and the resemblance he shared with the man Carlos had morphed into during her dream unsettled her to no end.

Carlos frowned. "Sandro. I didn't expect to see you here tonight. You don't usually make appearances at these types of social gatherings. To what do we owe the pleasure?" Carlos inclined his head, and though his voice betrayed nothing but courtesy his eyes were suspicious.

"You're not the only one with a penchant for history, or with a taste for beautiful things," the man answered as he turned the weight of his full gaze toward Trina. "Speaking of beauty, aren't you going to introduce me to your lovely companion?"

Trina could see Carlos's jaw clench. The undercurrent of hostility between the two men was palpable, and she couldn't help but wonder where it stemmed from. She gave Carlos a puzzled look as she waited for him to introduce her.

"Sandro, this is my friend Trina Markham. Trina, this is an old…friend, Sandro Mendoza."

Carlos's stilted introduction was polite but strained, and she had caught the other man's cocked eyebrow at being dubbed an *old friend.* However, Carlos was nothing if not gracious, and she would be the same.

"It's a pleasure to meet you," she said, extending her hand. Sandro slid his fingers beneath the soft curve of her palm, lifting her hand to his lips. Trina stiffened, taken aback by the gesture. She was immediately uncomfortable. When Carlos kissed her hand the gesture was simple yet unbelievably erotic, but this felt off. For some unknown reason the man made her skin crawl and she had to resist the urge to pull her hand away.

Sandro kept her hand in his. "And how are you enjoying the show, Ms. Markham?" he asked, his lips twitching a little as if he could sense her discomfort and enjoyed it.

Straightening her shoulders, Trina eyed him boldly. "Very much, Mr. Mendoza. Carlos's collection is as beautiful as it is vast, and he's extremely knowledgeable about every one of his pieces," she said, successfully extracting her hand from his.

Carlos hadn't taken his eyes off Sandro. They had narrowed to mere slits as if he were trying to read the man's thoughts, and if Trina didn't know better she would have sworn she heard him growl.

"I brook no argument there, Ms. Markham," he said with a smile that didn't quite sit true on his face. Sliding his eyes to the side, he met Carlos's glare and chuckled. "In that, it seems he and I are of like minds. Our natures are such that we both have appetites for the rare as well as the beautiful. However, that wasn't always the case, eh, Carlos? It's nice to see that you've finally improved your…*tastes*."

Carlos took a step forward, clenching his fists.

"Touchy, eh?" His gaze fell back to Trina. Cocking his brow, he smiled knowingly. "Well, I'll have to try to remember that in the future."

Sandro's veiled threat wasn't lost on Carlos. "Aren't you going to introduce us to *your* companion, Sandro?" he said before the man could turn and walk away.

Sandro turned back toward Carlos, his eyes narrowing for a moment before he plastered another not-quite-right smile on his face. Glancing dismissively at the golden-haired beauty on his arm, he shrugged. "There's no need, really. She's merely decorative and of no consequence to me, unlike your lady friend," he said pointedly.

Trina gaped. Shocked to her toes by the man's outright disdain, she couldn't help but look at the pretty blonde. Pretty didn't go far enough. The woman was absolutely stunning, from her curvy body and flawless face to the thick mass of gold crowning it all. Everything about her was perfect—until Trina looked in her eyes. They were vacant.

"Goodbye, Sandro. I hope you enjoyed yourself tonight." Carlos's words were gracious, but he made it clear the conversation was over. His face and his tone were flinty as he spoke, almost as if he were gearing up for a fight.

"Oh, yes. It was very...enlightening. By the way, my boys wanted me to say hello if I happened to run into you tonight."

"Yes. It was, to use your word, enlightening when last I ran into them. Please remind them for me of my last invitation."

"Oh, we haven't forgotten your hospitality, nor will we. Until we meet again, then," he said with a flourish, but his eyes stayed on Trina.

Trina took an unconscious step closer to Carlos. There was something about Sandro that had her body's alarm system blaring. He was handsome, but his underlying cruelty was palpable and Trina shivered instinctively.

Sandro walked away with the blonde in tow and Trina let out the breath she didn't realize she been holding.

"Carlos, who the hell was that? I don't mean to be rude, but there's something definitely not right with that guy. Talk about your tense situations. What did he mean by that bit about never forgetting your hospitality? It sounded more like a threat to me."

Carlos exhaled, shaking his head. "Sandro and I go way back. We met in Spain when I was first…" he hesitated for a moment. "Well, let's just say when I was much younger than I am now. We used to run with the same crowd, but then we had a falling-out over a mutual acquaintance and haven't seen eye to eye since."

Carlos scowled at the empty spot where Sandro had stood. His mood had soured and Trina felt a little awkward just standing there.

"I bet your disagreement was over some hot little *chica,*" Trina teased, elbowing him lightly in the ribs trying to make him smile.

It worked and he gave her a half smile. "No, it wasn't. But it doesn't matter anyway. It was long past. Unfortunately, my problem with Sandro now is that I don't agree with the way he chooses to live his life. I know that on the surface that makes me sound like a snob, but trust me, it's much more complicated than it seems."

"I know. What was all that business about his date being of no consequence? Can you believe the way he treated that poor girl? Either she's really as dumb as the stereotypes say, or she has absolutely no self-esteem. I can't imagine allowing anyone to speak like that about me. I feel bad for her. She looked completely clueless."

Carlos didn't comment.

"Come on, let's get out of here. If you like Spanish antiques I've got a few at my place that might interest you," she said, seeing his face cloud over again.

"Well, I wouldn't exactly call you an antique, *querida,* but interest me you do," he said with a chuckle.

"Very funny," she said tugging on his arm. "Let's go." Linking her arm in his, they made their goodbyes and headed out.

Chapter 8

Carlos turned onto Trina's block, and luck was with them as they found a parking space two doors down from her brownstone. Trina talked, trying to keep Carlos from dwelling on what happened at the museum.

"My great-grandmother's family was originally from Spain, though I'm not really sure from where. She left when she met my great-grandfather and the two moved to England when they married. Her stories about what it was like for her growing up filled my whole childhood. Her horses and her dogs, how she loved the sea and the smells of the square on market day. She sort of romanticized the Spanish culture for me, so when I had the opportunity to search for some of her original furniture, I jumped at the chance."

Trina unlocked the front door and they went inside. The house was dark so she went ahead, turning on the lights as Carlos took off his coat and draped it over the railing. The banister was polished mahogany and it shined like black ice.

The whole house was warm and inviting. He inhaled, taking in all the different scents lingering throughout the house. Trina's was the most prominent, but there was another, much older and much more faint, but familiar. It puzzled him.

He took another step into the foyer and stared, open-mouthed. Intricately carved tiles formed a mosaic pattern on the floor he recognized as one from the Alhambra Palace in Granada, Spain. He smiled at the memories it brought back.

Trina came back in after turning on the lights in the kitchen and parlor. She saw the look on his face as he stared down at the floor.

"Nanita loved visiting Granada as a child. She told me she used to run ahead into the palace when her family would visit there on holiday and dash from room to room and courtyard to courtyard. She'd run her fingers over the tiled walls and fountains imagining she was a Moorish princess, eating pomegranates and dates as her suitors filed past," Trina giggled as she reenacted her great-grandmother's childhood fantasy for Carlos.

"It's beautiful. Did your great-grandfather have it copied for her?"

"Yes. He loved her very much. It was obvious, even to a kid, although I have vague memories of family arguments, ugly moments. My great-grandfather was a good man, but family drama claims he wasn't the love of her life, that Nanita had been very much in love with someone else, but something happened and they couldn't marry. From what I gather, she never quite got over it, even though she did learn to love my great-grandfather. He understood her."

Trina led Carlos into the parlor and stood in the middle of the room, her arms out to her sides. "Well, this is it. These are the pieces I was able to find. What do you think?"

Carlos looked around the room. It was obvious from the way the polished walnut gleamed that Trina truly loved these pieces from her family's past. He looked at the ornately carved writing desk in the corner with its pawed feed, the Spanish *baqueno* chest with its ivory and ebonized wood, and finally the *papelera,* or Spanish secretary, with all its little hand-carved drawers and ivory inlays. But it was the small religious box sitting on top of the mantel that caught his attention. He walked up to the fireplace and lovingly ran his fingers over the carved images of St. Francis of Assisi and St. Anthony, and the delicate ivy and flowers intertwined around the top.

"I knew someone many years ago who owned something similar to this," he said, his voice almost a whisper. Lost for a moment in a memory, he cleared his voice and looked over at Trina. "The furniture is impeccable, Trina. You must have been ecstatic to find pieces in such good condition."

His reverie wasn't lost on her and she wondered what he too had to leave behind in his life, just as her great-grandmother had to do.

Taking him by the hand, she led him back into the foyer. "Come upstairs. There's one other thing I want you to see."

She didn't say a word as she led him upstairs into her bedroom. Carlos sat on the end of her bed as Trina lifted the top lid to her standing jewelry case and took out a wide, black velvet box. She brushed her hands across the top as if dusting it off before turning around with it.

She walked over and sat next to him, putting the box gingerly on his lap. "Go ahead, open it," she said excitedly. "It's really old, but totally cool."

He hesitated a moment, and Trina nodded, pushing the box toward his hands. "It's okay, go ahead. I want you to open it. I know you'll appreciate it for what it's worth."

Carlos ran his fingers over the velvet. The clasp on the box was beautiful in its own right and he gently pushed the little gold release. The box opened a crack and he carefully lifted the lid. Staring back at him was a gorgeous antique tortoiseshell mantilla. It was in perfect condition, not a scratch.

"Beautiful," he whispered. "Where did you get this? Was it your great-grandmother's?"

"No. I found it in at a flea market downtown, if you can believe that. I bought it for a song—they didn't even know what it was. I had it appraised. It's genuine and it's more than two hundred years old."

"Try it on."

"What? No. I wouldn't even know how to fasten it in my hair. Besides, I'd be too afraid I'd snap it in two, it's so delicate."

"Allow me," he said and before she knew it, he'd gathered her hair and pulled it back, fastening the antique to her hair like it was something he did every day.

"You, *señorita,* are the most beautiful thing I've seen in a long time," he said, leaning over to kiss her gently. "See for yourself if you don't believe me."

Carlos turned her around to face the large, full-length pedestal mirror on the other side of the bed. He grabbed the delicate lace wrap she had worn with her dress and carefully draped it over the mantilla.

Trina's eyes widened at her reflection. The warm glow from the floor lamp shimmered against the bronze satin of her dress, and her hair cascaded down her back in soft curls. The mantilla fit perfectly, and the way the lace fell around her shoulders made her feel like she was meant to wear it.

Trina stood, trailing her fingers along the fragile edge of the lace. Carlos stood behind her, and when she looked at their mirror image, it was as if they belonged to another time and place. His fingertips brushed against her neck as he gently moved back the lace. Leaning down, he kissed her bare skin, his lips traveling the length of her shoulder. His arms came around her waist and she leaned against him as his mouth continued to feather kisses along her neck.

She turned in his arms and her lips found his. His arms were still around her waist and back, gripping the satin of her dress as his mouth devoured hers. She met his kiss with a hunger all her own and gasped when he finally broke away.

Carlos reached up and undraped the lace shawl, tossing it casually over her bedroom chair. Taking the mantilla from her head, he let her hair fall around her shoulders in loose waves, running his fingers through the curling mass. His hands lingered for a moment as her pulse beat erratically beneath her soft skin before placing the mantilla back in its box and resting it on her nightstand. He didn't say a word as he went about it, then just as quietly turned back to Trina and gathered her into his arms.

Kissing her, he laid her on the bed, his hand traveling the length of her leg passed the curve of her hip, sliding once again around her waist. Trina sighed, sliding her foot in, her silk stockings rubbing softly against his pants. Her fingers trailed along the edge of his shirt as she bent her knee, the smooth satin of her dress slipping past and pooling at her hip exposing the thin lace of her thong.

Carlos ran his finger under the thin edge of the dainty elastic and with a single twist tore it in two. Pulling the shredded material from under her, his fingers trailed along her delicate skin, the rough edges of his fingers brushing between her legs, and she moaned.

"I want to look at you, Trina. I want to see all of you," he said, his voice thick.

Trina turned her head away, her hair fanning out against the pillow. She smiled secretly; her body humming with pleasure, but not only from his touch. His words made her feel beautiful, wanton, and more desirable than she'd ever felt and the fact that he wanted her so much made her almost giddy.

Trying to be sexy, she slid off the bed. Still facing him, she moved a few steps back and turned around. Reaching behind her, she slowly unzipped the strapless satin, letting it fall to her hips. She shimmied out of the rest till it fell to her feet. Standing there in just her thigh highs and heels, she stepped out of the pool of satin and turned to face him.

Carlos got off the bed and went to her. "*Dio*. You are exquisite," he whispered as his hands skimmed her narrow waist and cupped her breasts. He leaned over and licked the puckered nipple on one, while his hand teased the other. Trina arched her back and moaned low in her throat.

Carlos stepped back and shed his own clothes. With a sweep of his hand, he cleared her dresser, lifting her onto the polished surface in a single move. He sucked and teased her breasts while his hands explored every inch of her body. Her skin felt like electric satin as she shivered under his touch.

He kissed her, his lips and tongue teasing her mouth as he slid his arm around her. His free hand glided slowly over her breasts and belly before stopping at the soft curls between her legs. With feather-light strokes, his fingertips circled and grazed her sensitive skin till she arched into his hand, craving more.

With an almost violent stroke, he delved into her slick cleft, his fingers pushing deep and hard. She was panting as her hips struggled to match his pace from her high perch. Shoving her knees apart, he dipped his head between her legs and tasted her, his tongue laving and swirling till she grabbed his hair in her fists and ground herself further into his mouth.

She came hard as his tongue delved over and over, and as her body rocked with the aftershocks, he picked her up and carried her to the bed. He knelt in front of her, his cock long and thick as she crawled toward him. He fisted his hand around his shaft and squeezed.

A tiny pearl shimmered on the edge of his head, and with a wicked smile, Trina licked it clean. She sucked in his head and swirled her tongue under its ridged edge, and as his breath hitched sharp and quick, her lips twitched slightly in a tiny smile.

She slid her mouth entirely around his cock and slowly took it fully into her throat, sucking and squeezing till he growled. He flipped her onto her stomach, his voice jagged as he whispered in Spanish, pulling her hips up and back roughly, and then entering her with a single thrust. Pumping his hips, his balls slapped against her swollen sex. He rode her hard and fast and she met him thrust for thrust until she cried out, climaxing again.

Carlos felt himself tighten and his head bulge as he pounded faster, harder. His face contorted and his fangs lengthened as the need for her blood swelled along with his cock. He snarled, and in the last moment turned his head, struggling against his nature so as not to reveal too much too soon as he exploded, pouring himself into her.

It was too late. Trina pulled away from him, her eyes wide with terror as she choked on her scream. She had seen his face change in the same mirror he had turned her toward only a short while ago. Instead of seeing something out of a dream, it was something out of a nightmare.

Shaking her head in confused horror, she scrambled back toward the headboard. Her eyes so full of desire only moments before now looked at him in fear as his come dripped down her thighs.

"What the fuck are you? Get out! *Get out!*" she screamed, picking up the lamp from the nightstand and swinging it back and forth in front of her. *"Get out of my house!"*

Carlos's face looked human once again as he pleaded with her. "Trina, let me explain...please, don't be afraid!"

Her words were already a tidal wave slicing through his head. She had rescinded her invitation and pain ripped through him like a dull blade.

He doubled over in agony, clenching his fists as he tried to reason with her. "It's not what you think. I need to explain." As she stood on the bed with her eyes wild, he knew it was no use. She was terrified of him and he had no one to blame but himself. Gritting his teeth against the pain slicing through his body, he grabbed his clothes and stumbled out of the room.

Cowering against the wall, Trina followed behind him, still desperately gripping the lamp. She held her breath as she watched him. Carlos seemed wracked with pain, and it was obvious in the effort it cost him just to try to speak.

He struggled into his clothes, and even as he did, it was almost as if something propelled him toward the front door. Their eyes met for a moment, his filled not only with physical pain, but also with a sad regret. Trina's heart squeezed even as her eyes filled with tears, but she was too afraid to do anything else.

She lurched toward the door and threw the dead bolt as soon as he was on the front step, then sank to the floor, shaking. Gulping down air, she tried to calm herself, but was frozen, too afraid to move as she shivered from the shock and the cold.

One word kept running through her mind. *Vampire*. Crying, she thought about calling 911 or at the very least one of her friends, but who would believe her?

Trina curled into herself, sobbing as she rocked back and forth, trying to wrap her head around what had just happened. "What the hell did I get myself into? He's some kind of a monster, for Christ's sake, he had fangs! And his face…what the hell was that? God help me, what have I done?"

What had she missed? There had to have been some kind of telltale sign that Carlos wasn't all he seemed. This was New York City, with all types of crazy, underground fetishes. Her mind raced. Didn't she just watch a show on the History Channel with about modern-day vampirism? Hadn't they called themselves *sanguinarians* or some such thing?

She thought back to everything she'd experienced with Carlos over the past few days, everything she'd felt. There wasn't anything even remotely unusual to give her pause. Her own wanton behavior was the only thing that was unusual; her own gut telling her Carlos was the one haunting her dreams. Was she really that desperate that she'd misread her own body's alarm signals as romantic folly?

She was still on the cold tile in front of the door, her teeth chattering when she finally roused herself. She made herself get up and go back upstairs, but she couldn't face her own room. Practically sprinting past her bedroom door, she turned instead and went into her great-grandmother's room.

The familiarity of Nanita's room comforted her immediately, from the soft fragrance of her lavender and vanilla sachets, to the handmade quilts folded neatly over the edge of the bed. Nanita's own scent still hung in the air and as Trina breathed in, she suddenly felt homesick in her own home.

Trina caught a glimpse of herself in the dresser mirror, naked and disheveled. She grimaced. Her head was in turmoil. She was afraid and angry, and though she didn't want to admit it, somewhere inside she was heartbroken as well. Looking at herself in the mirror, she suddenly felt dirty. She hurried into the bathroom and turned on the shower, trying to wash away all traces of Carlos, but her mind wouldn't let her. She would never reconcile it all, but at this point, she was too tired to try.

Exhaustion crept over her as she dried off, and she wrapped herself in her great-grandmother's soft fleece robe. Curling up on her bed, she sank into a troubled sleep, hoping for the first time in weeks that it would be dreamless.

***

Trina slept fitfully. Disjointed images passed through her mind, taunting her until she woke in a cold sweat. Blinking, she shook off the last remnants of her broken sleep and looked at the clock. Three a.m. She exhaled and sat up, rubbing her face. Wide-awake she knew sleep would just continue to elude her. Not that closing her eyes at this point held any appeal.

She went downstairs to the kitchen, purposefully skirting the door to her bedroom as she passed. She filled the teakettle, lit the burner, and stood numbly waiting for it to boil. She hadn't even bothered to turn on the light, and as the kettle whistled, she fumbled with the teabag, burning her fingers as she poured. She sat down, stirring honey and a little lemon into her mug, too dazed to do anything else but stare into space.

She sipped her tea and glanced at the phone, almost as if she expected it to ring. When it did, she practically jumped out of her skin. For a split second, she thought it might be Carlos, but she'd never given him her home number. Looking at the clock, she was suddenly apprehensive, knowing at this hour it was probably someone calling about her great-grandmother.

"Hello?" she answered, her voice slightly panicked. "What's happened?"

"Ms. Markham? It's Jeannette. I'm sorry to call you this late, but it looks as if your great-grandmother's had a stroke. She's unconscious right now, but responsive. The doctors are doing tests to determine the severity of her condition, and said they would explain things further once you arrive. As she never signed the Do Not Resuscitate order, they need to know what you want them to do in the event that she…" Jeanette trailed off, her voice thick with emotion. She dropped the professional nurse persona and started to cry. "Trina, honey, how quickly can you get here? I think she's waiting for you. She's hanging on for some reason and I think it's because she wants to say goodbye. Please get here as soon as you can."

Trina just stood there mutely, holding the phone to her ear.

"Trina? Did you hear me? Do you understand?" Jeannette asked, her voice urgent.

Trina's throat worked as she swallowed back her tears. "I understand. Thank you, Jeannette," she answered, her voice breaking. "I'm on my way. Please…tell my…tell Nanita I'm coming."

She hung up the phone, all thoughts of Carlos gone as she flew up the stairs. Rushing into her room, she threw on the first clothes she could find and was out the door in minutes, her great-grandmother the only thing on her mind.

***

She flew out of the cab in front of the facility and rushed through the double doors. The night guard nodded to her as she hurried past toward the elevators. It seemed an eternity for the lift to reach the right floor, but finally the doors opened and Jeanette was waiting there for her.

"Where is she?" Trina asked as the two walked quickly down the silent hallway.

"She's in her own bed, Trina. They moved all the monitors in there to try to make her as comfortable as possible. She's quiet and she's breathing on her own. She's responsive to the stimuli tests and her heart and brain waves are strong, yet the doctors can't seem to figure out why she's comatose. It's almost as if she's made up her mind that it's her time to go."

Trina looked at Jeanette in shock as they continued down the corridor. She tried to process the woman's words, but she couldn't believe what she was saying. There was no way it was possible. The two had just had a spa day together and had torn around town shopping for her date with Carlos. Trina swallowed at the thought of him, then forced his image from her mind.

When they reached the door, her hand froze on the knob. She wasn't sure she could deal with whatever she found on the other side.

"Go on in, honey. It's okay. Just talk to her. I know she'll hear you. It's what she's been waiting for," Jeannette said with a reassuring smile.

Trina nodded and took a deep breath as she turned the knob, pushing the heavy, wooden door open. The room was dim and the only sound the hum of the machines monitoring her great-grandmother's vital signs. Quietly, she closed the door and took a couple of steps into the room.

"Nanita, it's me. I'm here," she said tentatively, walking up to the bed. She looked at the old lady. Jeanette was right. She looked perfectly at peace, as if she was sleeping. Tears formed in Trina's eyes as she watched the old woman's chest gently rise and fall.

This was impossible. Just the day before she was laughing, forcing Trina to try on dress after dress and teasing the hairdresser till he blushed pink enough to match his hair. She put her hand on her great-grandmother's forehead. It was cool and the skin smooth. The old woman sighed at her touch and Trina jumped at the unexpected sound.

"It's actually amazing that she does that. She's quite an anomaly, your great-grandmother. She's confounded everyone around here."

Startled, Trina's head whirled around at the quiet, female voice behind her. "Dr. Harris! Are you practicing stealth as part of your bedside manner these days?" she said with her hand on her heart.

"Sorry about that. I didn't want to disturb you, but Jeanette told me you were here. Did she fill you in on what's been happening?"

"Yes, sort of, but she said you would explain it further when I got here."

"Well, the bottom line is there's no concrete medical reason, short of extreme old age, to explain the comatose state your great-grandmother is in right now. There was no stroke as we originally thought. CAT scan and MRI images show no damage to her brain tissue, and her brainwave function is perfect. As you just saw yourself, she responds to touch. She also responds to voices, as well as to all the stimuli tests we've done. But we still can't figure out why she's unconscious."

"Jeanette said it was almost as if Nanita decided it was time," Trina said in a whisper. "This doesn't make any sense."

"At her age things can change from day to day, sometimes even minute to minute," the doctor said, putting her hand on Trina's shoulder and giving it a gentle squeeze.

"Talk to her, Trina. Tell her everything you want her to know. I can't prove it medically, but my gut tells me she understands and she'll hear everything you have to say. If nothing else it will make you feel better," she said with a final pat before leaving the room.

Trina pulled Nanita's soft chintz bedroom chair over to the side of the bedrail and sat down. She took the old woman's small hand in hers and ran her fingers over the delicately wrinkled skin. It was just as soft as she'd always remembered. For some reason the memory of holding her great-grandmother's hand on her first day of kindergarten flashed through her mind, and a single tear fell from the corner of her eye. She wiped it away with the edge of her knuckles and as she sniffled, she caught the faint scent of her great-grandmother's perfume.

"Nanita, you have to wake up. I need you. There's so much I have to tell you, so much I need to ask and I don't have anyone else I can talk to. Please, Nani, if you can hear me…" Trina stopped and took a deep breath, trying to calm herself. Falling into hysterics wasn't going to do either of them any good.

"Dr. Harris says you're a mystery. She says they can't figure out why you're…sleeping like this." She couldn't bring herself to use the term comatose. "But that's nothing new to us is it, Nani? You've been a mystery all your life. I know how much my mother and grandmother hurt you—that they could turn their backs on you simply because they thought you too eccentric.

"The things you believed embarrassed them. And to some extent I'm just as guilty, and I'm sorry. I never meant to hurt you, especially since now I know you were right. But I need to know how you know. I've found some of the things from your past, the things you were forced to leave behind, but I'm as much in the dark now as ever and twice as confused."

Trina gripped her great-grandmother's hand so hard she could see her fingers turning white. She exhaled, and released the pressure on the old woman's hand, bringing it to her cheek. She rubbed the slightly gnarled fingers against her skin.

"It's just like you always told me. Things aren't always what they seem in this life. I just never understood what you meant, never believed you—until now. I don't know what happened in your life that made you realize there are things out there beyond our comprehension, but something happened to me, Nanita, and it happened tonight. You're the only person I know who will believe me, the only one who won't think I'm crazy. I need you to help me to understand."

The old woman sighed again and this time her eyes opened for a fraction of a second. In that instant, her gaze fell on Trina, and as their eyes met, they held for that split second before they closed again.

"Nanita!" Trina jumped up. Searching her great-grandmother's face, she looked for any sign of lingering sentience. But the old woman had slipped back into unconsciousness just as fleetingly as she had left it.

Trina ran to the door to call Jeanette, but she wasn't there. Glancing back at her great-grandmother, she hesitated, afraid to leave her for a moment before she rushed down the hall toward the nurses' station. Finding it empty, she darted around, but soon realized all the rooms on the floor were dark.

Annoyed, Trina headed back to Nanita's room. This was bizarre. She looked up at the fire alarm strobe, thinking maybe she'd missed some kind of a drill, but it too was silent. She shivered, and gooseflesh began to spread across her arms. Even beneath the sleeves of her blouse, the hair on her arms stood on end. The air around her seemed to shimmer with faint electricity, and she began to sense something wasn't right; something beyond the fact the place seemed deserted.

Rushing down the corridor, she picked up her pace as anxiety and adrenaline flooded her system. She pushed open the door, half-expecting to find her great-grandmother sitting up, and the other half expecting the monitors to be flat lining. Everything was as she left it—a peaceful yet eerie quiet, like the kind that always comes before a storm.

***

Carlos drove in a black rage, pushing his Jaguar to the limits as he flew up First Avenue. "Stupid ass," he muttered to himself as he blurred past the buildings lining the streets of pre-dawn Manhattan.

He'd put too much trust in merely satisfying his thirst before spending time with Trina. There was something more to this than he had anticipated. The force of his initial reaction to her should have tipped him off that this ran deeper than just a craving for blood and sex. He had disregarded it.

In more than two hundred and seventy-five years he'd never felt like this. He craved Trina, all of her. Even his feelings for Isabel had paled with the advent of his preternatural life. In the beginning, he still loved her, but it was more a kin to nostalgia than anything else. The memory of her had brought him both solace and pain, but never once had he craved her existence.

He had never used their blood tie to try to interfere with Isabel's life. He had buried it, along with most of his human memories, so much so that any link they shared was long gone. Isabel had survived the injuries he had inflicted, that much he knew—but beyond that he had no clue of her life, and she hadn't crossed his mind until just a few days ago when he'd tasted Trina's blood.

He pulled up to the steel gate adjacent to his townhouse and hit the remote. He drove into the courtyard hidden to the side of the building and parked. The house was dark and he wondered briefly if Julian and Melissa had stayed the night or had headed back to the main house. Either way it didn't matter, he wasn't in the mood for company.

He silently made his way up to his room, his expression making it clear to anyone that it would be best if they kept their distance. Walking straight into the bathroom, he stripped, turning on the shower. In the stillness, the jets of hot water sounded like a roaring waterfall as it cut through the silence. Steam curled through the air like misty tendrils coating everything in dampness.

Carlos picked up his shirt to wipe the mirror and caught the scent of Trina's perfume still lingering on the fabric. He buried his face in the soft material and inhaled, his body reacting immediately, growing hard at the scent and his teeth tingled in unspent need.

"Jesus Christ!" he swore, tearing the shirt in two and crumpling it into a ball. He threw it at the door and it hit with a soft *whoompf*. "What the fuck is *wrong* with me?"

With a scowl, he pulled open the seamless glass door and stepped into the warmth of the shower. Closing his eyes, he let the hot water pound on his head while he tried to relax and think.

"Carlos?"

His eyes flew open at the sound of the soft voice in his head. It was very faint. He closed his eyes again and listened, focusing his senses.

"Carlos…your promise. You said you'd come if I called…"

He rubbed his eyes. Surely, this was some trick of memory. There was no way on God's earth that Isabel could still be alive.

He reached out with his thoughts. "Isabel?"

"Yes…come quickly, Carlos. I haven't much time."

"How? Where?" He voiced out loud as he flew out of the shower, his mind spinning with the improbabilities.

Half dressed, Carlos raced out of the townhouse, throwing the rest of his clothes onto the passenger seat of his car. It was near morning, but he didn't care. If it took all day, he didn't care.

For the first time in centuries, he focused his vampiric senses on Isabel's trace. It was faint, he could barely taste it, but it was enough for him to follow. He flew up the FDR Drive, alert to every nuance inside his head as the weak thrum guided him. As he neared the hospital facility, it suddenly grew stronger, like the pulsating beat from a racing heart.

Running through the lobby Carlos was nothing but a blur as he passed security. With a flick of his hand, he threw up wards obscuring everything, and took the stairs at preternatural speed, pushing his way through the doors to the resident's floor. Wards in place, he walked slowly down the hallway, reaching out with his senses. She was here. The pulse of her trace beat loudly in his head.

He felt a sense of comfort and peace flow past him and was surprised. The place wasn't what he had expected. It was beautiful, decorated more like a posh hotel with every amenity than a health care facility. He could still smell the old age, illness, and death all around him, but it wasn't overpowered by despair. Instead, the place smelled of hope.

"Isabel?" He reached out again with his mind. He stopped in mid-step and turned toward the door on his left. Placing his hand on the knob, he turned it clockwise. As he pushed it open, unexpected warmth tingled along his spine. He had found her.

The tiny woman lying on the bed filled him with awe. She had changed so much, yet an overwhelming desire to hold her in his arms washed over him, but she looked too delicate for even the simplest touch.

"Carlos. At last…" her voice whispered through his mind.

"I'm here, *mi vida*, just as I promised. But, Isa—how is it you're still alive?" he asked as he came toward the bed. The smell of death was strong all around her as he took her small hand in his. The feel of her skin was soft, and he could still sense the faint spark of their connection as their hands touched.

"Your blood, my love. That's how I come to still be here." Her voice was as frail as she was as it vibrated in the air between them. "When you gave me your blood to heal me all those years ago, you also gave me another gift. Don't you remember what you said to me? I asked if you were angel or demon, and you replied you no longer knew, but that I was going to live. You prayed I would be happy."

Carlos thought back to that horrible night. He remembered the manservant had told him something about the blood extending a human's lifetime. But this? Never in his long existence would he have guessed he meant this prolonged a life.

"I've lived a few lifetimes thanks to you, Carlos. I've witnessed so many things, both wondrous as well as monstrous. It's been quite an adventure, but now my time has finally come."

"Isabel," he hesitated. "Your life…has it...have you been contented?" Carlos's voice rang from his mind, heavy with questions too difficult to ask aloud.

Throughout his existence, he had convinced himself Isabel's life had been happy, that she had lived it to the fullest. Faced with the reality that she had lived for as long as he had, it followed suit she had probably spent most of it alone. She was inevitably the one left standing graveside as she buried loved ones and friends as the years went by.

Carlos turned his head unable to face the sadness he expected to hear in her voice as her thoughts continued to drift through his head. With his jaw clenched, he cursed himself and that night.

"Carlos," Isabel whispered. "I have known great happiness as well as great sadness in my long life, but such would be the case if I'd had but one life to live. The greatest gift you gave me was Jeffrey. When you entrusted me to his care, he became both my truest friend as well as my truest love. We eventually married, reinventing our lives as time required. We had many children, and yes, we had the sad burden of burying almost all of them as the years passed. I lost him more than twenty years ago, but the last of our family remains with me and for that, I am blessed. Through you I have had a love that truly spanned the centuries, and for that I will be forever grateful."

Carlos leaned on the bed and carefully placed a kiss on her wrinkled cheek, lingering for a moment as he breathed in her scent, committing it to memory.

"You know, that's not exactly how you promised you'd kiss me goodbye," Isabel said aloud, her voice thin and a little weak, but her eyes sparkling with mischief.

Carlos grinned, and his shoulders slumped a little in relief. Isabel was still dying, but at least now, he'd be able to ask her forgiveness and fulfill his promise the way he envisioned it.

"You haven't changed a bit, *mi vida*, have you?" he said as he brought her hand to his lips.

"You must be as blind with old age as I am if that's what you think," she said with a weak smile. "But, I guess you'll always see me as I was…but you see, Carlos, I have changed. I haven't been the polite, quietly demure young girl you once knew in a very long time. The years have made me independent and strong, and quite frankly I like the person I've become."

He smiled. "So do I, *mi vida*." Leaning forward, he ran his finger along the thin gold chain hanging around her neck. Gently he picked up the delicate locket that lay across her breast.

"I told you I would always keep it with me," she whispered, covering his hand with hers.

Reaching into his pocket, he pulled out the fragile miniature she had given him so many years before. Holding it in his palm, he lifted it for her to see. "As did I," he said his voice thick. "And I always will."

Her hand still covered his, and he closed his eyes for a moment. He took a deep breath, and when he opened them again, he stared down at her with one question burning on his lips. "Can you ever forgive me?"

She tilted her head, looking at him thoughtfully for a moment. "There's nothing to forgive. We each live the life God has ordained, regardless of what kind of existence that turns out to be. I truly believe he has a plan for each of us, and that there are reasons certain things are left as mysteries. What happened to you was not of your making…and don't look at me like that! Jeffrey told me everything. He told me how much you struggled so I might live. He told me you fought to keep whatever humanity was left to you. It's obvious to me now that you never lost that battle, and for that, I am grateful. My memories of you are of a good and decent man, and it's clear to me those qualities followed you into this existence. It's who you are, Carlos, and who you'll always be.

"Your wish for me was that I live and be happy, and now it is also my wish for you. Still, if my giving you absolution affords you the release you need to find that happiness, then so be it. I forgive you."

Carlos clenched his jaw against the blood tears that threatened, but a single drop managed to escape down his cheek. "Thank you, Isa." A huge weight suddenly lifted from his chest, and he felt light. Wiping his eyes on his shirtsleeve, they both laughed at the mess it made.

"Comes with the territory," he said with a shrug, cuffing his sleeve.

Isabel smiled tiredly, then closed her eyes. The air around them had changed subtly, and Carlos knew her time had come. He wanted to do something for her, ease her in some way, but didn't know what he could do.

"Isabel, do you want me to take you somewhere? You don't have to stay here, *mi vida*. I'll take you wherever you want to go."

"No, Carlos, I want to be here. I still need to say goodbye."

He wondered for a moment to whom she still needed to say goodbye, then remembered she said she still had family and he couldn't help but wonder about them. Instinctively he inhaled, and the scent that registered through the haze of death and illness hit him in the stomach, knocking the air from his lungs like a punch to the solar plexus.

"Trina," he whispered.

Isabel eyes flew open. "Trina?" She looked at him now, her eyes narrowing. "Carlos, how do you know my great-granddaughter?"

Carlos's mind whirled as all the puzzle pieces fell together. The familiarity, the way his mind danced with memories when he tasted Trina's blood. His face was incredulous as disbelief flooded through him. Of all the people in the world, how could it be? Maybe Isabel was right, and they were all just part of God's greater plan.

"Carlos, you're not answering me. How do you know Trina?"

Grinning, he walked back and forth like he couldn't contain himself. "Isabel, I had no idea she was your great-granddaughter, but now everything makes sense," he said, as he paced. "Now all the little things that didn't fit, all the little clues…maybe I just wasn't paying close enough attention."

He turned suddenly and came back to the edge of the bed, taking Isabel's hand. "We only just met this week—and Isa, she's unlike anyone I've ever met. I think I love her."

He looked at the old woman with such intensity it was as if he was seeing her for the first time. "Don't look at me that way, Isabel. I'm no monster, and I have no intention of hurting Trina. But if you want me to leave here and never see her again, then I will respect your dying wish."

What he didn't tell the old woman was that Trina might have already decided that for them. He opened his mouth to say something else when the door opened.

"What are you doing here? Get away from her! Help. *Help!*" Trina yelled as she picked up an empty bedpan and started beating Carlos over the head with it.

He threw his hands up in front of him, trying to fend off her assault. "Trina, stop it…it's not what you think. Stop, you're going to hurt yourself."

"It's not what I think? That's what you said earlier this morning when you suddenly grew fangs! What are you doing here? Are you stalking me, hunting me and my family?"

She gasped, "Oh, sweet Jesus…no! *Nanita!*" Trina ran to the old woman's bedside. She searched her face and neck, looking for any signs of attack. She took her great-grandmother's hands in hers and turned them over, inspecting her forearms and wrists when suddenly the old woman jerked her hands back.

"Trina, stop it! Carlos is right," she said, smacking Trina's hands away. "You need to calm down and let us explain before you make yourself crazy. I'm fine. Carlos would never hurt me."

Trina's eyes few open as she looked from one to the other. "You two know each other?" she asked, her mouth hanging open in shock.

"Yes, *mi niña,* I have known Carlos for quite a while. More than two hundred years, in fact, and no, I am not insane, nor am I delusional as most people have thought," Isabel said huffily. "I heard you what you said to me when you thought I was unconscious. I realize now what happened to you last night was…*Carlos*."

"What's going on? Can one of you please explain it to me? Nanita, you're talking about centuries here, and myths and folklore. It's impossible!"

"Trina, it's not impossible. It's no different from what I've been claiming your whole life. Everyone, especially members of my own family, thought I was insane, and that your poor great-grandfather loved me too much to have me committed. The truth is both your great-grandfather Jeffrey and I were almost killed by vampires centuries ago. He was given blood so he could continue to serve his master, and I was given Carlos's blood that I might live."

Trina sat on the end of the bed, her shoulders slumped and her jaw slack.

Carlos reached for the bedpan still in her hand, and Trina jumped. He took it from her slowly, not wanting to upset her any further, and placed it on the nightstand. "I know how bizarre this feels, Trina. It feels pretty much the same way for me. I never imagined Isabel would still be alive. There's much more to this story than either of us can tell you right now, and Isabel doesn't have much time left," he added gently.

Trina's eyes flew to her great-grandmother. She got up and went to her side, taking the old woman's hands in hers. Kneeling down, she rested her head on her great-grandmother's arm. "Nanita, none of this makes any sense. The doctor said there's no reason for this. The tests are all normal. I don't understand."

"*Mi niña*, you have been such a joy to me since Jeffrey died. It's finally my time, sweetheart, and no test, no doctor, is going to find the answers as to why. I'm just sorry this is how you must learn about your legacy."

"My legacy? This is my legacy? That I have vampire blood running through my veins?"

"No, honey, you don't have vampire blood in your veins, but because of my connection to Carlos, you carry some of that within you. Myths are based on truths, Trina, but don't believe everything you've heard, because most of it is exaggerated."

Isabel unclasped the locket from her neck and handed it to her. "Open it."

Trina held the locket in her hand, and looked at Carlos before pressing the release beneath the gold filigree. The locket sprang open, and a small key fell out onto the bed. Isabel picked it up and held it out to Trina. "This key opens the side compartment on the *papelera* you found in England. I was afraid it had been lost forever, but God works in mysterious ways. I believe you were meant to find it and bring it here, just as I now believe Carlos was meant to find you.

Open it, Trina. Inside are all my diaries. Read them and know the truth. Don't be afraid, *mi niña,* and never be afraid of Carlos. It is because of him that I'm still here, and that you were born."

Trina looked at the tiny portraits inside the locket and had to blink back her tears. The images were so innocent. Two young lovers whose story had played out in ways neither could have imagined. She put the key back inside and snapped the locket closed. "Okay, Nani, I'll read them. I promise."

Isabel breathed a sigh of relief. Her eyes looked from one to the other, and she reached out taking hold of each of their hands. "Take care of each other," she whispered, bringing their hands together. "I love you both." And without a sound, her hands fell limp.

Trina let go of Carlos's hand. Silent tears ran down her cheeks as they stood on either side of the bed. It was time. All she could do was watch as he leaned down and kissed Isabel's pale lips, just as he had promised. Her chest rose and fell once more, and all the joys of her life were there for him to taste as her last breath washed through him.

Chapter 9

The sun sank below the horizon, and as the sky blurred to indigo Trina stood at her great-grandmother's graveside. Clutching a single white rose, she stood stoically, even as she struggled to hold onto the last shreds of her composure. It was twilight, and her only consoling thought was that she had honored her great-grandmother's dying wish—one of them, anyway. Somehow, she had managed to convince the pastor of the Immaculate Conception Church on 14th Street, to hold her funeral services at sunset, instead of at the Catholic standard of ten a.m.

The events of the past week seemed surreal, but at least now, she finally understood the old woman's odd request. Carlos stood graveside as well. He was on the opposite corner from Trina, a poignant reminder of just how surreal her reality had become. She could feel his eyes watching as she struggled to keep it together, but she just didn't have the strength to meet his gaze.

As the priest offered his last benediction for Isabel della Cortes Markham, Trina's heart skipped a beat. He closed his bible and stepped back from the edge of the grave, motioning to her that the ceremony had come to an end.

With a nod, she stepped forward, leaning on Louie's arm for support. Her hands shook as she laid the rose at the head of the polished mahogany casket, and her breath caught in her throat with the finality of the symbolic gesture. All at once, it overwhelmed her, and she could feel the weight of Carlos's gaze grow even more intense as he witnessed her distress.

Louie's arm tightened around her waist and Susan stepped up, sliding her arm around Trina's shoulders. Her whole world had unraveled, and no one but Carlos understood the extent of just how much.

Initially she had gone numb, dealing with the assisted living facility, the funeral home, and the church as if on autopilot. Carlos had given her space. But even through the haze of her grief she couldn't stop thoughts of him from lingering on the periphery. Trina knew it was only a matter of time before she had no choice but to face him.

Susan's offer to let her to stay this past week was a godsend, giving her the distance she needed to just breathe. Trina had even joked it had more than made up for all the times she had covered for her at the club. But as much as she dreaded it, she knew it was time to go home.

The line of mourners passed, each placing their flowers on the casket and each one touching her hand as they left. Susan and Louie had gone to wait for her in the car, leaving her alone with her thoughts. She stood there in the encroaching darkness, and a terrible loneliness slowly dragged itself across her heart.

"Trina?" Carlos's deep voice called softly from behind.

"Go away, Carlos. I can't deal with all of this and you right now," she said.

"Not a chance, *querida*. For a week now, I've left you alone. We need to talk."

"You're right, but not right now. I need to go home. Hell, I haven't been there since …" Her voice broke and she couldn't finish. With a ragged breath, she just stared at the raw earth surrounding great-grandmother's grave.

"Look at me, Trina," he said as he gently turned her toward him. He put his fingers under her chin and lifted her face so she had no choice but to meet his eyes. "I'm sorry for the way everything came to light, but you have to believe me, it was never my intention to hurt or deceive you. I had no idea of our connection, and would have eventually revealed what I am to you in time."

Trina's tears were cold on her face and exhaustion gripped her. "I believe you, Carlos, I do. But regardless of that, I don't see how this can be set to right. I mean, I still can hardly believe you are what you are. That all of this is true. I know you loved my great-grandmother and that she loved you—but it's over now, all of it."

"You don't mean that. Too much has happened, and it's happened too fast. You need time to think, to come to grips with it all. Have you had a chance to read Isabel's diaries?"

"No, not yet. Like I said, I haven't been home."

"Read them. Just promise me that when you do you'll call. Whether you believe it or not, we need to work this out. Together."

"I promised Nanita I would read her diaries, and I will. Still, I don't know whether or not my feelings will change after I do—about you or everything else," she said with an unhappy shrug. Her narrow shoulders slumped a bit, and she suddenly felt tiny under the burden she'd been carrying all week.

"Just read them, Trina, and maybe after you do you'll understand."

Trina could only nod, and when Carlos bent to kiss her goodbye she didn't flinch or pull away, but she didn't respond either—regardless of how her blood sang in her veins when his lips touched hers.

He left without saying another word, and all Trina could do was watch as he walked away, her heart even heavier than it was before.

***

Susan poured Trina another drink and sat back down on the couch across from her. Four empty bottles of merlot stood side by side on the coffee table like a row of dead sentinels, and whether it was from the wine or sheer exhaustion, the tension that had followed them home from the cemetery had finally seemed to dissipate. No one was feeling any pain.

Drumming her fingers on the side of her wine glass, Susan glanced at Louie and winked. "So, you little minx, just when were you planning on letting me and Louie in on your big secret?"

Taken completely off guard, Trina's eyes flashed in momentary panic. "What secret? What are you talking about?"

Louie smirked. "Oh, I don't know," he said with his finger on his chin for effect. "Maybe the one about our resident choir mistress getting her pipes cleaned on the sly?"

"What?" Trina sputtered, choking on her wine.

Holding his wine glass by its stem, he swirled the ruby liquid around, eyeing her over the rim of the cut glass. "You know exactly what we're talking about. We know who he is, honey. Susan never forgets a face—especially when it's attached to a good tip. She elbowed me the minute he walked up, chirping in my ear like an annoying seagull. But what I want to know is why you didn't introduce him to us after the service."

Still coughing, Trina wiped the back of her hand across her mouth. "Louie, please. I love you, but no questions tonight."

"Not a chance, honey," he said folding his arms unrepentantly in front of his chest.

Trina caught her breath, then exhaled. "That's the second time someone's said that to me tonight," she mumbled. Both of her friends sat there expectantly, and she couldn't help but wince. "What? There's really not much to tell. I met him at the club. We've seen each other a couple of times, but that's all," she hedged.

Louie blinked. "That's all? Honey, I could come up with a better story than that even on my worst bad hair day. You go from living like a nun to hooking up with a hottie that can barely tear his eyes from you, and you expect us to let you off the hook with that?" he questioned, cocking one brow.

"Louie, lay off. The poor girl's had a rough week. It's obvious she doesn't want to talk about it. Although, I do think it might take her mind off things if she told us a bit more about him…like say, his name, or maybe how they met? And for the record, Louie, when I say *us*, I really mean *me*," Susan said deliberately slanting her eyes toward Trina. "You know, Trin, I'm the one who should be put out considering I saw him first."

Trina shook her head. "Nice, Susan. Too bad no one ever told you passive-aggressive is an undesirable trait in a friend." She sighed. "Since I know you two will only nag me till my ears bleed, I might as well tell you. His name is Carlos. We met at the club the same night I threw that redneck asshole up against the mirrors. He witnessed the whole scene, along with everyone else in the gallery that night," she added dryly.

"Anyway, the two of us fell into talking. It all happened so fast. One minute I'm dealing with a handsy, out-of-town drunk, and the next I have a date. At first, it seemed too good to be true—*he* seemed too good to be true. It was like Carlos had stepped out of a dream or something. But then it got complicated," she said wistfully. "You guys know me. Never in a million years would I fall for someone that quickly. But I guess that's what happens when you let your guard down." Trina's voice was soft but it rang with regret.

"And…?" Louie prompted.

"And nothing. I really can't get into it, but let's just say the whole situation gave new meaning to the words *extraordinary* and *ironic*. Especially after I found out he knew my great-grandmother."

"He knew Isabel?" Susan replied her eyes owlish in surprise.

"Yep."

"*Jesus*, how? Is he a doctor?"

"No," Trina answered with a quick shake of her head. "The details are kind of fuzzy. I'm not really sure how they originally met, or how the whole thing came about, but somehow he was there with us at the end. Nanita regained consciousness right before she died and was lucid enough to recognize us both. The strange part is that she seemed overjoyed we had met, like it was some sort of predestined karmic reckoning. She even clasped our hands together and gave us some kind of blessing."

"Wow. Weird, *huh?*"

"You have no idea."

"So are you going to see him again?" Louie asked.

"That's just it. I don't know if I want to."

"For heaven's sake, why not?" Susan posed. "I mean he's gorgeous, and based on the wad of cash he threw my way, he's gotta be loaded. Aren't you even the slightest bit curious?"

Trina just shrugged. "Of course I am, but like I said, it's complicated. The situation is much more involved than anything a simple case of curiosity could resolve."

"I don't understand. Is he married?"

"No. It's nothing like that. Let's just say his lifestyle isn't exactly one that I'm comfortable with."

"Oh, please! Comfort is subjective. And whose lifestyle is completely normal, anyway? For that matter, what's normal? I mean, *jeez*, take a look at us…take a look at me!" Louie exclaimed, leaving his characteristic sarcasm behind for once.

Trina opened her mouth to say something, then thought better of it. There was no way in hell she could tell them the truth of the situation.

"Louie, that's not it at all. You know me better than that. I'm the last person who'd sit in judgment over anyone else's choices. This is different. I wish I could explain it more and maybe someday I will, but right now you guys are just going to have to trust me on this."

"Sweetie, I'm sorry, we didn't mean to pry. You'd never guess just by looking at him that Carlos was some kind of deviant," Susan said, concerned.

"He's not a deviant, Susan, he's just…different."

"Yeah, well, *different* is what makes the world go 'round. Take a walk on the wild side for once in your life, Trina, if for no other reason than to find out if that boy is as hot in the sack as he looks!"

Rolling her eyes, Susan pushed herself up from the couch. "And he's back! Such warmth, Louie. It never ceases to amaze. We'd better go before you really *do* make Trina's ears bleed," she said, and steered him toward the hall.

"Hey, she's the one with the pornographic dreams, remember?" he said with a sniff.

Laughing, Trina walked them out onto the front porch. "He may have a point," she said, giving Susan's shoulders a squeeze. "I don't know how I would have made it through this week without you guys." Pulling her sweater tighter around her waist, a shiver passed through her from more than just the crisp night air.

"Call me if you need anything, and remember my door is always open if it gets too creepy being alone around here." Susan winked.

Louie blew her a kiss from the sidewalk as Susan walked down the steps after him. "Anytime, girlfriend, and all kidding aside, you should give him a call. But in case you don't, you can always give him *my* number!"

"Ha! Not a chance!" Blowing them a kiss, she waved, watching the two weave unsteadily down the street until they turned the corner. She closed the door and leaned her head against the heavy hardwood. She was lucky. Friends like that were a blessing, but there was still no way she could let them in on her family's little secret.

The house seemed so still. She knew it was no quieter than it had been for the past month, no emptier, either. Tonight it just felt that way. Moving into the parlor, she stood just inside the doorway, consciously squelching the urge to pick up the phone and call Carlos. "Thanks a lot, Louie," she muttered. But regardless of her friend's advice, the truth was she hadn't been able to get him out of her mind all week.

To keep herself busy, she grabbed a tray and carried the empty wine bottles and half-empty glasses into the kitchen, piling everything into the sink. Standing there in the dark, she gripped the edge of the stainless steel. What now? She turned, pressing the cool, hard edge of the granite counter into the small of her back. The mahogany steps down the hall were shadowed in the ambient light, beckoning her to go upstairs and lie down. But the last thing she wanted was to face the reminders waiting for her in her room, regardless of her exhaustion.

She hadn't been home, not even for her own clothes. She had sent Louie to get them, which explained some of the over-the-top outfits she'd been running around in over the past week. Bracing herself, she walked through the darkened hall, and as she made her way upstairs she could almost hear her great-grandmother's voice telling her to stop being so silly.

She opened the door to her room, expecting an onslaught of memories. But instead of chaos, everything was in its place, including the black velvet box holding her antique mantilla. Someone had known enough to put it back in her jewelry case. *Someone*. It didn't take much for her to guess who.

She kicked off her shoes and sat on the edge of the bed. There was no rhyme or reason to this, no matter how she tried to figure it out. If the myths were true, then Carlos couldn't have come back. She had told him to get out. That meant one thing—he had sent people to clean up their mess. Shuddering at the thought of strangers in her house, she realized she no longer had a clue as to what was truth and what was fiction come to life.

She tossed her stockings into the hamper, and unzipped the back of her black dress, hanging it on the door with the rest of her dry cleaning. At her dresser, she took off her earrings and the rest of her jewelry. It was then she noticed her great-grandmother's locket lying on the mirrored tray. Carlos must have left it for her.

One of her oldest memories was of sitting on Nanita's lap and playing with the delicate gold. Never in a million years did she think something so innocent would hold the key to so much. She opened it, and her eyes met the tiny images inside, their surreal reality blatant and heartbreaking all over again. This time one thing was missing—the key to her great-grandmother's writing desk.

She searched the floor and the dresser, but it was nowhere to be found. Still in her bra and panties, she flew down the stairs and into the parlor, her mind in a spin. He wouldn't, would he? Why? Didn't he say he wanted her to read the diaries?

Trina snapped on the light and sure enough, there was an envelope with her name on it sitting on the beveled edge of the *papelera*. She tore it open and the key fell into her hand. With shaking hands, she opened the enclosed note. Written in elegant old-world script, she knew it was from Carlos before she even read the first word.

Trina,

I understand how overwhelmed you must feel at the extraordinary revelations to which you now find yourself privy. It is understandable after the shock from this past week that you would want to be alone, but I feel compelled to tell you just how astonished I am to find myself linked with you through such an unprecedented chain of events. Your memories of our time together may be filled with fear and disbelief, but mine are bittersweet…a mixture of unbelievable pleasure, hope, and sadly, regret. As you read Isabel's diaries, questions are to be expected. I want to be there to answer them the moment they spark in your mind. That way there will never be any doubt about who and what I am and how I feel about you. There is so much you don't know…so much you can't yet comprehend. When you are ready, I will come.

Carlos

Trina sat speechless in the glow of the antique Tiffany lamp. This was monumentally unfair. Hadn't she just finished convincing herself not to see him again? Carlos might not have known her very long, but it was clear he knew her well. And as for questions—was she really that transparent?

Tears threatened, stinging her eyes. "He's a vampire, Trina…a vampire," she repeated to herself. But her words were hollow. His heartfelt honesty ran through her head, clouding her thoughts even as her great-grandmother's words came back to strike a chord. *Don't be afraid, mi niña, and never be afraid of Carlos.*

Trina sniffed, wiping her eyes on the back of her hand. Complicated? Yeah, right—can anyone say understatement?

Taking a deep breath, she marshaled her thoughts. The diaries. They were what mattered now, regardless of the muddled mess churning inside her. Reading them, keeping her promise to her great-grandmother—that's what she was determined to do and all else be damned.

She carefully inserted the tiny key into the archaic lock, silently praying the mechanism would still work after all this time. Holding her breath, she turned the key, listening for the telltale click. She couldn't help but smile as the tumblers engaged and the door came ajar.

Amid a layer of dust and the scent of antique leather were at least two dozen or so leather-bound journals stacked neatly into the narrow space. Faded dates were scribbled along the spines, the oldest ones barely legible. Trina carefully pulled the bottom volume from the stack and opened the delicate cover. All she could do was stare. Written on the fragile vellum of the first page was the undeniable truth. *El Diario de Isabel della Cortes—el año de nuestro Señor, 1740*. The Diary of Isabel della Cortes—the year of our Lord, 1740.

Chapter 10

Pouring herself another cup of tea, Trina climbed into one of the parlor chairs and wrapped a soft woolen throw around her shoulders. Resting her cup on the antique end table, she settled in to continue reading. She marveled at the sense of personal history these journals held, but also at the painstaking work that must have gone into making each handcrafted sheet. She turned the pages almost reverently, afraid they would crumble in her hand if she moved too quickly.

They were yellowed, and on most the ink had faded, but as she ran her fingers over the delicate handwriting she could picture Isabel in her mind, youthful and vibrant, sitting with her quill in hand as she documented the extraordinary.

Between the faded ink and Isabel's long, looping script, translating her native Spanish was a daunting task. Her chronicle began shortly after she was married, describing in detail the two years it took for her to completely regain her strength, and how Jeffrey had kept his promise to Carlos and cared for her.

As Trina read each of the slender volumes, she could hear Nanita's voice in her head, her soft accent rhythmic and musical in her mind as she told her story. It was well into the morning as Trina continued to turn page after page, book after book. She was compelled to hear the story through to the end. Without realizing it, she eventually found herself skimming past the mundane accountings of Isabel's daily life and searching for any mention of Carlos. It wasn't until she picked up the seventh diary that she found what she didn't even realize she was looking for.

The 18th of April, the year of our Lord, 1781

Easter is but a week off, yet the air is damp and cold, as I go about the streets of London in preparation of the day. The people here are pleasant, and though they have long since accepted me as one of their own and no longer mind my accented English, I am nonetheless homesick.

Perhaps it is the spring or the want of it in this cold, wet place that makes my heart yearn for the warmth of Spain. It has been years since Jeffrey and I arrived on this rocky shore—just one year after that fateful night when I lost Carlos to the demon that so violently took his life, and in return had him lust for mine.

That night would have forever remained a poignant blur if not for Jeffrey's accountings. Perhaps that terrible night burns so brightly in my mind because of the recent association with which we now find ourselves graced.

After years of quiet solitude from the nightmare of his time in the service to Sir Robert Mayfair, Jeffrey has once again unwittingly made the acquaintance of a nightwalker. Even as I grant the incontrovertible truth of their existence, a part of me still tries desperately to deny them—even as they move among us cloaked in their inhumanity. The marks Jeffrey and I carry have since faded, but to the elders of their race they remain a herald of our past encounters.

Oh, rightly, I am sure my beloved Jeffrey would think me uncharitable in my opinions, for this new acquaintance is undeniably a man of genteel grace, and manages somehow to remain a practitioner of human compassion—however inhuman he may be. His name is Dominic De'Lessep, and although he boasts centuries in age and experience, he looks to be no older than we. But then, neither Jeffrey nor I resemble our true ages for almost the same reasons.

While Dominic candidly admits he has in the past been guilty of the same kinds of behaviors we are wont to fear, he has for some reason befriended my dear husband, assuring him he has regained his humanity in the only way left to him—to revere the human race and to seek his sustenance amongst the animals of the field and wood. He believes this is his way to redemption. And although he forces none of this enlightenment on others of his kind, instead leaving each to his own devices, he chuckles over the fact that some of his brethren have found his philosophies novel, even eccentric.

I am loath to admit a fondness for him has managed to find its way past my fears, and so it has come to pass that an unusual comradeship has formed. It was from him that we recently came to learn of Carlos and what became of him. And as I have never held Carlos culpable for his attack on my person, I was thus grateful for the news.

Dominic joined us at nightfall, after our evening repast. And as we sat by the fire I commented on the unusual chill for a Palm Sunday, and spoke of my yearning for the warmer climes. It was at this point that he embarked on an amusing tale about one of his expeditions south. He spoke of a young nightwalker who he encountered during his travels, one so despairing of his nature that he brought himself to near starvation before succumbing to his need for blood. He said he stood by and watched as the man reduced himself to pure need, then ravaged those in his wake, crying with such despondency in the aftermath of his actions that it touched Dominic's heart.

Dominic went on to say it was obvious the young man was newly born to this existence, and that he wore the marks of one turned against his will. He found himself intrigued by the young one's struggle against the violence and bloodlust that surely raged through him, for those turned in violence and lust forever lose any connection to their former humanity. My heart bled, for at that moment I somehow knew the young nightwalker of whom he spoke to be none other than Carlos.

Dominic spoke of how he invited the young man to share his lodging against the coming dawn. The two fell easily into conversation, their exchange lasting well past sunset the following evening. It was there that Dominic learned of Carlos's past and his connection to us. From then the two traveled together, Dominic as teacher and Carlos as student—learning from Dominic how to rebuild and strengthen the threads binding himself to his remaining humanity.

Although their encounter occurred decades in the past, I am not ashamed to confess I sobbed in Jeffrey's arms, grateful that Carlos had managed stay true to the decent man I had loved—a man Jeffrey remembered as one to be respected for his integrity and struggle, yet feared for the fragile veneer that held him so tenuously to his humanity.

It gave us pause, realizing that although Dominic and Carlos had both been changed unalterably, their strength of will and truth of character had overcome even their most heinous of fates. The true nature of their virtue enabled them to remain forever the men God had intended them to be.

My prayer is that wherever Carlos may be, and on whatever journey his life has taken him, that he is contented. And that somehow, some way, he will know I forgive him.

Trina sat there in stunned silence as the late morning sun filtered through the sheers, bathing the parlor in a clean light. Patterns of sunlight dotted the floor, and as she watched them dance, she understood the cliché of how everything looks clearer in the cold light of day.

There was still so much to learn, so many questions she wished she could ask. Isabel's clear, steady hand had already given Trina more than she had hoped for. Isabel's words had pulled away the veil of doubt and shame. Through her words, she had relived Isabel's pain, her fear, her doubts—and finally, her forgiveness. She now knew exactly what had happened to her great-grandmother, and who was responsible. What she didn't know was why.

Although she had searched as she read the first time through, Trina could only find disjointed references to the events that brought Carlos to his fate. Perhaps Isabel didn't know the full story, or perhaps it was just too painful to recount. She wrote that Carlos had forged a bond with Dominic, that he had been the one privy to the story—immortal confidants, with her and Jeffrey as their common connection. But that was all. Trina knew there was only one person who could tell her the truth of what happened and that was Carlos himself.

Closing the last journal, she placed it with the others on the end table and stretched. She had read for seventeen hours straight, stopping only to eat and to pee. Her back was a mess from sitting for so long and it cracked as she stood up. Even during her worst final exams, she had never pulled an all-nighter like this. Well, at least she didn't have to go into work this evening. Rick had been really good about giving her some time off and she knew Susan and Louie would cover her shifts.

Yawning, she glanced down at the pile of journals stacked neatly in front of her. She was tired and bleary-eyed, but she hadn't felt this good in a long time. It was as if everything that had unraveled this past week had managed to weave itself back together. The threads of her life had come together in a tapestry that spanned the centuries, and Trina knew she would never be the same. She was connected to Isabel, to her family and her past in a way that just couldn't be explained—and for the first time in her life, she knew who she was.

She picked up the journals and locked them carefully back into their hiding place. Opening her great-grandmother's locket, she hesitated as she went to put the key inside, looking at the tiny images of Carlos and Isabel as it lay open in her hand. There was only one loose thread that remained. Trina knew she needed to either snip it clean, or weave into a place in her life. But which? She snapped the locket closed, slipped it into her pocket, and headed upstairs. She had a lot to think about.

***

Holding a half-empty cup of coffee, Trina picked at the Styrofoam until the sidewalk at her feet looked like it had been dusted with tiny white balls. "Just walk across the street and ring the goddamn bell, Trina. It's not like he doesn't already know you're here," she said under her breath.

Self-conscious, she kicked at the white mess with her heel. "Great, now I'm talking to myself in a random doorway." Without thinking about the condition of her cup, she took a sip of her coffee. Her eyes flew open and she turned awkwardly from side to side looking for a place to spit. "Ew!" she sputtered, wiping loose pieces of Styrofoam from her tongue.

Scrubbing the front of her jacket with a napkin, she glanced at the elegant wrought-iron balustrade lining the curved stone steps of Carlos's townhouse. "Classy, Trina," she muttered, grimacing while she continued to scrub.

All afternoon she had grappled with whether or not to call, arguing with herself as she showered, and even as she tried to catch a little sleep. As the afternoon wore on, curiosity triumphed over caution and she decided to take her first steps onto the wild side. Louie would be so proud. But even as she told herself it was nothing more than a need to finish what she started, she couldn't help the nervous quiver that ran through her lower belly as she stood there looking at his house like some kind of stalker.

She had expected her call to go straight to voice mail, and when Carlos picked up, she wasn't sure who was more surprised. Here she was, and anticipation flooded her system like a drug. The butterflies in her stomach had somehow morphed into a swarm of bees, shooting tiny stingers of nervous pain into her abdomen as she walked across the street and up the stairs to his front door. "The better part of valor and all that jazz," she mumbled as she rang the bell.

Trina's heart did a little flip-flop as he opened the door and smiled. He was even more beautiful than she remembered. It was sunset, and the reflected glow made him seem even more real, yet unreal.

"You have no idea how happy I am that you're here, that you decided to call," he said, taking her hand. His eyes pierced hers, and no sooner did their hands touch then she knew he was aware of all she'd learned, that she knew what he'd done to Isabel.

He looked at her in amazement, as if surprised she hadn't run screaming for her life. Trina had taken it in stride, and she wondered if he felt her determined curiosity, as well as her budding compassion. If he guessed every one of the hundred questions racing through her mind, despite her underlying fears.

"I can understand your apprehension in coming here this evening. There's really no reason for you to be afraid. Except for the housekeeping staff there's no one here but me, and I promise I'll be on my best behavior." He crossed his heart and flashed a reassuring smile. "Please, come in."

Trina face flushed with embarrassment. "I know that, Carlos, and I appreciate the welcome. It's silly how I can't help my nerves sometimes, especially when I'm out of my comfort zone, and this whole situation qualifies more as *Twilight Zone* than comfort zone," she said with a nervous chuckle.

Not quite knowing what do next, she quickly leaned up and kissed his cheek.

In a flash, Carlos's arms circled her waist. "How I managed to be blessed enough to find you, I will never know," he said, pressing his lips to her temple.

Trina felt a slash of guilt, despite the warmth flooding her lower belly. This wasn't what she had come here for. As attracted as she was to him, if she wanted any sort of answers, she was going to have to make sure they kept it light, and that meant keeping Carlos at a distance. A tiny sarcastic voice in the back of her mind whispered, *"Yeah, right…good luck with that."*

She put her hands on his chest and gently pushed herself back. "Carlos, please. I shouldn't have done that. The last thing I want is to send you mixed signals, especially from someone as mixed up as me. I came here to talk. I have so many questions, and I need to understand why things happened. Hopefully, you'll be able to fill in the blanks." She tried to sound as apologetic as she felt. "Maybe it would have been better if I had waited longer to call."

He took her hand and kissed it, and the gesture made her heart jump remembering the last time he'd done that. Breathing in his clean, sexy scent, she closed her eyes. *God help me. Did he have to smell so damn good?*

"Of course, please forgive my…enthusiasm," he said, but she couldn't help notice the small smile that tugged at his mouth. He affected her and he knew it. "Let's go into my study. We can talk there."

Trina could only nod as she followed him inside.

The foyer was sumptuous, with its thick Aubusson carpet and carved wooden staircase. Paintings as tall as her lined the walls, and an antique, beveled glass chandelier hung from the ceiling in front of a stained-glass window looking out onto the street.

"Are you hungry? Rosa, my housekeeper, is a fabulous chef. I can have her whip something up, or we could order in pizza if you'd rather something quick," he offered as he led her into the study.

She smiled tentatively as she took in the rich décor. "Funny, I never took you for someone who orders take-out…I mean, I didn't think…I mean before…I mean when I thought you were…" she stuttered, feeling her cheeks start to burn again at her own incoherent rambling.

"That's quite all right, *querida,* I understood what you meant. No harm, no foul." He chuckled.

Carlos was nothing if not gracious, and here she was acting like some kind of driveling idiot. *Get it together, girl, this is what you wanted.* Sitting down on the soft leather couch, she took a quiet breath.

She'd rather starve than feel like an imposition, and as if he knew it, he took his cell phone from his pocket and handed it to her. "I have the pizzeria on speed dial. Just press seven and tell them the order is for Salazar. If my guess is correct, with the kind of questions you have waiting for me we're going to be here a while."

Trina hesitated. "No, that's okay…"

"Go ahead," he insisted. "After all, I still owe you a dinner, right?"

Trina gave him half a smile. He was referring, of course, to their date at the Met. The same night everything hit the fan. Well, at least now everything was out in the open. With a nod, she took the phone and dialed. He sat down next to her on the couch, with his arm across the top of the pillows. And so it began.

***

Carlos inhaled. A metallic tang of anxiety had saturated the room when Trina first arrived, but now all he smelled was pizza and her overwhelming curiosity. She had calmed down completely, and he was amazed at how well she managed to pocket her fear. He paid the delivery guy, and carried the food into the study.

She helped herself to the pizza, and he watched the sway of her hips as she walked back toward the couch.

"Sure you don't want a slice?" she asked, swallowing a mouthful of stringy cheese. "It tastes like they didn't use much garlic."

Carlos took a bottle of merlot from the wine rack to the left of the sideboard and meticulously cut the thin metal wrapping from around the neck. "That's a fallacy. Garlic doesn't affect me one bit."

"So, what does affect you, then?"

He winked, twisting the corkscrew into the center and pulling it from the bottle with an audible pop. "Well, you, for one," he said, pouring the wine into a glass and handing it to her.

"That's not what I meant and you know it," she said, taking a sip and peering at him from above the rim of the crystal.

Carlos's lips curled upward as he leaned against the back of the bar swirling his wine. "Then you'd better qualify what you mean by 'affects' me." His gaze pierced hers, and he couldn't resist the play on words.

Trina shifted in her seat, and he caught the faintest trace of arousal mixed with the wine's oaky bouquet. "I thought you said you'd answer anything I asked. I want to know these things, so come on…if garlic doesn't bother you, then what about the other things? What things are myths and what will actually *'dispatch the undead'*?" she asked, doing her best Dracula impression.

He raised an eyebrow at her. "Cutting right to the chase, eh? Well, I hope you'd at least get to know me better before you try to 'dispatch the undead'," he mimicked.

Considering her for a moment, he sipped his wine before answering. "Fire, decapitation, the sun…although that one lessens as we age. That's about it."

"What, no stake through the heart? No holy water?"

"Funny…you're a funny girl."

He sat down next to her on the couch. Was it simple curiosity, or was there a method behind her litany of questions? She said she came here looking for answers, but was this all what she wanted? Vampire 101? Carlos looked at her, and her quiet probing eyes. "No. You would literally have to cut out my heart…as opposed to just breaking it."

Trina didn't answer. A transitory shadow passed her eyes, and she appeared lost in thought, like she was filing everything away somewhere behind those vivid green eyes. In that moment, Carlos sat listening to her heartbeat, wishing he could read her better.

She frowned down at her hands. The silence between them was thick, and Trina reached for a cloth napkin to wipe her mouth. When she turned, her eyes met his again and they were tender. "I don't know what to say, except I would never intentionally break anyone's heart."

"I know that, *querida*…and I didn't mean to make you uncomfortable. Forgive me?"

Trina blushed. "I'm not uncomfortable, Carlos. I'm just trying to take it one step at a time."

High color stained her cheeks, and the rosy tone was almost as delicious as the scent of the blood causing the sudden flush. "I know that too, and I'm glad. Back to questions, then?" With a smirk, he freed the cloth napkin from her unconscious vise grip and wiped the corner of her mouth. "Missed a spot."

She exhaled a chuckle. "Sorry, I guess I had more of an appetite than I thought. So, right…back to my questions. What were you saying about the sun? Do you burst into flames as legend says? And what happens as time passes? Do you age at all?"

He smiled at her tenacity. "When one is first turned, the sun is a deadly thing. Even so, it's like anything else in life. You can build up a tolerance for it as your blood ages and becomes stronger. I have met elders of my kind who can walk in the full sun of midday and not have it affect them in the slightest."

Trina got up for a second slice of pizza and refilled her wine glass. "What do you mean by build up a tolerance? The more time passes, the more human you become?"

"No. I'll never be human again, but what it does mean is that I can partake of certain things. You said one of the things you found unusual about me when we first met was that I didn't eat. That's true, but not because I can't eat. It's because my body won't metabolize the food. Human food makes me slightly ill, like I've ingested something my body considers foul. Kind of like what would happen to you if you ate dirt."

"But you do drink," she said, indicating his wine. "Doesn't that bother you as well?"

"It used to, but the older I get, the more I can tolerate. My body doesn't seem to mind liquids, the more organic the better. I couldn't drink a Coke, for example, but mineral water is fine, especially since water is a key component in blood. I seem to be okay with certain naturally fermented alcohol as well." He shrugged. "It really doesn't do anything for me, though. I do it more to keep up appearances."

"What about what you mentioned before, about the sun? Is that something you can tolerate?"

"Are you trying to ask me in a roundabout way how old I am? After everything we've been through this past week, just ask. You already know almost everything there is to know about me." Carlos kept a smile on his face though he knew his statement wasn't quite the truth.

"All right," she said playfully, and with a sly look, grabbed a book off the coffee table and placed his right hand on top. Feigning a serious expression, she cleared her throat. "Sir, for the record, will you please state your full name and your age."

Chuckling, he answered. "I was born Carlos Antonio Jose Salazar, in the year of Our Lord, 1711, in Valencia, Spain."

At the look on her face, he nodded. "That's right, Trina. I may have said I was twenty-six years old, but the truth is I have been so for two hundred and seventy-five years. The last time I celebrated my birthday as a human, it was 1737. Which makes me over three hundred years old."

The full impact of the term *immortal vampire* and its dreamlike reality must have hit her at that point, and she suddenly grew very serious. "How did you...die?" she asked, hesitating as if the words were somehow stuck in her throat.

"I'm sure you've heard of the Spanish Inquisition. It began in 1478 under Isabella of Castile in her quest to purify Spain of its heretics. Tomas de Torquemada was her first inquisitor-general. There have been many parodies over the years, but the truth of the tortures and atrocities carried out in the name of God remain true nevertheless.

"Most people felt they were carrying out God's work and labeled Torquemada 'the savior of Spain.' Torquemada was evil and reveled in his power. He did unspeakable things to innocent people, and though many people believed his actions and ideology were neither condoned nor continued after his death, the truth remains they were still very much in practice up until the year I died. A fact that is both sad and ironic.

"We believed this was not what Christ intended and certainly not the kind of thing he would have wanted done in his name. We tried to help as many people as possible escape."

Trina sat, her face amazed as he spoke about his life and how his people had banded together to form a kind of underground movement against the abuses carried out in the name of God and the church. Carlos was eighteen years old when he began his crusade, and for eight years, he and his group managed to smuggle people out of Spain to safety.

As Carlos spoke, he kept his voice calm and an iron grip on his rage and regret. He spoke as if a narrator, retelling an event from history.

"I was on a mission to procure passage to the east for a friend. His name had been reported to the inquisitor's guard, it was only a matter of time before he, and his family were arrested. Passage of this nature was usually procured in places that were less than savory. I had my usual contacts in the various bars along the coast and made the customary inquiries. It wasn't long before I had a lead on a ship willing to take on passengers of this kind. I met with the captain's agent and handled the negotiations late one night in the port town of Cadiz." Carlos closed his eyes.

"The Captain asked about my accommodations for the night and I told him I would probably be spending the night with my horse. He asked if I would like to join him and his crew on the ship, and I welcomed the chance at sleeping in an actual bed. It was aboard this ship that I met the man who changed my life…who took my life."

Carlos recounted the events, speaking quickly and without emotion. Trina was riveted by the images he conjured, and though she knew the story wasn't going to end well, she had asked him the question. That he was willing to tell her meant the world, and she knew it was something she needed to hear.

"I awoke that first sunset to what I am. It's taken centuries, but I have come to terms with who and what I am, trying to live this life by honoring the human one I once possessed. I know Isabel's diaries told you what I did to her, so to spare us both the pain I won't reiterate the story. But I've lived with that regret from sunset to sunset until she finally forgave me. For many years, I wandered, living on the fringe of humanity as well as on the fringe of my own kind. I drove myself to near insanity. If it hadn't been for another immortal, I would never have found any peace. He gave me a way to live my life again."

"You're talking about Dominic."

Carlos was astounded. "How do you know about that?"

"Isabel's diaries. Somehow, he and Jeffrey knew each other and became fast friends. He eventually told them about meeting this young nightwalker, as Isabel referred to your kind. As Dominic told them the story, they came to the realization it was you. Isabel wept for what happened to you, but wept more that you stayed true to the man she knew and loved. She wrote that she hoped you were happy and that she never held you responsible for what happened. She forgave you, Carlos, a very long time ago."

Carlos hung his head, drained. He looked weary. He'd kept his emotions in check as best he could, but she felt his pain regardless—his revulsion at his own lust, at his own cravings, and his overwhelming regret.

Trina knew he had evolved in this life, in all the centuries that had ensued. The man he had been, the one who had been willing to risk death to save those suffering unjustly, was still there in the man sitting next to her today. The fate that had befallen him may have changed his body, but it hadn't changed who he was, of that, she was sure—just as she was sure her feelings for him had somehow changed.

She was falling for him.

She lifted his bowed head so she could look into his eyes, then kissed him passionately, driving her hands into his hair, crushing his mouth to hers. Stunned, Carlos's fingers gripped her shoulders. He hesitated for less than a moment, then held her fiercely, kissing her back. He felt his body harden with such need that he picked her up and carried her down the hall to the stairs without breaking their kiss. He took the stairs three and a time, kicking open the door to his quarters.

He stripped off Trina's clothes and climbed over her, crawling up her body sensuously, like a cat rubbing her sensitive skin and teasing her with light licks and tiny bites till he reached her mouth. He devoured her lips in another kiss.

Trina's hand wound around his neck and she arched back. Carlos trailed kisses down her throat and through the valley between her breasts. He cupped their heavy weight in his hand and suckled, teasing and biting one with his mouth as his thumb teased the other.

She arched her back even more, moaning as his tongue teased her nipples into hard peaks. Wrapping her legs around his waist, she pushed wildly against him—trying for more friction, frantic for release.

His hand drifted across her belly and worked his way down to the fluffy, dark curls at the juncture of her thighs. Trina parted her legs for him as she bucked up against his hand, urging him to enter her, but he pushed her hand aside.

"Patience, my love. I'm not finished," he said, lowering his head and blowing gently on her curls and sending little tingles down into her core. He continued to kiss her and play, as his fingers lightly brushed her sensitive, swollen bud in light, languorous strokes until Trina thought she would cry with need.

"Is there something you want from me, Trina?" he asked as he continued to tease her. At the sound of her growled response, he plunged his fingers into her wet, slick sex, using his thumb to rub her taut nub in vigorous circles.

Raising her hips, she bucked against his hand. He felt her stomach muscles bunch as the muscles of her inner walls began to squeeze and contract as she reached climax.

Panting, she reveled for a moment in the aftershocks, then pushed his hand aside.

"My turn," she said, her eyes never leaving his as came up on all fours. Ordering him to strip, she straddled him, sliding her body over his torso, letting her sensitive breasts rub against the rough hair of his chest. She teased his nipples with her teeth and buried her face in his stomach, licking a trail down through his nest of black curls to the base of his member. Thick and swollen, the sight of his sex was just as intimidating as it was the very first time.

Carlos was average height, about five feet, eleven inches, with a lean and well-muscled body. Strong thighs and a defined back supported his broad shoulders and solid abs, but when he stood in front of Trina, naked and aroused, the only thing she could see was his massive erection—long and thick with a bulging head that looked like it would tear her apart. She couldn't keep her eyes from it. Luckily, for her, Carlos knew how to use it, wielding nothing but pleasure.

Trina stroked and suckled and Carlos's body grew rigid. She licked the full length of his hard, silken shaft, sliding his head, swollen and pulsing, into her mouth. Carlos breathed in sharply and held his breath for a moment. He fisted the hair at the back of her head urging her to take more of him, deeper, faster. He made a noise between a moan and a snarl, and when Trina looked up, she saw his face had changed. He was close to climax. She pulled away from him and he roared in protest.

"Do you want me, Carlos?" Trina asked her face intense and her voice breathless. Carlos flipped her onto her back and with one furious thrust, buried himself within her soft, swollen folds. He was fighting for control, holding back, and Trina could see him struggling with his darker side.

"All of me, Carlos. Not just my body, my blood too. Take all of me now!"

Carlos plunged into her body once again and sank his fangs deep into her neck.

A flood of pleasure and pain mingled in a sweet rush and it pushed Trina over the edge. She cried out as she climaxed again, screaming Carlos's name. He hissed at the sound of her cry, pumping his hips furiously one powerful thrust after another.

The tension reached its peak with his body buried deep within her sex and his fangs buried deep within her neck. He released her throat and with a guttural roar reared up as he climaxed, his seed exploding hot and deep within her.

As the last spasms shook them, he held Trina tight, closing her wounds with a flick of his tongue. They collapsed together, spent and happy, in a tangle of sheets that smelled of sex, sweat, and blood.

***

Carlos ran a bath for them while Trina went to pour herself a glass of orange juice from a tray he had sent up to his bedroom. Chuckling, she walked back into the bathroom, carrying her glass.

"What's so funny?" he asked with a confused smile as he swirled scented herbs into the bath water.

"This," she said, raising the glass. "The Red Cross always makes you drink orange juice after you donate blood." She took a large gulp and then set the glass down, perching herself on the edge of the vanity.

"Oh," he said regretfully. He looked at her, his face a little ashamed. "I'm sorry, Trina."

"I'm not," she said emphatically. "That was one of the most wonderfully intense experiences of my life. So don't you go and get all maudlin on me. I asked for it, remember?"

He took a deep breath, then walked over and wrapped his arms around her. "I'll try to remember that." Kissing her gently, he took her by the hand and led her over to the tub. "Come on. The water is perfect."

They eased their way into the steaming, fragrant water. Trina loved the fact that the Jacuzzi was big enough for the two of them.

They made love again amidst the churning bubbles of air, but slowly this time, languorously, making sure they enjoyed every delicious moment together.

Trina lay back against his chest as he played with the bubbles, drawing lazy circles over her full breasts. "You never answered my question," she teased, playing with his fingers as they swirled over her body.

"What question?"

"About the sun. Are you old enough yet to come out and play in the sunshine with me?"

"You just love being the comedian, don't you?" he said with an exasperated sigh, but Trina felt his lips curl into a smile as they grazed her cheek.

"Well?"

"Yes. I can walk in the sun, but only when it is not very strong."

"You mean like early morning or late afternoon? What about overcast days?"

"Yes, to all of the above."

"That's great! This means sometimes we can spend the night and the whole next day together!"

"Let's not get too carried away. It's not as much time as you'd think. I still have to be very careful and make sure I have cover available to me at all times. Sunscreen is not going to help me one bit if the weather suddenly clears or we misjudge the time of day. So don't go planning any picnics on the beach for us just yet," he said, laughing at her enthusiasm.

"I won't, but don't rain on my parade, okay?"

"Rain on a parade day would be a good thing for us."

Trina went to splash him playfully but instead he grabbed her hand and kissed it. "I think maybe we should be getting out soon. Your hands are all pruned and the water is getting cold."

They toweled off and slipped into a couple of thick terry robes hanging from the back of the bathroom door. Trina picked up her glass and walked over to the dresser to pour herself some more juice. Feeling a little lightheaded, she grabbed a couple of cookies too. *God bless the Red Cross,* she thought, munching her way through the sugar cookies.

Trina sat down next to Carlos as he flipped through a DVD case looking for something for them to watch.

"I think it's time you met my family," he said, suddenly but with complete nonchalance.

Trina turned to look at him in utter surprise. "You have a family?" she asked incredulously.

"Well, what did you think? That I've lived all these centuries alone like a hermit?"

"No…yes…no…Oh, I don't know. I know you mentioned it when you drove me home that night, but afterward…I guess I thought you only said that to be polite," she said, embarrassed.

"I have a house full of people who rely on me and on whom I rely. They are my family."

"Why haven't you brought them up before?" she asked, a little perplexed and at the same time a little hurt. "Are they all vampires like you?"

Carlos almost cringed at Trina's last question. This was it. The moment he had been dreading almost as much as he had dreaded her finding out his true nature. "I didn't mention it before because you really weren't speaking to me, remember? However, to answer your question, no, they're not all vampires, although the ones that are have been with me for many, many years. The others, well, they're like…like…" He hesitated, not sure what to tell her. He couldn't very well tell her that in his world they were referred to as pets. She'd never understand. To a vampire, pets were more like wards, not like dogs or cats. Maybe she'd understand if he put it to her that way.

"Like what?" she asked, confused at his hesitation.

"More like foster kids."

"Oh," she said.

Carlos knew by her tone, and how she chewed on her bottom lip, that she was turning his words over in her mind. He could almost hear those wheels spinning and the questions forming, but he beat her to the chase. "Why don't we get dressed and you can see for yourself?

I promise, no dungeons with chains, no coffins or large harpsichords playing eerie music."

Trina just smirked and slapped at his shoulder. She leaned against him and he put his arm around her shoulders. "No, not tonight. I'd rather stay here with you, just us. It's too soon, anyway. Maybe in the next couple of weeks or so. I'm off on Sundays. We can do it at some point then. All right?"

Carlos leaned over and kissed the top of her head. "Whatever you wish," he said, brushing the side of her cheek and her ear with his index finger. His relief was palpable. At least now, he'd have the opportunity to prepare not only his family, but himself as well.

"Carlos?"

"Mmmmmm?"

"Your foster kids, wards...or whatever... Do you and the other vampires feed from them?"

Carlos's body froze. Just when he thought he'd dodged a bullet for a couple of weeks, that damn mind of hers. He took a deep breath and told her the truth. "Yes, *mi vida*. We do. It's a very common thing in my world."

"Is sex a part of it when you drink their blood as well?"

He cringed, he should have known. There was no going back now. "At times, yes. But it is not something that is necessary, although the person…ah…donating their blood does get pleasure out of the experience."

"Oh."

Carlos turned so they were sitting face to face. He wanted to see her, to look into her eyes as he spoke. "Trina, I have shared many experiences with many different people, vampires and humans alike, over these many centuries. You can't have expected that I was a celibate nomad for almost three centuries, could you? I have loved in the past, but there has been nothing, and no one, that has made me feel the way you do. Since we have been together I have shared blood with those in my family, but that is all. Blood is required for my life. Unfortunately, you are going to have to realize and accept that even though you are giving me your blood, it will not be enough. It would weaken you too much."

Trina began to protest, but Carlos interrupted her, placing a finger on her lips. "There is no other way. The only being with enough blood strength to sustain me would be another vampire, and I don't think you are ready for that yet. Are you?"

Trina shook her head. She looked sadly at Carlos and cuddled up next to him, resting her head on his silent chest. He stroked the back of her hair, whispering reassurances into her still-damp curls.

"Come and meet my family, Trina. See the way we are together. I know then all your worries and apprehensions will be put to rest." Carlos kissed her hair again. He sincerely hoped he was right.

Chapter 11

Trina stood in the spray of the shower letting the water cascade over her head and shoulders. It felt wonderful. She felt wonderful. These past three weeks had been the happiest of her life so far. With her iPod plugged into the speakers on her nightstand, music filtered into the bathroom behind the sound of the running water. She sighed contentedly, singing along to Faith Hill's *Breathe* playing in the background as she finished rinsing the last of the shampoo from her hair.

With her eyes closed, she smiled to herself as she pictured his face, his incredible mouth, his laughter. How his smell made her want to tear her clothes from her body, and how his kiss always made her forget where she was or what she had to do.

Behind her lids, she could see Carlos clearly, remembering everything they had done and all the places they had been. How he looked in the candlelight at dinner as he kissed her hands across the table, or with the wind in his hair as they walked the beach just before sunset. Or how he had awakened her body like no other had before.

She leaned against the shower's tiled wall and out of the direct spray. The water from her hair fell in tiny rivulets between her breasts and she ran her thumbs gently over her nipples, picturing his mouth, when she heard the phone ringing.

"Shit," she said, exasperated, as she turned off the water and stepped out onto the bathmat. "Hang on. I'm coming!" she yelled to no one, grabbing a towel and running to answer it before it stopped ringing.

"Hello?" She huffed, a little out of breath, and struggled to keep her towel in place.

"Are you all right, *mi amor*? You sound a little winded."

"Carlos. Yeah, um, sorry. I was in the shower. Is everything okay?" Heat rose in her face like she'd been caught doing something she oughtn't. "I thought we were meeting at the club tonight. I'm working, remember?"

"We are. It's an hour's drive to the house, so I wanted to remind you I'm picking you up around ten."

Trina chewed on her bottom lip. Just the mention of meeting Carlos's family sent her nerves into overdrive. *Shit*—and a minute ago she'd been so relaxed. "Ten o'clock. Got it," she repeated.

"Your enthusiasm is staggering. Are you still nervous about meeting everyone? Trina, how many times do I have to reassure you?"

"Sorry, I can't help it. This isn't exactly your average come meet the family scenario."

He chuckled. "I'll grant you that, but I promise you have nothing to worry about. Dress casually. Prozac optional. I'll see you at ten."

Trina hung up the phone. "Can't wait," she muttered, heading back into the bathroom.

***

The gates to the estate swung open as Carlos pulled into the drive. Trina had made small talk the whole ride out of the city, chatting nonchalantly as she tried to keep her mind off their destination. However, the farther north they traveled, the quieter she became, barely saying a word as they navigated the streets of the sleepy hamlet of Verplanck, New York.

Pulling through the gates, he slid his eyes sideways and caught her fidgeting again. "Will you please relax? They're going to love you. Besides, what can they say? I'm the head of the house, remember?"

"I remember," Trina said dryly. "Let's just hope they're not planning a coup."

Carlos laughed. "There's my girl. I was wondering when she was going to show up. I told you, nothing to worry about."

Trina pushed at his shoulder and laughed uneasily. She was going to a visit house full of vampires and vampire wannabes with her vampire lover. Nope, calm just wasn't in the cards tonight.

"*This* is your driveway?" she commented as they wound their way around toward the front of the house. It was more like a private road, and she could only assume the little cottages they passed along the way were for the staff.

As the house came into view, she was dumbstruck by its sheer size. Flanked by large oaks and sitting at the pinnacle of a circular drive was a stunning Georgian brick colonial. The word mansion didn't go far enough. She counted eleven chimneys, the largest of which were on either end. One side of the house was a glass conservatory, and the other a large veranda that sparked the imagination back to a bygone era. As they pulled in toward the front, she caught a glance of the river and the breadth of the property leading toward the dock. The place needed its own ZIP code.

They got out of the car and walked hand in hand to the front door. White columns supported an ivy-covered portico, and a graceful arch of stained glass welcomed them as they walked past toward the entryway. "Nice digs. And to think you were impressed by my little townhouse in the city," Trina said with a smirk.

"If you remember correctly, I think it was you I was impressed with," he said, lifting her hand to his lips.

Trina felt one kind of tension leave her body, only to be replaced by another. She closed her eyes as the touch of his lips sent shivers through her. Would she ever get used to the way her body responded to his? God, she hoped not.

"Hello? Anybody home?" Carlos called as they walked into the foyer.

Trina plastered her best smile on her face as she waited for the "family" to make their appearance. Her anxiety had renewed itself and she swallowed hard against the butterflies winging around in her stomach. This was it. Fidgeting with the buttons on her jean jacket, she smoothed her hair twice.

"Càlmase! El olor de su miedo me està quemando la nariz." he whispered.

Normally Trina found it very romantic whenever Carlos spoke to her in Spanish, but telling her that the smell of her anxiety was starting to burn the inside of his nose left a lot to be desired. "Terrific. Why don't you just add to my nervousness?" she whispered back sullenly. "Maybe we should just leave this for another night."

"What, and deprive the rest of us from finally meeting the one person who's managed to enthrall our fearless leader? Aw, love, you can't possibly be that cruel, now can you?" a deep voice said from off to the left.

Trina turned. The subtle British accent belonged to a young man, and without a second look she knew he was also a vampire. With his arms crossed casually in front of his chest, he leaned against an open set of French doors, his foot propped indifferently against the molding. His relaxed pose made it obvious he was part of the family, but Trina guessed that behind his casual demeanor he was shrewdly evaluating her.

The young vampire was slightly taller than Carlos, with light sandy hair and green eyes, and though he seemed to be somewhere in his mid-twenties, looks didn't mean a thing. For all Trina knew he could have been older than dirt.

"Why don't you introduce me to your lovely lady, Carlos? Although I must say I feel as though I already know her, since you've done nothing but chatter on about her for the past three weeks."

At his words, Trina knew her face was a wash of color, and with her auburn hair, it never failed to make her feel like a walking tomato.

Pushing himself away from his perch, he smiled and walked over. Trina could feel subtle changes in the air, and even without the benefit of vampiric senses, it was obvious he was up to something.

"Trina, this is my brother, Julian," Carlos said, shooting him a look.

Trina looked from one to the other. They held no resemblance whatsoever. After the brutal way Carlos was changed, she couldn't believe he would turn on one of his own. Or would he? As much as she knew, she was still pretty much in the dark when it came to vampires and their nature. "Your brother?"

Carlos kept his eyes on Julian, his stare flinty. "Not in the human sense. Technically, we are maker and progeny, as I turned Julian over a century and a half ago. But in our world he's my blood brother, the same as the others in our little family."

The other man kept his eyes on her, his amusement evident. Extending her hand, Trina murmured, "Nice to meet you," but instead of shaking her hand, Julian swept it up in his, turning it over and exposing her wrist. Trina gasped as Julian's fangs descended, his lips brushing the delicate skin directly above her pulse, lingering just long enough to cause Carlos to step forward.

"Julian…enough," he said, putting a staying hand on his brother's wrist.

His brother simply shrugged. "Can you blame me? You of all people can appreciate just how delicious she smells."

Carlos's eyes narrowed, and even though he spoke to Trina he kept his scowl focused Julian. "Not to worry, *mi vida*. Julian's just doing this to aggravate me. He means you no harm and he's going to stop right now. Aren't you, *hermano*?" he said to his brother through clenched teeth.

Chuckling, Julian's grin said it all. "I'm sorry, Trina. I just couldn't resist getting a rise out of *el Jefe* here. He's been driving everyone to drink ever since he told us we were to meet you tonight. I'm sure I don't have to tell you how obsessive he can be."

Carlos frowned.

Trina knew he was as worried as she about how tonight would go, regardless of his perceived nonchalance. If they traumatized her, he'd never forgive himself. The tension coming from Carlos was palpable, and he looked like he was ready to bite Julian's head off—literally.

She burst out laughing. The mental image Julian had conjured in her mind was just too ridiculous, and his brother smiled brilliantly at the success of his plan to break the ice, even if it was at Carlos's expense.

"Relax, Carlos, it's all in good fun, eh?"

"Mmmmmm."

"Come on, Trina. Let's leave Grumpy here to hang up the jackets. I'll introduce you to the rest of the family," Julian said, swinging his arm affably around her shoulders.

Carlos trailed after them. Glancing back, Trina shot him a sympathetic smile. His family was going to have fun with this, and it was clear he was to be the guest of honor at their version of a vampire roast.

"Everyone, this is Trina," Julian announced as the three of them entered the room. All at once, everyone started to clap. Trina flushed, clearly embarrassed. Of all the things she had imagined could happen when she finally met Carlos's family, this was definitely not on the list. She looked at Carlos for help, but all he could do was shrug.

"Take a bow, love, 'cause you deserve it," Julian quipped. "Somehow you've managed to get Sir Serious to actually smile on more than just Christmas and Boxing Day."

Trina smiled and curtsied with flourish and the clapping grew even louder with the addition of some whistles and hoots. Even more embarrassed, she started to laugh as Carlos came up next to her and took her hand. He brought it to his mouth and kissed it yet again, smiling himself. "See? I told you you'd be a hit."

Before long, Trina's nerves dissipated. Introductions were made all around and soon they were all talking and laughing as they each shared funny and somewhat embarrassing stories about Carlos. But it was obvious to her just how much they all loved and respected him.

Miguel was one of the younger members of the family. He had been eyeing Trina thoughtfully for most of the night, watching her interact with everyone. He seemed fascinated by her and when the conversation finally came to a natural lull, he spoke.

"I'm sorry, *mija*, but I need to ask. You really had no clue that Carlos was...different from you when you first got together? He told me you instinctively fought against his glamour. How is this true?"

Trina considered Miguel for a moment. "I had no inkling about Carlos at the beginning. The only way I can explain it is that I didn't want to see it. I'm not usually an obtuse sort of a person. My curiosity typically gets the better of me, but for some reason I didn't recognize the warning signs. I guess I wasn't meant to, otherwise I wouldn't be here. But now that I think about it, the no-heartbeat thing should have been a dead giveaway." She tapped on Carlos's chest. "No pun intended." Leaning up, she gave his cheek a kiss. "But my subconscious figured it out long before I did. I kept having these incredible dreams after our very first meeting…the one by the back stairwell."

Carlos's head whipped around. "You remember that?"

Trina nodded. "My memory of it had almost completely faded. A few blurry, incoherent images were all I could conjure, if that. But everything came flooding back the first time I gave you my blood. My memory of those loathsome teenagers, and what they did to that poor girl is clear as day, as is my memory of how you saved her. If you hadn't messed with my memory, I don't think I'd ever have fallen in love with you. I would have been too afraid."

"Afraid? Of me?" Carlos asked, pulling back slightly.

"No, not you. But of your kind." Her eyes swept the room and all the faces watching her. "I would have thought you the exception to the rule, Carlos. That most of your kind was like those two monsters. But after listening to my great-grandmother, and hearing you talk about your family and now meeting them, I realize your race is not so very different from the human race. Each has both good and bad.

"But to answer your question, Miguel, I'm not really sure what you mean by glamour. My head got a little fuzzy and my heart started to race when he first introduced himself to me, but then again he annoyed me as well, so maybe that's why I was immune to his tricks."

Miguel just chuckled. "Yeah, I know all about how irritating *el Jefe* can be at times. But perhaps there's something to your theory—anger as opposed to fear. Makes me wonder," he said contemplatively.

Miguel, like Julian, had joined Carlos about one hundred and fifty years or so prior. The two seemed contented with their nocturnal bachelorhood and spent a good portion of the evening razzing Carlos about his new ball and chain and other various forms of imprisonment.

Trina just laughed at their good-natured ribbing. It was clear to her that they were truly brothers, and Carlos was the elder of the group.

Margot and Trevor, however, were older than the younger two by more than one hundred years. Carlos had found them in France. They had been traveling as servants to Thomas Jefferson and his party, as they looked to garner France's support for the American Revolution against England. Both had fallen ill with smallpox and were left without much hope. Carlos found them in the care of nuns at a local hospital, a mere hair's breadth away from death.

The last member of Carlos's family was Eric. He joined the get-together well after everyone had settled into talking and getting to know one another. For some reason the introduction didn't go as smoothly as the rest, making her feel slightly awkward. Eric looked uncomfortable when he greeted her, seemingly ill at ease whenever he glanced her way.

Trina didn't need her degree in psychology to see there was much more to Eric and his story. Although he was slightly more relaxed with the others in the group, he still held himself apart. With questions in her eyes, Trina looked at Carlos.

He took Trina's hand and led her out onto the veranda. It stretched across the side and back of the house and the two walked its length in the moonlight.

"Eric is the newest member of the family. He's had the hardest time of all of us adjusting to his new life. You see, he was turned against his will, not unlike what happened to me. It's because of our similar stories that he and I have managed to bond," Carlos said in answer to Trina's unspoken questions.

"Every one of us is tied to each other by blood. Julian, Miguel, Margot, and Trevor all belong to me because I changed them—it was their choice, of their own free will. But Eric, he is tied to us through the sharing his blood, which for a vampire created without compassion and trust is nearly an impossible thing to do.

"You see, we each carry the mark of the one who made us—our sire, so to speak. So to be sired out of lust or cruelty or both leaves us with only those feelings from which to draw upon. The other emotions we experienced in life die along with our human bodies. Eric and I are very similar creatures. It's taken me centuries to recover from all I lost that night in Cadiz. Eric is still struggling to find what he lost. We all help in any way we can."

"He resents me," Trina said. "It's obvious, and from what you just told me I can certainly understand why. You're his touchstone, and he's afraid I'll take you from him, that he'll sink back into the kind of cruel depravity that created him. I don't want him to feel that way. I want him to know that in loving you, I want to help him find himself as much as you do."

He looked at her with eyes both astonished, as they were tender. That she could feel sympathy for someone like Eric and not be afraid? It was unheard of. Eric was frightening, volatile, especially when he felt threatened. Trina never ceased to amaze him, not just her intelligence, but also her inexhaustible capacity for compassion. Her trust in his ability to keep her safe ran deep into her core, and he knew that trust was something he would never betray. Words failed him, so he placed his hand on her cheek and kissed her softly.

"Well, what do you think, now that you've met everyone?" Julian asked as the two walked back inside.

"Well, I haven't met everyone yet. I haven't met the kids," Trina said, a little confused. "Where are they? I assumed when you spoke of them that they were older, more like teenagers. How come they're not around?"

The five vampires all turned at once to look at their leader with baffled expressions.

"Trina, if you're talking about our pets, they don't socialize with us. They have their own quarters and only join us when they're summoned," Julian said matter-of-factly.

Closing his eyes, Carlos groaned inwardly. *It had been going so well.*

"Pets? You call this group of kids your…pets? I hope that's just a term of endearment." She looked from face to face, but seeing their collective bewilderment made her turn to Carlos for an explanation. "Carlos, I don't understand. You said they were like foster kids. I assumed they were part of your family. Taken care of, cared for."

"They are cared for, love. But if I'm reading you correctly, just not the way you thought," Julian said.

"Shut up, Julian," Miguel interrupted sharply. "Let Carlos handle this."

Julian just shrugged and leaned casually against the wall.

"Carlos?" Trina pressed.

"Trina, I explained this to you. How we share blood…and other things with them. However, they aren't part of the family unit per se. It just isn't done."

"What do you mean, 'just isn't done'? Is this some common vampiric practice, keeping humans on call for…whatever?"

"It's very much a commonplace thing in our world. But it's not what you think. Pets are selected based on need, and are always given a choice. I don't permit anyone to be admitted to the ranks without first receiving a straightforward explanation of what is to be expected. The entire family also has to be in agreement."

"You make it sound so diplomatic," she said derisively. "Call them up here. I want to see for myself what your idea of 'cared for' looks like. Better yet, I want to see how and where they live, especially since they're *not* considered part of the family."

"All right. I'll take you to see for yourself. In fact, we'll all go."

Julian stood up. "All right? Since when do we let humans sit in judgment over something they can't possibly understand?" His gaze shifted to Trina and their eyes locked. "Sorry, luv, but that's the ice-cold truth of it. Just because you're bumping uglies with Carlos, it doesn't entitle you to pass sentence on our way of life."

"Julian!" Margot hissed.

Eric's eyes were daggers. "No, Margot, he's right. Don't we have enough trouble with our own kind and their ideas of how vampires should behave? My day-to-day life is hard enough. I'm not going to sit here and let Carlos's blood type of the month tell me how to live my life."

"Enough," Carlos said tightly. "I never ask anything of you, but now I am. I want solidarity here. And Trina is not my 'blood type of the month', Eric, and I don't appreciate you referring to her that way. It's disrespectful, not only to her and to me, but to you as well. We're not the monsters others of our kind have painted us to be, and that's the whole point of this."

No one dared argue with that. One by one, they got up, some with perplexed and worried looks, others with amused indulgent expressions, but Carlos looked stoic and unapologetic as he led the way.

Trina expected to go up the main staircase into the living quarters where she assumed all the bedrooms were, but instead they headed down the hall toward the kitchen. At the end of the hallway, there was a nondescript door. Carlos opened it and a light came on, illuminating another stairway leading down to a lower level.

They descended two by two and turned at the bottom of the stairs into a large great room. The ambiance was that of posh private club with just a hint of college dormitory. The couches and chairs were soft buttery leather, the color of tobacco. There was an entertainment unit that housed a large flat-screen TV and countless DVDs. There were books by the score, a pool table, air hockey and foosball tables, and a gaming station with a Wii and an Xbox and every other conceivable type of video game spread throughout. The room had everything except windows. Trina counted six bedrooms off the great room, as well as a kitchen that seemed stocked with enough food to feed a small army.

"Pretty cool, huh, Trina?" Julian said with an impertinent wink.

Miguel just shook his head at the Brit vampire. "You never learn, do you?"

"What? What did I say?"

"Enough," Carlos said, his face grim.

"Well, where are they?" Trina asked, resentment filling her voice. This was not going well. Carlos had lied, or at the very least bent the truth. He may have explained things, but he was guilty of omitting the most important facts.

"Niños, vengan aquí!" Carlos called out into the great room.

One by one, the bedroom doors opened. Teenagers, girls and boys alike, filed into the room and a few actually sighed. But they broke into eager smiles when they saw the vampires and immediately began to pair up. Carlos raised a finger, stopping them.

Trina was speechless as she looked at their faces. They were all so young. Most were thin and pale, but she had to admit none of them had that desperate, haunted look she'd seen on the faces of the runaways in Penn Station and around Times Square. For the most part, they seemed healthy; except for the few, whose bodies still held the scars from what she could only assume was their time on the streets.

Somehow, she instinctively knew none of these kids had been harmed since Carlos had taken them in. Well, not outwardly anyway. In her heart, she knew they were probably all better off here, than where they had come from, but consensual or not, this was tantamount to blood slavery. Or at the very least, indentured servitude.

Trina gave Carlos a pointed look before she turned to the kids. "I just have one thing I'd like to know, if you wouldn't mind. Do any of you ever want to leave here, maybe go back home?"

They all looked at Trina like she was crazy. "Why would we want to do that?" one of the girls asked, her expression as baffled as the others.

Trina was speechless for a moment. She didn't know what to think or how to feel. Her mind had run with possibilities for weeks about how tonight would play out, but this scenario was one she hadn't envisioned. She looked at Carlos, not knowing what to say. "I think you'd better take me home now. I have a lot to think about," she said quietly before walking past him and the others and up the stairs to wait for him by the front door.

***

Trina closed her front door and slumped against the doorjamb. She had just told Carlos she needed to be alone. Again. The words tasted like bitter bile on her tongue, as if they had become the pattern of their relationship, and it broke her heart. Once again, she had too much to digest, and there was no way she could think straight when he was around.

She snapped on the lights and walked past the parlor and up the stairs to her bedroom. The house seemed empty, mirroring how she felt inside. Was this to be her fate? Always back in the same lonely place in her life, again and again?

Everything had been going so well. She had in fact, liked all the members of his family, and was sure they had liked her as well, even moody, brooding Eric. She truly wanted to help him, and looked forward to getting to know them all, especially Julian. The memory of how he had gotten such a rise out of Carlos, and how the camaraderie between the two of them had been almost infectious, broke her heart. This was just a mess.

She went into the bathroom to wash her face and brush her teeth. She slipped on pajamas but couldn't bring herself to go to bed. It just seemed too big, too empty with just her in it.

Trina walked back downstairs into the parlor and turned on the TV. She sat and blindly channel surfed, not really paying attention. This wasn't helping much. She had to face her situation and decide what she wanted to do. Julian was right; she had no right to tell Carlos how to live his life. She wasn't a vampire and hadn't a clue as to what the protocols were to their…what was it, anyway? Lifestyle? Culture? Whatever it was, she didn't have a clue as to what was considered acceptable or not.

She went into the kitchen and poured herself a glass of wine. Grabbing a bag of chips, she headed back into the parlor and turned off the TV, turning on some music instead. The words to Beyonce's *Sweet Dreams* poured out of her IPod like a slap to the face. Sweet dream or beautiful nightmare? *I don't know myself anymore,* she thought miserably.

For the past three weeks, she wore a secret smile every time they played that song at the club. It was to the point that Susan had started referring to it as Carlos's song. Now it seemed more a melancholy lament.

Trina knew she could accept almost everything about Carlos personally; she'd even taken the fact of him being a three-hundred-year-old vampire in stride. The fact that she found that just a little exotic and intoxicating was a plus.

His family wasn't an issue either. It was their basement harem she just couldn't reconcile, no matter how much she wrestled with the idea. Even the fact that most of those kids were better off with Carlos than in their own families wasn't a good enough reason to condone it. Bringing each one of those kids into his home may have started out as well intentioned, but it was clear—at least to her—that the benefits the vampires gained from having them there on a permanent basis had far outweighed any initial benefit to those kids.

It was too inequitable and she knew Carlos knew it as well. Those kids could be so much more with the right kind of help from him and the other family members. If only she could make them see that. Trina knew she couldn't accept things the way they were, and she was going to have to tell Carlos.

Chapter 12

It had been almost a week since Trina had been to the house and Carlos hadn't heard from her. He resisted the urge to pick up the phone and call out of respect for her wishes, but it was killing him. Every instinct told him to claim what was his, but what was left of his humanity prevented him from doing just that.

Every member of his family had been tiptoeing around all week. *Approach with caution* had become the unspoken mantra of the house as Carlos stalked around, scowling, and snapping his teeth at the slightest thing.

The nourishment he took was minimal and came from bagged blood he had gotten from a local blood bank. The idea of any kind of intimacy, even for the sake of sustenance, was unthinkable to him at this point.

He sat in the great room listening to music with Julian when Melissa, one of Julian's favorite pets, came in. She casually draped herself across Julian's lap. Carlos shot Julian a warning look, then leaned his head back, barely acknowledging the two.

The unspoken tension in the room ratcheted up a couple of notches, and Melissa went to get up and leave, but Julian pulled her back down. "Don't worry, Mel, Carlos doesn't mind if you stay. Do you, bro?"

Carlos just grunted in response. He knew exactly what his brother was up to.

Julian smiled at Melissa and kissed her as he moved her hair away from her neck. She sighed when he drew from the vein that throbbed directly under her pulse as they cuddled together on the couch.

Melissa's face was languorous, her eyes half closed in an obvious state of semi-arousal. Carlos tried to ignore them and the strong scent from Melissa's pheromones. He opened his eyes to say something just as Melissa slid her hand down Julian's chest and massaged the bulge in his jeans.

That was bad enough, but when she undid the top button of Julian's fly, Carlos lost it. "Goddamn it, Julian! Get out! That's what you have a bedroom for! Either take it there, or take it elsewhere…now!"

Julian sealed the small wound on Melissa's neck and stood up with her. He threw her over his shoulder, and above the sound of her giggles, politely told Carlos to go to hell.

"I'm halfway there already, my friend," Carlos whispered under his breath.

His cell phone rang, and just as he was about to let it go to voice mail he saw Trina's name come up on the caller ID. He flipped open the phone and closed his eyes.

"*Buenas noches, mi vida,*" he said. "I'm glad you called. I've missed you."

"I've missed you too, Carlos, more than you know."

His silent heart jerked at the flash of hope in her words. "Trina, I'm sure we can work this out. It's understandable how you feel but I'm sure, given time, you'll see this arrangement benefits all involved."

"I'm sure you believe that. Unfortunately, I don't."

His gut clenched. "Trina…"

"No, please, this is hard enough for me as it is. The bottom line is I cannot reconcile myself to the fact that you keep those kids for the reasons that you do. I understand the logistics of it, of how it benefits you and your family. I can even see how it has benefited the kids. But regardless of how you dress it up or how pampered and well treated they are, the reality is they're nothing more than your blood slaves."

"That isn't fair. Every one of them can leave if they choose. They are here of their own free will."

"Really? What have you left them fit for? They have no education, no idea of how to function in the real world, no concept of how to take care of themselves or how to make a success out of their lives. You've made them helpless, however well intentioned you were when you brought them into your home."

"What would you have me do, then?"

"Let them go."

"I can't do that. The decision affects more than just me."

"I'm sure your family members are resourceful enough to be able to find alternative means of…sustenance." The word left a bad taste in her mouth.

"Trina, be reasonable, this is who we are. This is our life, our way."

"Then it's not a life for me. I'm sorry. I love you more than you know, but I can't be with you if this is your choice."

"Trina…"

"I'll love you, Carlos, always," she whispered, crying as she hung up.

"Trina!" he yelled into the phone, but the line was dead.

Carlos threw his cell phone against the wall smashing it. Throwing his head back, he roared in such anger and pain that the windows shattered. There was no question, everyone in the house cringed at the sound. A collective gasp clamored in his ears, and rang of disbelief and worry. Never before had they heard such anguish from him, and he didn't have to guess what they thought. This was bad. Very bad.

He stormed out. The screech from his tires carried for miles as he peeled down drive, but everyone in the house waited for the proverbial dust to settle before they came to access the damage.

"Jeez, do you believe this?" Julian said, staring at the mess, splintered glass and wood all over the floor and on the bushes outside the windows.

"I didn't even know we were capable of that kind of power. I mean, I know we're strong and all…but this…it's kind of creepy, man, if you know what I mean." Miguel said as he looked at the glass strewn across the floor.

"You think?" Julian smirked. "I think we'd better tape up what's left of this now, 'cause it's getting close to dawn. We can leave the rest for Marta and Pietr tomorrow."

Marta and Pietr were the human caretakers who looked after the house during the day. They knew the people living here were different, and it wasn't unusual to see them cross themselves each time they came and left the premises. Rosa outranked them, and when push came to shove, Carlos left it to her to deal with the help. However, unlike Rosa, they had no clue as to what the residents were, and the family wanted to keep it that way. But Marta and Pietr were astute enough to keep any suspicions they might have to themselves, and in return, Carlos made sure they were well compensated.

"Can you just imagine what they'll think when they see this?" Miguel laughed. "They think we're freaky enough as it is."

"You got that right," Julian said, tossing Miguel the roll of tape. "I'll tell Melissa to let Pietr know first thing in the morning that he needs to have the windows fixed ASAP. I don't know about you, but after this display I don't want anything else to set Carlos off, at least not until he can get a grip on all this."

"Amen to that, brother," Miguel agreed.

***

Carlos needed the wind; needed to feel it whip across his face, sear his skin. He was a mess—a churning cauldron of feelings so alien to him that his first instinct was to escape. Without a thought to where he would go, he jumped on his bike and took off. Speed. He needed speed and wind.

At the end of the drive, the gates were already open. "Julian," he muttered, and without missing a beat, he revved the bike's throttle, raised his arm in silent salute to his brother's quick thinking, and tore onto the street.

The little town of Verplanck was a ghost town at this time of night. Carlos blurred through the quiet streets until he wound his

way around to the highway. He drove south toward Manhattan, his thoughts racing faster than his Harley Davidson.

As he drove, Carlos's mind replayed the things Trina had said. Her voice had sounded ragged, as if she had been crying. Her sadness was evident even through the phone. If she was as miserable as he was, then why was she doing this? He didn't understand. In his world, he had already changed enough. What more did she want?

He raced through the tolls without stopping. The alarms blared behind him as he passed, but he dared anyone to try to stop him. He flew down the Westside highway and into the city. The streets here looked desolate, empty except for a few streetwalkers looking to turn one last trick and a couple of drunks looking to score. Carlos didn't give them a second glance as he sped across 57th Street.

He turned onto Broadway and headed toward Midtown and Times Square. There would be people there, and for a moment he considered stopping, but decided he really just wanted to be alone. Winding his way around past the New York Public Library and over to the East Side, he stopped at the light at 33rd and 3rd and revved the bike's throttle. It had to be close to three a.m. at this point, and dawn was a few hours or so away. With a wry smile he turned south and headed toward the Brooklyn Bridge and the Long Island Expressway. He still wanted the wind, but he wanted the sun as well.

Carlos found himself at the end of the Expressway in no time at all. He had been driving completely alone for what seemed like hours, with nothing but the flat expanse of the road ahead of him and the trees whizzing past on either side. Finally he turned onto the only road that remained, and headed toward the Eastern Long Island beaches.

Sprinkled between the sprawling estates were family farms, wineries, and quaint little cottages. As the sky began to lighten, Carlos pulled into one of the more secluded beachside motels.

The motel was actually a series of tiered rooms, each with a perfect view of the ocean. Carlos parked and got off his bike. Stretching, he took a deep breath and held it for a moment. Sea air.

There was nothing else like it. His estate in Verplanck had a small cove beach and a dock on the Hudson River, but it wasn't the same.

Taking another breath he spotted the little check-in hut at the end of the path. It was at the base of the stairs that led up to the rooms. He walked toward it and rang the bell.

"Good morning," the night clerk said with an affable chuckle. "Either you're very early, young fella, or you're very late!"

A kindly old gentleman with a large white beard and an easy smile, he had a sailor's skullcap pulled over his shaggy head, and Carlos had to stifle a chuckle. All that was missing was a pipe, and he'd be the perfect picture of a salty seadog.

"No, just couldn't drive anymore tonight. Would you happen to have a room available?" Carlos asked, having already seen the vacancy sign out front.

"Sure do," he answered, "but during the season we only rent for three consecutive nights or more. Sorry…this time of year it's that way all over the island."

The old guy shrugged apologetically, and Carlos smiled. "That won't be a problem," he said, signing the register.

The guy handed Carlos the key and as he walked toward the door called after him. "If you need anything, my name's Hank." Carlos nodded his thanks and headed out into the pre-dawn air.

The sky was beautiful. It held an aura about it, a glow that undeniably heralds the imminent arrival of the sun. Carlos headed down to the beach to watch. He sat on the edge of a moss-covered stump at the end of the planked walkway, and listened to the sound of the waves as a light ocean breeze tickled his hair.

The sky turned a beautiful array of pink and orange as he sat and watched the dawn crest the edge of the horizon. The view as it swelled over the ocean was magnificent. Carlos never tired of watching the sunrise, especially after centuries of having to hide from it.

As the light began to spread its warmth across the sand, he chuckled to himself. *Age certainly has its privileges.* Reaching out, he let the first rays of the morning touch the tips of his fingers. He smiled as he watched the light play on his skin and laughed recalling the first time he realized it would no longer kill him. It had happened quite by accident. Expecting flames or at the very least searing pain, he remembered being stunned when all he felt was a strong heat, like sitting too close to a fire.

The years since had made him almost impervious to the early morning rays, so he sat without fear watching Earth awaken. He watched as surf fisherman set their poles in the sand and early-morning joggers ran along the beach. He laughed at the beachcombers with their funny headphones and cumbersome metal detectors.

By now the sun had fully cleared the horizon, turning the sky from pink to blue and the ocean from black to navy. It climbed steadily on its course across the sky and Carlos knew it would become deadly for him soon. He got up and turned to walk back toward the motel, glancing over his shoulder for a last look at the ocean.

Fatigue crept up on Carlos like thick smoke as he put the card key in the slot and unlocked the door to his room. Watching the sunrise had centered him, given him the time to settle himself and think calmly. His anger and frustration had dissipated with the brightening sky, and now he needed sleep.

He threw his jacket over the rattan chair alongside the tall reading lamp in the corner of the room, and then pulled the blackout curtains closed. He took off his shoes and lay down fully clothed, with his arm over his eyes. His kind usually didn't get headaches, but Carlos could feel one building at the back of his skull. With the emotional rollercoaster he'd been on, he wasn't surprised. He closed his eyes and let his exhaustion flow over him like a wave, pulling him under. He was going to be here a while.

***

Carlos still hadn't returned home. The windows had been replaced, and though there was no physical trace left to the shattered mess, remnants of it still hung in the air. Everyone was anxious, still tiptoeing around as if Carlos was just in the next room.

"Where do you suppose he went?" Margot asked as she and Trevor sat on the couch listening to Miguel practice his twelve-string.

"He could have gone anywhere," Trevor said idly. He was sitting with his arm around Margot's shoulders. She played with his fingers, keeping tempo with the lively song Miguel was playing. Are you worried for him, love? He just needs time to think."

"No, I'm not worried about him," Margot said. "If anyone can take care of himself, it's him. It's just I have this feeling..."

"What?" Trevor asked, paying more attention now.

"I'm afraid he won't bounce back from this. I'm afraid Trina has left a hole in his heart bigger than anyone's ever left before. I mean, in two hundred years, do you ever remember seeing him this happy or this miserable? I don't."

Miguel stopped playing and both men turned to look at Margot. Her gut instincts about each of them had always been correct. She had always been a little freaky that way, even during her human life. Trevor told them stories of how she was the one who always knew if they were being cheated at the market. That she had been the one who told Jefferson the French would help his cause, but not to be fooled into thinking it was out of fraternity rather than avarice.

If Margot had been born in modern times she would have been called an empath. She could always tell what a person is feeling and why, and subsequently what those feelings were going to affect. Margot was the reason Carlos had accepted Eric into their home. Her intuition assured them he could be healed and that he'd be an asset to the family, regardless of his time with Sandro and his proclivities.

"What are you saying, *mija*? That Carlos isn't going to recover from this?" Miguel was afraid of how she would answer but more afraid not to know.

"No, that's not what I'm saying, but it's a possibility. Things are changing, Miguel, and not just for Carlos, but for all of us. And it's only going to get worse before it gets better. There's a storm coming, I feel it, and it's coming from outside our family. It's going to test us, pit us against one another."

"Are you're telling me this storm is going to happen and affect all of us simply because one human girl can't deal with our way of life?" Miguel yelled, and the sound of his raised voice brought Eric and Julian into the room.

"What's going on?" Julian asked, his eyes moving from Trevor to Miguel, "And why are you yelling at Margot? Haven't we got enough to worry about with Carlos, without the rest of us sniping at each other?"

"That's just it, bro. Margot's got one of her gut feelings again, and this time it's about Carlos and Trina. That it's bigger than them," Trevor said, trying to explain.

"I don't understand," Eric said, confused. "What does Carlos's love life have to do with us, other than having to put up with some drama? It'll all blow over and Carlos will move on."

"That's the point, Eric. Margot is saying not only will he not move on, but that something is going to happen because of it."

"Well, we'll just have to prevent that from happening, talk some sense into them. If Carlos just changes Trina, then she'll be one of us and just have to deal with things the way they are," Eric said.

"It's not that simple." Margot answered delicately, knowing how sensitive Eric was about the entire concept of conversion. "Carlos would have to change Trina with her consent. It would have to be done right or otherwise she…" she trailed off.

"Or she'll end up like me, right?" Eric said angrily.

"Eric…I'm sorry."

Trevor was indignant. "What are you apologizing for? You're right and Eric knows it. He may not like the truth, but that's too bad. If Carlos takes Trina's life from her, the way his was taken from him or the way Eric's was taken, then we'll be left with another cruel vampire wreaking havoc on humanity. We'll be responsible for her actions, and it will be left for us to either rehabilitate her or destroy her. I'm sorry to put it so bluntly, but that's the truth of it no matter how much you want to sugarcoat it."

"All right, everyone stop it. This is getting us nowhere. Carlos has never done wrong by us before. We'll just have to trust his judgment and wait and see," Julian said, leaving his wiseass attitude aside.

***

Carlos sat sipping his wine as he watched the sunset over Montauk harbor. He loved this time of day and how the sun turned a bright orange red, throwing the last of its rays onto the water. He'd been coming to Gosman's Dock since the 1950s, when it was just a chowder stand.

He'd been gone for almost a week and knew his family was wondering what had happened to him, but he also knew they trusted him. They knew he'd be back, eventually.

He sighed and ran his hand through his hair. The wind off the water was light and felt good on his skin. The scent of the salt spray mingled with the bouquet of the wine and had him sighing again. He was relaxed, or as relaxed as he could be. He felt much better now that he had made his decision. The hard part was going to be breaking it to everyone else.

With their faces pictured in his mind, he knew exactly who would say what. Julian, of course, would be the most vocal and the most argumentative—and he would be the one to blame Trina. Carlos couldn't allow that. This was his decision.

He had already checked out of the motel. All clothes and toiletries he'd purchased this week he'd left for housekeeping to dispose of or keep. He was heading back but wanted the sun over the water one more time before he left.

Carlos poured himself another glass of wine, polishing off the bottle of Cabernet Sauvignon. He turned the bottle over in the ice bucket just as his new cell phone buzzed.

"Hola?"

"Carlos? Jeez, man, where have you been?"

"Julian. How are you?"

"How am I? How are you? Where are you?"

"I'm fine and I'm glad you called. I'll be home tonight. Can you make sure everyone is around? I need to speak with you all."

"Sure, no problem. You sure you're okay, though. You've never been gone this long without at least a phone call and Margot's been having some vivid dreams. Her gut's been going haywire and the longer you're gone, the worse it's getting."

"Dreams? What kind of dreams?"

"Dreams about you and about us and some kind of fight, both from within and without."

"Huh. That's strange."

"To be quite honest that's the only reason I called. She's driving us all nuts. Every time one of tries to leave the house she makes us go out in pairs."

Carlos laughed aloud at that. "Leave it to you to complain for completely narcissistic reasons."

"What time do you think you'll get here?"

"I'll be leaving shortly. Depending on traffic, I should get back around midnight. Can you get everyone to stick around till then?"

"Believe me; once I tell Margot you're on your way, she's not going to let anybody leave."

"Good," Carlos said with a chuckle. "See you later tonight."

***

Everyone heard Carlos's bike pull up to the house. When he came up the stairs from the garage Margot was waiting for him. "Hey little one…just where I expected you'd be," he said giving her a quick peck. Stepping back, he leaned against the doorframe and studied her face. "Julian tells me you've had a hard time sleeping. There's really no reason for you to worry. I'm fine, *mija*, trust me."

Margot nodded and started to say something when Carlos put his hand up to stop her. "Wait. I want to hear everything you have to tell me, but right now I need to grab a quick shower and unwind from my ride."

She just nodded again, watching as he passed. Climbing the stairs, he could feel her eyes on his back and the worry coming off her in waves. He turned and winked. "Get everyone together in the kitchen.

I'll be down in about twenty minutes." With a single nod he went up to his room and closed the door.

***

"I'm leaving," Carlos told his family as he leaned against the granite counter next to the sink. Julian stood up with his hands on the table, ready for an argument, but Carlos stopped him before he could speak.

"This is my choice. No one else's," he said pointedly. "Truth be told, I've been restless with the way things have been for a long time, long before I met Trina. I need to get away for a while. I need to figure out where I'm going, where my life is headed. Don't worry, I haven't deserted you. I'll stay in touch and come home from time to time."

"Why, Carlos? Why now? You can tell us this is your decision, but the truth of the matter is if Trina had no problem with the way things are, you'd be sticking around."

"Julian, please…"

"No! I know you like I know myself, so don't try to hide what's going on. We all knew you were restless, Carlos, but to think you might run? Never in a million years."

At the sharp intake of breath at the table, it was easy for everyone to see Julian had gone too far. Carlos had never run. Ever. He'd been there for each one of them when it certainly would have been easier to just cut and run.

"I'm sorry you feel that way, Julian. I am telling you the truth when I say this decision is mine and mine alone. It's true that if things with Trina had turned out differently I might have decided to stay, but it would have only delayed the inevitable. I would still have left. The only difference is I would have taken her with me."

"Where are you going?" Margot asked in a small voice.

"I feel like I need to go back to the beginning, *mija,* back to where my life changed. I know you all think I'm some kind of rock, but I have my own set of demons to face," Carlos said softly.

The weight of their eyes bore into him. How could he tell them what churned in his gut? What had plagued him since the realization of what he was took root so many centuries before?

When he was alive he lived by his sword, fighting for others in the name of God and what he believed was right. There was never a question it was the reason God put him on Earth.

Since then he still fought for others—for his family, saving each one of them from certain death. But had he given them life? Or had he just bartered one miserable existence for another?

Julian said they knew he was restless. Over the years he'd tried to hide it from them, from himself as well—trying on various excuses and rationalizations as to why he felt such regret and listless boredom. His longing for absolution haunted him, yet whatever resolution he found it was never enough. Even the long-awaited forgiveness Isabel granted him on her deathbed afforded only temporary peace.

Trina's words haunted him this past week. Was his *mutually beneficial* way of life truly that, or had he just bought into his own self-delusion? Were all vampires opportunistic predators? Base, self-serving creatures, regardless of lifestyle? Was he? Was the life he'd created nothing more than a carefully constructed veneer of selflessness? Truth was he didn't know, but perhaps going back to the beginning would help him find the answers. And maybe even a way back to Trina.

He walked over to where Margot sat nestled in Trevor's arms. He put his finger under her chin and lifted her face so her eyes met his. "I will always be here for you, for all of you," he said, looking around at each of his family members. "I'll only be a phone call away."

The room was silent except for the soft sound of Margot's sniffling. Miguel got up and handed her a box of tissues from the counter. She blew her nose so loudly the unladylike honk was just the comic relief they needed. Laughing, the tension in the room soon disappeared.

"There's one more thing, though," Carlos said, clearing his throat after everyone relaxed. Their immediate apprehension told him they were expecting the other shoe to drop, and he didn't disappoint.

"I'd like you to let the kids know I am releasing them from their blood bonds. They are no longer tied to this house, or me. Of course they can stay as long as they want, no strings attached and under no obligation. This can still be their home if they wish."

"And you can still stand there and tell us that Trina had nothing to do with all this?" Julian yelled his face a picture of anger and resentment.

"Julian, this is *my* decision. How many times, in how many ways do you want me to say it? I am bored with all this," he said sweeping his hand around the room. "There has to be more to my existence than just collecting bodies."

"You're *bored?* Gee, thanks, *Dad,*" Julian answered.

"Whoa, dude, that was so not cool," Miguel said, shaking his head.

"I meant that I'm bored with me, with my life—not with the people in it," Carlos said tiredly. "It really doesn't matter who you blame. This is my wish, and I hope you will respect it."

"Of course we will respect your wishes. But I do have one question: How are we to protect the ones who choose to leave?" Julian asked, still bristling.

"You don't," Carlos said in an expressionless voice.

"What?"

"You heard me. You don't, because you can't. If they come back to the house, offer them whatever help you can, but you can't follow them around. It's not practical, nor is it fair. I will give them my protection while they live under this roof, pay for their needs and wants while they prepare themselves for the outside world. If that means paying school tuition or helping them learn a trade, so be it. But the minute they choose to leave this house, they choose to leave my protection."

"So you are encouraging them to stay?" Margot asked.

"It is the best way for them to ready themselves for life on the outside, but the same way I gave them the choice to come here, I offer them a choice again."

Margot got up and flung her arms around Carlos's neck, sobbing. "I knew you meant this in a good way, that you'd never just leave them to the fates."

"So, are we in agreement?" he asked them all as he disentangled himself from Margot and deposited her back into Trevor's arms.

They all nodded. Even Julian looked placated if not completely relieved, but then again he was never one to embrace change.

"You do all realize you will have to make other arrangements in terms of blood exchange. The kids are no longer here in that capacity, even if they ask. Is that clear?"

Eric, who had been silent throughout the entire exchange, shrugged. It didn't affect Margot and Trevor as they provided for each other, and Miguel looked excited at the prospect of hunting. Only Julian grumbled.

"Come on, bro, you and me out together trolling the clubs. It'll be fun," Miguel said, clapping Julian on the back. "Melissa will still be around, you'll see, so cheer up. This is a good thing. We were all getting too lazy anyway. Hell, if vamps could get fat, some of us would be totally porked out!"

At that, Trevor spewed his drink across the table, hitting Eric dead in the face. His stunned look had everyone roaring with laughter and Trevor mumbling apologies as he tried to mop up the mess on the table and Eric's shirt. Even Eric cracked a smile.

"So where are you headed, Carlos, or don't you know?" Margot asked.

"Spain, *mija*, back to where it all began."

"When?"

"Tomorrow, late afternoon. I leave for the airport before the sun sets."

"So then, this is goodbye," she said softly, knowing they all would still be asleep when he left.

"Yes," he answered gently.

Margot hugged him again, but Carlos saw the worry written across her face. He hadn't forgotten about her dreams or their inherent warning, but tonight had been emotional enough to go into theoretics.

"Don't worry about your dreams, *mija,* I trust in the strength of our family. Whatever is coming we will handle together. Like I said, I am only a phone call away."

Margot let out the breath she had been holding. "I love you, Carlos," she said, sniffing again.

"I love you too, *muchachita.*"

Trevor grabbed Carlos in a bear hug. "Take care of yourself and don't worry. We'll keep everything running smoothly until you come back."

Carlos nodded, clapping the big man on his back. "Thank you, Trevor. Just make sure you take care of my little girl, eh?" He let go, giving Margot one last kiss before she and Trevor headed out for the night.

One by one he made his goodbyes, until Julian was the only one left with him the kitchen.

"It's just you and me now, Carlos. So tell me. Why? Or do you think I won't understand?" He stood with his back against the granite counter, his eyes accusing.

Carlos exhaled. "I've already told you."

"To face your demons…yeah, I get it. What I want to know is what demons? What could be plaguing you after all this time? We've been together for a century and a half. What?"

"Why?"

"What do you mean, why? I think I deserve an answer, that's why," Julian shot back.

"No, Julian. I'm not asking you why you want to know, I'm telling you that's what I need to go and find out. *Why?* What was the meaning behind my being turned, the purpose for it under God?"

"Oh, for God's sake! Seriously? After all this time? Do you really think taking a stroll down memory lane is going to do the trick? Everyone from your days as a man is dead, and the immortals you know haven't any more of a clue than you do. What happens if you don't find your answer, if you can't find the true meaning of life? What then? Do you just end it all and go into the sun?"

"Don't be such an asshole, Julian. I'm not on a quest for some guru to tell me the meaning of life. I'm on a quest to see if I can find some meaning *in* my life. From the beginning I thought if I continued to live for the greater good, and looked for absolution for my sins, it would be enough. It isn't. I need to know there was a purpose to all this, to understand why so I can endure the endless years spread out in front of me."

Julian was silent.

"I don't know what answers I'll find, if any. Margot says there's a storm coming. I've felt it too, and the one thing I know is I'll either come out of it contented with the existence I have or come out dead."

The tiny muscle at the corner of Julian's jaw worked back and forth, like he was fighting with what to say. He exhaled and pushed himself away from the counter. Grabbing Carlos in a bear hug, he whispered. "Whatever the storm, whatever the outcome, we will weather it together."

Julian let go of Carlos's shoulders as abruptly as he had grabbed them. He turned to leave without saying another word, but not before Carlos caught the red tinge of blood tears on his cheek. "Goodbye, *hermano,*" he murmured as he watched his brother leave.

Alone with his thoughts, he headed up to his room to pack, when a sudden urge to see Trina once more overwhelmed him. He changed direction and sprinted out the front door, but stopped halfway to his car. An annoying little voice in his head screamed: *but she doesn't want to see you!* Closing his eyes, he exhaled tiredly. *And didn't you just ask everyone to respect your wishes?* The voice was right, it would only cause them each more pain. Carlos turned and walked back into the house and straight upstairs.

Julian watched from the second-floor window of his room as Carlos turned and headed back to the house. He shook his head. "His decisions, my ass!" Julian muttered. Whatever Carlos said, Trina was the reason behind his sudden need for enlightenment. He exhaled sharply, letting the curtain fall back into place.

Chapter 13

Trina kept her smile cemented in place as she worked, the pounding in her head keeping time with the music blasting from the speakers on the dance floor. She walked around clearing empty glasses, filling orders, and trying hard not to look as desolate as she felt.

It had been almost two weeks since she spoke to Carlos, and her heart was still breaking. She had no choice. She knew she had no right to ask him to change his way of life, but he had no right to ask her to accept it. They were at a stalemate and this was the only solution.

She went past the corner table where she and Carlos had first met. She closed her eyes and took a deep breath before turning and asking the group sitting there if they needed anything.

"You okay, honey?" Susan asked as she came up behind Trina.

Trina nodded, but knew she wasn't fooling anyone. "I'm good, thanks. If you wouldn't mind, can you bring this table some more pretzels? I'm going to take my break."

"No problem. You sure you're okay? You want me to come with you?"

"No. I'm fine, really. I just need some air."

Susan eyes were skeptical. "Okay. But remember, I'm here if you need me."

"I know," Trina said, flashing her friend what she hoped was a convincing smile, patting her arm before walking toward the employees' lounge,

"Where are you going?" Rick asked as Trina passed the bar area.

"Break."

"Trina, we're really busy. You can't leave Susan alone on the floor."

Trina looked at Rick as he and Louie tended the busy bar. He was right. The club was hopping tonight and they were already down a server as the newest girl, Debi, had called in sick. Susan had covered for her a lot. It was ironic because in the beginning it had been Trina covering for Susan all the time.

Pull it together, Trina. The breakup was your decision...

"You're right, Rick, I'm sorry. I'll get back out there. I just need to change my shoes."

Rick nodded and Trina rushed past him, through the doors that lead to their lockers. Sitting on the bench she traded her black platform pumps for a pair of black Nike cross trainers. She knew the manager liked his girls to wear heels, but tonight she didn't care. She hurried and tied the laces and rushed back out to the floor.

The rest of the night went by in a blur and she was grateful to be so busy that she didn't have time to feel sorry for herself.

"Why are you still so down? I thought you were the one who wanted to stop seeing Carlos," Susan said, unloading a tray of dirty glasses and empty bottles onto the bar.

"I know. But it's not as cut and dried as it seems. The fault wasn't with Carlos himself. He was wonderful. He still is. But there were things in his life that I…" Trina didn't finish. Susan was a friend, but she would never betray Carlos and his family that way. She'd caused enough hurt. Not that Susan would believe her anyway.

"What?"

"Nothing, never mind. It doesn't matter anymore, anyway."

"Jeez. Remind me never to share my deepest darks with you either," Susan said sullenly.

Trina was about to respond when she heard someone call her name. She turned and saw Margot standing by the stairs. She knew Margot had said her name quietly and that no one else had heard it but her. She guessed it was a side effect of sharing blood with Carlos.

"Excuse me," Trina said as she got up and walked toward the stairs. "Hi. Margot, right? What's up? Is everything okay?"

"Yes and no. Carlos is gone," she said, her voice flat.

Trina froze. She didn't quite know what Margot meant by gone.

Margot elaborated. "I mean, he's left the house. He took off for a week after you two last spoke. When he finally came home, he changed everything. He freed the pets—I mean, the kids—then said something about traveling. He's been gone a little more than a week. I just thought you'd like to know."

"He freed them? What do you mean?"

"He gave them all leave to go their separate ways, to leave the house and be on their own. He severed their blood ties. Some have already left but others are still at the house. Carlos said it was their choice and they could stay as long as they wanted, no strings attached."

"I see."

"Do you?" Margot asked, tilting her head to one side.

"What do you mean by that? It's for the best. Now those kids will have a chance at living a normal life. They can go to school, make a success out of their lives."

"Do you really believe the things that come out of your mouth?" Margot said, her voice dripping with uncharacteristic disdain.

"I beg your pardon?"

"You come into our home and meet us for one evening, then act as judge and jury when you really know nothing about us at all. You think because your life went one way that all kids will have the same chances that you had. That's a very noble sentiment, but that's not the way things are. Those kids had nothing before they met Carlos, and you know what? They still have nothing because you guilted him into putting them back on the streets. At least some of them had the sense to stick around."

"Why, so they can hope they'll be reinstated as your blood slaves?"

"You have no clue what a blood slave is or how they are treated in our world, so don't use labels you don't understand. Those kids are facing far worse out on the streets, especially since they all carry a blood mark."

"Mark, what mark?"

"You really are a naïve little girl, aren't you? Naïve and opinionated. Yes, a blood mark, and no, it has nothing to do with the arrangement we had with them. You do realize you carry Carlos's mark on you as well?"

Trina's hand instinctively went to her throat. She opened her mouth to say something, but she was too stunned to speak. She knew about the marks from her great-grandmother's diaries, but she had forgotten all about them.

"Yes, my dear," Margot confirmed. "Once you share blood with one of our kind you wear their mark, kind of like a beacon. Carlos will always be able to find you as we will always be able to find those kids—that is, unless they're taken."

"Taken? Wouldn't a blood mark protect you from that?"

"Usually, yes. But there are those of our kind who don't respect the old ways. We have codes of behavior that go back millennia, but of course that's all changing now."

"Changing how?"

"You are either born to our life or you are transformed into it, and there are proper ways to do it. Do you remember the comedy *Young Frankenstein*? Remember how Igor was supposed to obtain the brain of a famous scholar and scientist, but instead took an abnormal brain back to the lab? I know it's a silly analogy, but it's sort of the same. The transformation was flawed because Igor didn't follow directions. The same holds true for our kind. We have rules that need to be followed or the end result will be monstrous."

Trina swallowed. "You said you were either born to it or transformed into it. Are you telling me your kind can reproduce?"

"Well, don't sound so horrified by the thought, but yes, in some cases. But it is very rare."

Trina's head was spinning. Almost every preconceived notion she had was being stripped away, one by one. "How? You have no heartbeat, you're not alive."

"We are alive, Trina, we're just different. Our hearts work very differently than yours, but that doesn't mean they don't exist, don't beat. Carlos really didn't tell you very much about us, did he? But then again, you never really gave him the chance."

"I guess not," Trina said, chewing on her lip.

"I'm sorry for that. Maybe if he had, things would be different right now. It's too bad, really. I liked you. You brought Carlos to life…that is, until you broke his heart." She turned to leave.

Trina cringed, hearing the truth in her words. "Margot?"

"Yeah?"

"Thanks for coming to tell me. I really liked you all too."

Margot shrugged as if to say, *too late now*, and left without another word.

Trina turned to finish cleaning up her tables. She felt her coworkers' eyes on her as she did, but when she looked up everyone managed to look busy. She was glad no one was brave enough to venture a question, and she quietly finished up and left without so much as a goodbye. As she headed home she felt a sudden sense of foreboding and a single word ran through her head. *Fool.*

***

Trina crossed the street and headed the four shorts blocks down toward the subway. Normally the walk didn't bother her. The streets were usually deserted at this hour, but that was never a concern. In this town there was always someone around somewhere, and it was for that reason she suddenly found herself jumping at shadows. Since her abrupt introduction to the reality of the supernatural, she knew what could be lurking there, and these days that didn't mean your average run-of-the-mill mugger.

She found her eyes searching for other people as she walked, finding comfort in the predawn activities of the city's early morning work force. There was no other way to phrase it. She was creeped out. It wasn't just Margot's unexpected visit, or what she said that bothered her. It was something else. For some reason she felt like she was being watched, or tracked, and no matter how hard she tried to shake the feeling, she couldn't.

Maybe Carlos had set up some kind of surveillance to keep tabs on her. But Margot would have told her that. Wouldn't she have? The 14th Street subway was just ahead across the street. Without waiting for the light Trina bolted across the street and down the subway stairs. By the time she got to the platform her heart was racing, but when she saw Gus, the old homeless guy that called this station home, she couldn't help but feel like a complete idiot.

He was in the same place he was every night, in the same clothes, with the same shopping cart full of his belongings. Looking up from the crossword puzzle he no doubt fished out of the trash, he smiled. "Hey, Red, why so winded tonight? Devil got a hold of your tail or something?" he said with a wheezy chuckle.

"Gus," Trina said, trying to catch her breath. "Am I glad to see you! I'm okay, just a little spooked. Everything okay with you? Nothing strange happening around here tonight, right?"

"Nope. Same old, same old." He grinned flashing his two remaining teeth.

Trina exhaled. "Good," she replied, fishing a ten-dollar bill out of her jacket pocket. "Do me favor. Don't hang around here all night, okay? Go to a shelter or something. I can't explain it, but I've got a bad feeling I just can't shake."

Gus took the money and stuck it in the only pocket of his pants that didn't have holes. "Don't you worry about me, Red, I'll be all right. I think I may head over to one of the parks tonight. Weather's fine for once. I think spring is finally here."

"Just be careful tonight," she said, looking around distractedly.

The screech of the subway as it slowed into the station jerked her back to attention. She waved goodbye to Gus and stepped into the deserted train car.

Trina sat down, running a hand over her forehead and through her hair. The prerecorded voice announced the doors were closing, and she slumped back against the hard plastic seat, waiting for the train to pull out.

The train rattled along while she sat, angry with herself for her silly, irrational trepidation. "Get it together, Trina. You're acting like a neophyte fresh from the suburbs afraid of the big, bad city. Get a grip!" she mumbled to herself as they approached the first stop.

The noise from the tracks was almost deafening, when one of the interior metal doors to the rear of the car opened. Two young men stumbled their way through from an adjacent car. Laughing, they tripped over the threshold, barely grabbing hold of the hand straps as the train lurched around a curve. Trina could smell the booze on them from ten feet away. They made their way toward the center of the car, pushing and shoving each other as they went.

The conductor's voice crackled over the loudspeaker that 23rd Street was the next stop.

The car swayed down the track, and Trina got up to stand by the door, but pitched forward, losing her footing. As she reached for one of the poles near the rear door, a hand suddenly shot out from behind to steady her.

"Thanks," she muttered, gripping the pole. She realized both guys had moved, positioning themselves in front of the sliding doors. Perhaps they were getting off as well, but between what her gut told her and their body language, she guessed otherwise. The car was empty except for the three of them. With all that space, why would they block the door?

"Um, excuse me," she announced, maneuvering her way past. "This is my stop."

"I don't think so," the taller one said. He burped, and the smell of beer rushed from his mouth along with his words.

Trina's adrenaline went into overdrive. Hadn't she dealt with enough already? This was just one more hassle on a very long list, and compared to dealing with vampire politics, these pissants didn't even make the top ten.

Her mind ran through all her options. She needed to keep her wits. Regardless of how many drunks she had handled in the past, it was still two against one.

They were so drunk she could probably get away with swinging her bag at them. Suppose one of them caught it, then what? Knowing it was an easy error in judgment for any woman to make, she lifted her shoulder bag over her head and across her chest, freeing up her hands.

Thinking fast, she waited for the train car to sway again. Stepping lightly aside, she brought herself closer to the drunk on her right, but stayed in a defensive stance just in case. The station was close, and the overhead lights flickered as they approached. The train bumped its way toward the platform, gears grinding in a high-pitched squeal.

As she anticipated, the car lurched forward as the train slowed, throwing its passengers off balance. Planting her feet, Trina grabbed the drunk to her side and shoved him forward, making the most of the train's momentum. He crashed headlong into his friend and the two fell to the floor between two seats. The main doors opened and Trina walked calmly out onto the platform. "Drunken stupidity, zero. Keeping a cool head, priceless," she murmured to herself climbing the stairs to the street.

Still shaken, her adrenaline level evened out as she walked. She had three short blocks to go before she hit the perimeter of the park and home sweet home. For the first time in what seemed like ages, she glanced up at the sky. It was a clear night, and the crescent moon rode high in its blackness. Taking a deep breath, she chuckled. Gus was right—spring was definitely in the air, even if buried under a pervasive blanket of petroleum smog.

She turned the corner onto 19th Street and slowed her pace. Parked outside her house was a long black limousine. As she walked past, the door opened and a young man climbed out of the front passenger seat.

"Ms. Markham?" he inquired.

Surprised, Trina stopped and turned around. Immediately she knew he was a vampire and her guard went up. She may have been naïve when she first met Carlos, but she had since become a quick study in Vampire 101 and could spot one anywhere. "I'm sorry. Do I know you?"

"No, ma'am, but we have a mutual acquaintance. I've been sent to pick you up. We've been waiting for you."

"Mutual friend? And who's that, if you don't mind telling me?"

"Señor Sandro Mendoza."

Trina froze for a moment. Sandro was the man Carlos had introduced to her at the art exhibition. She remembered him clearly. He was condescending and cold, but it was more the woman accompanying him and her vacant eyes that Trina couldn't forget. At that point, she had been naïve to the supernatural world. But now? Admittedly, she knew more than she wanted to. Sandro was a vampire, and with the way her gut was twisting, she knew he probably wasn't at all like Carlos in that department.

"I'm sorry, but I don't know anyone by that name. I think you must be mistaken. If you'll excuse me, it's been a long night." Trina spoke rapidly, her words clipped. Stepping away from the young vampire, she did her best to hide her rising fear, but knew too well he could smell it a block away.

"I'm sorry, Ms. Markham, but this isn't an invitation you can refuse." He held open the rear door to the limo like any experienced chauffeur, except instead of touching his cap, he hissed baring his fangs.

Trina backed away, a scream tearing from her throat. In a blur of movement, the vampire was at her side, his fingers locked around her forearm. Pivoting instinctively, she kicked him hard, driving the thick rubber toe of her sneaker deep into his groin.

The vampire doubled over and she took off running, no time to ponder the sensitive areas of a male vampire's body. Taking her stairs two at a time, her fingers dug unsuccessfully in her purse for her keys. *Shit, shit, shit!* Adrenaline surged, almost blinding her. Finally finding her keychain, she fumbled with the lock. *Get inside, now!* But a hand shot out from behind, grabbing her around the waist.

Without thinking, she lifted her knee, stomping down and driving her heel into the vampire's instep. White-hot pain reverberated up her shin from the impact, but he didn't budge. Instead, he squeezed her chest, compressing her lungs. She tried to scream, but all her air was gone.

Her vision blurred and Trina knew she was going to pass out. The lights went on at the house next door, and she heard voices. For some reason the vampire let go. Throat raw and head ringing, she dragged in a lungful of air. *So close—*

Her knees buckled and she felt herself falling before everything went black.

***

Cognizance took hold slowly. A sense of movement edged its way into Trina's consciousness. Her mind registered the steady hum and vibration of a car in motion, but not much else. Chilled, she shifted slightly, turning instinctively toward what little warmth she felt to her side. Inhaling, she wrinkled her nose. The air smelled metallic, like fresh blood and oiled leather.

Her head hurt. It throbbed and tingled at the same time. An odd prickly sensation fanned out along her scalp from where it ached. She opened her eyes, allowing her vision to adjust. Her head was resting on the bulging bicep of a rather large man. Shoulder to shoulder with him, her direct line of sight fixed on his flat washboard stomach. She tried lifting her head only to find his square jaw, complete with five o'clock shadow, pressed solidly against her temple.

Clarity flooded her mind. Somehow, she was in the backseat of the limo that had been parked outside her house. She had no idea where she was or where she was going, but one thing was clear—the man to her right was a vampire, and for some reason he was licking her head.

She jerked her head away, reflexively wrenching her body to the left. "Ew! What the hell do you think you're doing?" He let go and Trina scooted across the leather seat, putting as much distance between them as she could.

"Relax cupcake. You were already serving, so I just helped myself," the burly vampire stated licking his lips.

Trina's mouth dropped. "And what the hell does that mean? If you think I'm going to serve you anything, your brain is deader than you are!"

She knew she didn't stand a chance against him, and she cringed as he hissed, gnashing and snapping his teeth.

"That's enough theatrics, Terrence. Remember, Ms. Markham is our guest." A voice from the front of the limo chided. The interior of the car was dim. Even the ambient glow from the floor's running lights had been muted, and the windows were so darkly tinted, no light from the outside could penetrate.

The limousine was an ultra stretch, like the ones seen at Hollywood red carpet events. Trina peered into the interior's shadows, trying to pinpoint the voice.

The floor lights brightened a notch. It was still dim, but the soft suffuse light made it easier for her to see what was around, including the elegant vampire sitting toward the front of the large car.

"Allow me to introduce myself. My name is Maurizio. I apologize for the darkness. We don't often travel with human passengers, and as our eyesight is so much more acute…" he trailed off.

"Anyway, you'll have to excuse Terrence's behavior. His function in Señor Mendoza's household requires that he be…well, let's just say less than refined. You collapsed while we were delivering Señor Mendoza's invitation, and hit your head rather hard. *El Señor* would be quite upset if you arrived in less than perfect condition. Terrence was merely…tidying the mess." He paused for effect, giving her a cold smile. "And you'll be happy to note your head wound has completely healed. Regrettably, there's not much we can do about the blood on your clothes."

Trina's stomach flip-flopped. She suddenly wanted to shave her head, or at the very least scrub herself raw. Swallowing hard, she stared at nothing while her mind worked to wrap itself around what was happening. *Invitation? Try kidnapping.* She broke out in a sweat and her heart jackhammered in her chest, drawing leers and a lot of lip smacking from the big vampire.

Unconcerned, the other one ignored it, amusing himself instead with his BlackBerry. Trina sat white knuckled, hands folded in her lap and her gut churning. She was out of her league here. There was no way she could fight her way out of this. These weren't a couple of rowdy drunks from the club or creeps from the subway. These creatures radiated ruthlessness, and based on the way they spoke it wasn't hard to guess where she and the rest of humanity ranked in the pecking order.

Could this be Carlos's doing? Was this some kind of vampiric payback for breaking up with him? Her mind revolted against the thought. Carlos was many things, but vindictive wasn't one of them. So what then? "Look…like I said, I think you've made a mistake. I told you before I don't know anyone named Mendoza. What could he possibly want with me?"

A single raised eyebrow told her there were quite a few things Sandro Mendoza could want from her. Crossing his leg casually over his knee, Maurizio walked his gaze from her breasts to her eyes. "Oh, but you do know Señor Mendoza. However, I'm not at liberty to discuss the whys and wherefores of your acquaintanceship. He wants that pleasure all to himself."

The lights went dark again, letting Trina know the time for questions was over. She had no choice but to sit and wait.

Carlos, please. I need you, her mind called out, putting everything she felt into her wordless plea. She carried his mark, or at least that's what Margot had said. Closing her eyes, she prayed silently, hoping Carlos's mark was more like OnStar than just GPS.

***

The car finally stopped and Terrence got out first, grunting at the driver as he pushed his way past. Sliding over to the door, Trina placed one foot nervously on the ground and peeked out. Much to her surprise, a human driver extended his hand and helped her out of the car. Touching his hat, he gave her a sad look before turning away, and Trina's heart dropped.

A light breeze played with her hair, as she looked around, trying to get her bearings. The driveway was long and narrow, and though she couldn't see a gate, she had a gut feeling the property was both very private and much secured. The house itself was an imposing edifice of dark stone. An enormous estate, seemingly built on a cliff overlooking the Hudson River. The downtown skyline was painted across the southern horizon, and Trina guessed they were somewhere on the New Jersey side of the river.

"Beautiful view, isn't it?" Maurizio commented from behind as he took her elbow. The man was even more elegant in the moonlight. His dark charcoal gray suit fit impeccably, like it had been made for him, and his crisp lavender shirt and violet tie completed the picture. He looked like he belonged on a catwalk during New York's fashion week.

Trina could only nod. The house reminded her of the old mansions that once lined 5th Avenue, the kind that belonged to names like Carnegie, Vanderbilt, and Rockefeller, urban estates as commanding as their owners. She swallowed, wondering what kind of commands were in store for her inside this particular mansion.

The moon was bright, but the river looked black despite its glow. *Not a good omen*, she thought crunching up the gravel toward the front door. Maurizio's touch was light on her elbow, steering her toward the house in an almost courtly manner. Still, she knew his fingers would snap her arm like a twig with the slightest provocation.

She was chilled, but it wasn't from the night air. Still in the jeans and T-shirt she wore to work, she zipped up her jacket; thankful she had changed into her sneakers. Looking out at the skyline, she closed her eyes and sent out another prayer. An odd feeling of comfort stole over her. Being this close to the city, if she got the chance to run, at least she wouldn't have to worry about getting lost. She shuddered, wondering if she'd feel quite as comforted if the only way out turned out to be the river.

A white-gloved butler opened the front door. "Mr. Maurizio, good. Señor Mendoza had me ready the SoHo Suite for Ms. Markham. All is prepared."

"Thank you, Cox. Is *El Señor* is his study, or is he otherwise occupied?" he asked, the stress on the word "occupied" raising the hair on the back of Trina's neck.

"No, Mr. Maurizio, the master is spending the night in town. He sent word he won't be back until sundown tomorrow. He asked that

Ms. Markham enjoy the house and his hospitality until he arrives. He sends his trust, as always, that you act as host during his absence."

Maurizio snorted. "On that, he can depend." With a dismissive nod, he led Trina to the right past the grand staircase. Trailing beside the vampire, she couldn't help glancing back over her shoulder. She watched the butler as he spoke with other members of the household staff…all human.

"Don't look so surprised, Ms. Markham. Señor Mendoza likes to keep human staff around for various purposes. When they get too old, too troublesome, or are no longer of service, he eats them."

Laughing at Trina's horrified look, Maurizio let go of her elbow. Across from them was a narrow but ornate elevator off the main foyer. Reaching into his inside breast pocket, he pulled out a security access card, like the ones used in offices all over Manhattan. "This house is wired for everything. You can't sneeze without us knowing it, so don't get any ideas. You are Señor Mendoza's guest until he decides otherwise." He swiped the card through an unobtrusive electronic eye, then tucked it back in his pocket.

"Where I come from that isn't exactly the definition of guest. It's more like hostage," Trina answered coldly.

"Perhaps, but it's a question of semantics. In our world, human definitions simply don't apply. Neither, for that matter, do human civilities. Be grateful for the courtesies bestowed on you. Take my word for it—they are not the rule."

The elevator door opened and Trina stepped in first, her arms folded over her chest. Maurizio pulled the antique-style, wrought-iron gate closed, and the elevator door slid shut in front of it. The lift moved silently upward and Trina's stomach clenched. There was no getting out of here.

***

The afternoon sun hovered in the sky already well past its zenith. Its light winked in through the curtains, glinting across Trina's face. Cracking one eye open, she hiked the covers over one shoulder and rolled to her side. Still half asleep, she snuggled further down into her pillows. After just a moment, her eyes flew open and she sat bolt up, letting the heavy duvet fall to her lap. This wasn't her bed and she certainly wasn't home.

The reality of what happened pushed all remnants of sleep from her consciousness. Closing her eyes, her hands went to her temples. Whatever peace she enjoyed was gone, and the terror and ensuing adrenaline from the night before took over again. She glanced down at her watch. Considering Sandro's entourage had hijacked her sometime around four thirty this morning, she wasn't surprised to find it well past noon.

Actually, it had been closer to dawn when Maurizio deposited her here. The thought lingered that perhaps that was the reason Sandro hadn't gotten down to brass tacks with her right away. Bleary-eyed, she curled back into a fetal position, staring numbly at the windows across the room. Of course, if Sandro wanted her dead he wouldn't need hours to do so. He was playing some kind of game with her. But why? If this was some bizarre version of cat-and-mouse, then who was the cheese?

A knock on the door had Trina sitting up again. The bedroom door opened and a maid came in, carrying fresh clothes. She didn't say a word. In fact, she didn't acknowledge Trina's presence at all. She simply set the clothes on the chair by the makeup vanity and left, her eyes never leaving the floor.

"This place is like something out of a horror movie," Trina murmured under her breath. Pushing the covers back, she got to her feet. Gooseflesh pimpled her skin as she stood there in nothing but her bikini underwear and matching camisole. Someone had undressed her and the realization made her wince.

Padding over to the chair, she picked up the blouse from the stack of clothes the maid had left. A gorgeous crème silk, jeweled halter-top—striking, especially in the way the lustrous material crisscrossed the throat. Very telling, since it was a gift from a vampire. Folded on the seat was a pair of black wash jeans, a black lace strapless bra, matching panties, and pair of soft-as-butter, knee-length leather boots. Black stiletto—of course.

Fingering the underwear, she dropped them back onto the neatly folded pile. No way. She wasn't a Barbie to be dressed up and manipulated. She was here against her will, and until she knew why, she was hanging onto whatever was hers.

Finding her own clothes on the bench at the foot of the bed, she gathered them up and headed into the bathroom. It was huge, with a deep enamel clawfoot tub that looked like it could easily hold three people. A long, carved chestnut vanity housed two handpainted Crema marble sinks set into rich Italian granite. The fixtures were all antique oiled bronze, and the room gleamed.

She walked to the back of the bathroom where a separate toilet room was off to the side, complete with bidet, yet her mouth dropped as she stepped down two marble stairs into a massive sunken shower.

The walls were tumbled Tuscan marble and inlaid with mosaics. Dropping her clothes on a built-in bench, Trina stripped and walked to the center. It was enormous, with at least ten different knobs and an electronic wall panel that looked to control everything from water temperature to steam.

Salon-quality shampoo, body wash, and conditioner were laid out, as were a set of washcloths and a natural sea sponge. Exhaling, she mumbled *eeny, meeny, miney, moe,* and turned a few knobs at random. Water poured from the rain head above, drenching her almost immediately, and she yelped in surprise as sprays shot at her from two different walls, the rush echoing in the expanse.

The warmth and pressure of the water felt wonderful, and she longed to just stand there and let it cascade over her body. But she was being watched, or so she'd been told. So rather than give them an eyeful or be caught unawares, she hurried, giving her hair and body a quick once over, and gave her underwear and socks from the bench a quick scrub as well.

Rinsing off, Trina wrapped herself in a long terry robe and towel-dried her hair. Sandro had provided for everything, but she wasn't having it. Rolling her underwear and socks in a hand towel, she squeezed out most of the water and hung them on the heated towel bar. Combing her fingers through her knots, she used the blow dryer on her roots, then on her under things.

This is as good as it's going to get. She reasoned with herself, looking in the mirror at her rumpled clothes and her bloodstained jacket. Beneath her jeans, her underwear and socks were still a little damp. Nevertheless, she grabbed her sneakers and headed downstairs, memorizing the layout as she passed. Wherever she looked, there was another security camera. "Either this guy has a lot to lose or he's just paranoid," she mumbled, finding herself on the landing above the main foyer.

"Can I help you with something, Ms. Markham?" a young man in a white serving jacket asked from the circular bend at the base of the stairs. He was holding a tray with a crystal decanter filled with some sort of red liquid and a single wine glass.

"Um, yes…I was looking for the kitchen."

"Of course, ma'am. It's downstairs to the left. Follow the main hall to the back of the house and turn left again. Mr. Cox is there. I'm sure he'll help you find whatever it is you need." With a nod, he headed in the opposite direction, and Trina's stomach convulsed as she thought about what was in that decanter.

***

"Leave the bandages and splints. Your forearm has a slight fracture, but your shoulder needs tending to first." Cox frowned. The gardener's arm hung limply at his side, his shoulder obviously dislocated. Handing him a piece of leather, he took the man's arm and moved it slowly till it rested at a ninety-degree angle against his belly. Sweat beaded on the gardener's forehead, running in dirty rivulets from his temples. Teeth clenched, he bit down into the leather strip.

Rotating the arm up and around, Cox cursed under his breath. The dislocation was bad, and the man screamed in agony, his neck muscles corded as he tried not to move. After a few tries, an audible pop followed by a tense exhale said it was well done. The gardener's shoulders slumped. It was obvious he was still in pain, but the relief on his face was palpable.

"Next time, Josef, use more care while on the ladder. The gutters aren't going to clean themselves, and *El Señor* wants them done today. I'll have Mario finish up. You need to be out of sight until you're healed. This is the third time you've gotten hurt while working the grounds. I'll cover for you this time, but once more and you'll to face the master…" Cox's voice trailed off, as if he couldn't bring himself to utter the words.

His full meaning wasn't lost on the poor gardener, and the man's face blanched. Trina froze in the kitchen doorway. She had seen and heard the whole exchange.

"Are you coming in, Ms. Markham, or are you practicing to be a door stop?" Cox queried, not bothering to look up while he finished splinting the gardener's forearm and tying off his sling. "There, I think that will do nicely."

Grabbing a brown apothecary-style bottle from the table, Cox uncorked the top. His nostrils flared slightly as he ran the edge of the glass vial beneath his nose. With an eyedropper, he extracted a reddish-brown liquid, holding it up to the light. At first Trina thought it was iodine or mercurochrome, but when he squeezed a few droplets onto a white tablet and gave it to the gardener to swallow, she wasn't so sure.

Firing off a string of instructions in what sounded like Russian, Cox sent the man on his way. With a sigh, he wiped his hands on a towel and turned toward Trina, a frown lining his mouth at her stained clothing. "I see you're not wearing what was sent up for you. Didn't the garments fit properly?"

"I wouldn't know. I haven't tried them on. I never really cared for trash couture, and since I'm not suffering from Stockholm syndrome like everyone else around here, I won't be participating in *El Señor's* little game." Trina walked over to the table. Picking up one of the extra splints, she played with it between her fingers.

"Stockholm syndrome. An interesting, if not exactly accurate, diagnosis. You can choose to play this any way you wish. However, I suggest you change your mind and wear what was given you. You cannot meet the master looking like a refugee from a downtown flea market. Trust me, Ms. Markham, the last thing you want to do is insult Señor Mendoza, game participant or not."

Trina didn't comment. She just looked at the butler, not giving him an inch.

Cox ignored her stare, continuing in his most *Remains of the Day* manner. "But in the meantime, I'm glad to see you survived the night. Can I get you anything? I'm sure you must be famished by now."

Trina's eyebrows shot up. "Survived? Well, that's reassuring. Thanks for the vote of confidence I guess…and yes, I am a little hungry, if that's all right with you." Sitting down, she still played with the splint, looking at the other first aid bits and pieces.

"Excellent," he turned, snapping his fingers. "Mary, will you be so kind as to prepare a plate for our guest?"

"Cox?" Trina glanced up.

"Yes, Ms. Markham?"

"That boy…his shoulder looked pretty bad. Don't you think you should have taken him to the hospital, or at the very least called a doctor?"

Lips pursed, he waited a moment before answering. "No, miss. In the seventy-five years I've been in service here, I've had to learn many skills. I endeavor every day to make myself indispensable to Señor Mendoza and his household because the alternative is unimaginable. I vowed many years ago that was never to become my fate. You're an astute young woman, so I'm sure no further explanation is necessary."

Mary put a plate of food in front of Trina. The woman actually curtsied, bobbing once before going back to her chores. "This place is like something time forgot," Trina said. "You do realize this is the twenty-first century. No one curtsies anymore, at least outside of Buckingham Palace."

Cox frowned. "I don't think you're in a position to judge. In case you hadn't noticed, this isn't exactly a standard household. It might be healthier for you to keep your inside musings…inside."

Trina picked up a fork, but her eyes were on Cox as she considered his words. "Point taken and I apologize. So, you've been here for seventy-five years. That's quite a long time, considering you don't look a day over thirty."

The butler opened his mouth, but Trina waved him off. "There's no need to explain. I know how it works. As you said, I'm a smart cookie, so it's not like you're spilling some deep, dark vampiric secret. Based on that, I suppose it's a fair assumption it wasn't iodine you dripped onto that pill?"

A small smile curved at the corners of the butler's mouth. "No, it wasn't."

"Then why the tablet? What's the purpose?"

Straightening his vest and jacket, the butler sniffed. "It's just how we do things. Staff isn't easy to find, nor are they easy to keep—and not for very long, as you can imagine. I'm sure you're acquainted with the healing quality of vampire blood when taken in small amounts. The tablets are simply generic aspirin. Nothing more than a vehicle to get my staff to take the blood. Otherwise…" His voice trailed off again.

"I understand. You use it to heal them so they won't be considered…expendable."

"Exactly, Ms. Markham. Plus aspirin is a natural blood thinner, so the healing components get dispersed more quickly."

"I see."

Cox fixed a penetrating eye on Trina, his expression both questioning and sad. "Do you, Ms. Markham? Not everyone here suffers from delusion, or Stockholm syndrome, as you so casually accused. We do the best we can every day with the circumstances dealt us. My hands are tied for most things, but I do still have some compassion."

Trina stood, pushing the chair back abruptly. "If that's true, then help me get out of here. Does your compassion go as far as that?"

The butler's eyes turned cold as the mask of his professional veneer fell back into place. "I'm sorry, Ms. Markham. Unfortunately, I cannot help you with that request. If it is the outdoors you crave, please avail yourself of the grounds. They are beautiful this time of year, and I'm sure Mr. Maurizio has arranged for someone to accompany you. Do take advantage of the fresh air and sunshine while you have the opportunity. Especially since *El Señor* so enjoys the smell of it on the skin."

Cox turned on his heel, leaving Trina standing alone in the kitchen with her mouth open. *Compassion, my ass!* No one here was going to risk themselves helping her. They were all too afraid, not that she blamed them. Chewing on her lip, she looked at the clock above the stove. Time—she needed time to think.

Chapter 14

*I*t was just before sunset as Carlos walked through the tourist-filled streets of Valencia. The temperature had been warm and the beaches crowded. The sidewalks teemed with people rushing back to their hotels, their arms laden with the day's purchases, and their faces tanned and brimming with anticipation for whatever the night would bring. It was high season, and the third largest city in Spain was overflowing with life.

So many things remained the same, yet so much had changed. The twists and turns of the medieval town were still dotted with narrow doorways and hidden courtyards, yet trendy boutiques intertwined with neighborhood shops gave them a cosmopolitan flair. Street vendors still gathered in market-day style, but alongside traditional food and wares were items manufactured in places like China.

Amazingly, the oldest part of the city had been encircled by a great loop of the *Río Turia.* Heartened that the ancient stone bridges had been preserved, Carlos laughed to himself at the now-dried riverbed. After centuries of fighting floods and constant rebuilding, Valencia had finally made peace with the river, now home to elegant landscaped gardens and footpaths.

He meandered through the maze-like streets, finding ghosts everywhere. Reflections of people and time past—no more than whispers on the breeze they smiled, as if to say, *"No pierda la esperanza"—don't lose hope—*then vanished into the twilight.

It was well after dark when he crossed into downtown. The city's nightlife was waking up, and the scent of food and fun permeated the air. Like any other large, vibrant city, Valencia was a Mecca for the vampire. Its bars and clubs were a calling card to others of his kind, but there was only one immortal Carlos was interested in seeing.

Dominic had settled in Italy in the 1950s, forgoing his native France for the splendor of the eternal city, and its rebirth after World War II. These days he rarely left his villa, content to live out his days quietly above the throng that was twenty-first-century Rome. However, at Carlos's insistence, he agreed to leave his refuge.

Carlos had been in Spain for almost two weeks. Starting in Cadiz, he worked his way up the *Costa de la Luz* to Valencia, retracing his own personal history. Since his last waking dawn over the Mediterranean, he hadn't returned. Memories best left behind made this the last place on Earth he wanted to roam.

There were ghosts in Cadiz as well—raw specters of the horrors that changed him, and shades of the life he could have lived. However, regret was a shackle he'd learned to cast off a long time ago. Dominic taught him that.

The reclusive vampire would be waiting for him, his rented villa transformed into a sanctuary worthy of the gods. Dominic was old school, to say the least. He was twice as old as Carlos, yet he refused to venture out in even the weakest of daylight. For him, the late afternoon sun was as safe as moonlight, but no matter now. The sun had set hours ago, and it was time. Carlos had come full circle. Just as he needed Dominic years before, he needed his old friend once again.

Carlos's hotel was ahead on the corner. A former palace, it once belonged to the Duke of Cardona, but had since been transformed into luxury accommodations. The valet had his Mercedes ready and waiting for him as he approached.

"Will you be returning late this evening, Señor Salazar?" the valet asked, handing Carlos the keys.

"Perhaps, Juan. But who can say when the moon promises to be so beautiful?" Carlos answered with a wink. Sliding into the driver's seat, he put the key in the ignition and quickly checked his mirrors before pulling out into the street. Honking once, he waved and turned at the end of the street toward the A-7 highway and the coast.

***

Dominic's villa was in Castellón de la Plana on the Costa del Azahar, just a short drive north from Valencia. The weather was fine, and Carlos drove with the windows down. A soft Mediterranean breeze made the air taste of home.

The moon rose, its crescent shape casting just enough glow onto the water for it to shimmer, the sound of the waves against the shore like a lullaby in Carlos's ears. Listening to the soothing sounds, his car was the only one on the road for miles.

Before long, he approached the villa. Pulling up to the gates, he could see the grand hacienda-style house ahead, its facade entwined with beautiful flowering vines. The gate swung open, and Carlos drove in.

Pulling around the circular front, he parked. The house was a beautiful two-story building with a low-slung red-tiled roof and a wide veranda. Opening the car door, his head swung around as two German shepherds bounded up to the car before he could even step foot on the ground.

"Max! Fritz! Sit!" a voice called from the tall cypress trees off the edge of the path.

Carlos grinned. Both dogs dropped to their hindquarters immediately. Getting out of the car, he leaned against the hood, waiting along with the dogs for their master to emerge from the hedgerow.

"Well, leave it to you to have the dogs greet me before you. Don't you ever travel without them?" Carlos shouted across the driveway.

Dominic came into view, walking through the arbor like a 1920s heartthrob. "I don't travel, but then again, you never would take no for an answer. Tell me, what's so important that we had to have this little reunion here? My villa in Rome is so much more convenient."

"Convenient for you. And you know why, or else you wouldn't have come."

Dominic *hmphed,* coming up next to the car. "You look awful. When's the last time you fed?" he asked, looking at his friend's careworn face.

Carlos shrugged. "Doesn't matter, really. You know at our age it's no longer a regimented requirement."

"Our age? Last, I checked you were still the young blood here. Nonetheless, you look terrible. You need to feed before we talk. I have a feeling you're going to need all the strength you can get." Pulling a cigar from his pocket, Dominic snipped the end and put it between his teeth. Lighting it, he puffed a few times till the end glowed red. "Go on, Carlos. There's fresh blood in the kitchen, Iberian ibex. I'll bet you haven't had that in a while. I'm going to finish this on the back veranda, and you can join me there after you've had your fill."

"No, Dominic. I'm fine. I'll feed later. Right now, I'd rather talk if you don't mind. So much has happened."

"Come then, leave your bags. Charmaine will see to them so we can talk." Clapping Carlos on the shoulder, Dominic led him around to the back of the house, speaking in rapid French to the maid as they passed.

"Cheese? You asked her for wine and cheese? Isn't that going to make you ill?" Carlos asked with a raised eyebrow.

Dominic smirked. "Probably," he admitted with a nod. "But the smell and the feel of it on my tongue bring me right back to my mother's kitchen in Provence. Like you, I have a taste for memories."

A large smile cracked across Carlos's face. Dominic knew him well. "Rum. You're right; I suppose I do at that."

The two walked around to the back of the house. A large white veranda spread out from the house like a carpet of sun-bleached stone. A striped canvas canopy billowed out above it, tied to beautifully curved columns. The view of the ocean was spectacular, and the sound as it crashed against the rocks was like a symphony in the night air.

They sat in deck chairs and Carlos inhaled deeply. "It's so beautiful here. Don't you miss the ocean breezes cooped up on that hill in Rome?"

Dominic puffed on his cigar. "Rome has its own special breezes, my friend. Why do you think so many senators lived in the Palatine?"

"*Hmph*. But that was two millennia ago."

Before Dominic could answer, Charmaine glided silently onto the veranda, her tray covered in cheese and fruit, and a bottle of red wine and two glasses. She placed it on the glass table to the front of the men's chairs.

His retort forgotten, Dominic took the bottle from the tray. "Thank you, Charmaine. Why don't you retire for the evening, my dear? You've done quite enough, and I'm sure Carlos and I can manage reasonably well on our own." With a quick pop, he uncorked the wine, giving her a wink.

"Very good, sir," she murmured, and left without saying another word. Dominic's eyes followed her as she passed through the open French doors.

The longing in his friend's eyes was apparent, and Carlos watched as he stared at the empty doorway. "You've got to stop torturing yourself. You've been in love with her for years, and don't deny it. You know it and she knows it, so why haven't you changed her?"

"For the same reasons you never changed anyone who wasn't near death. It's our rule, Carlos. The way we have chosen to live out this interminable existence. This isn't a life to choose when one has other choices. It's for the same reason you refused to change Isabel."

Carlos was silent for a moment. "I didn't change Isabel for many reasons, not the least of which being I didn't know how." He looked over at Dominic pouring the wine. "She lived, you know."

"I know."

"No, I mean *lived, lived*...as in she just died a few weeks ago. It was incredible. Suddenly her voice was in my head, reminding me of my promise to her. I swear, at first I thought I was delusional. But it's true."

"I know," he answered, handing Carlos a glass.

"You know?"

"Yes...I've always known."

"What do you mean, *always?* I know from Isa's diaries that Jeffrey had an acquaintance with you, but that was two centuries ago. Are you telling me you knew her not only then, but *now*?"

"Yes."

Carlos pushed himself up from the chair abruptly and walked to the railing. The breeze blew his hair back, and he breathed in its salty scent. Silently he looked out at the ocean, his thoughts in a whirl. Wheeling around he glared at his friend. "You knew where she was for all these years and never said a word. *Why*? Didn't you think I would want to know? I've silently agonized over Isabel for centuries. Didn't you think it might give me some peace of mind to know she was okay? That she was happy?"

Dominic slowly cut himself a piece of cheese, using the knife to bring it to his lips. "Yes…and no," he said, chewing thoughtfully. "I met Jeffrey before I met Isabel. But the moment I met her I could smell you on her."

Carlos snorted doubtfully.

"I know it sounds farfetched, but *Christ,* Carlos, our whole existence sounds farfetched. I'm well aware that nearly twenty years had elapsed since you had given her your blood, but I swear the smell was as fresh and as potent as if you had just done the exchange."

Walking to the center of the patio, Carlos raised his hands in a wordless gesture. "How? It makes no sense. The marks we leave when we feed fade over time. *We* retain the trace, the blood's signature, *not* humans."

"Don't you recollect what happened that night?" Dominic asked softly.

Carlos shot him a look. "How could I forget? That nightmare is forever etched into my soul."

Shaking his head, Dominic exhaled slowly. "No, Carlos, not the drama of that night. Remember the details. Focus on how the deed was done."

"All I remember is Jeffrey telling me that if a spark of life remained in Isa's body, a little of my blood would heal her."

"A *little* of your blood."

Confused, Carlos ran his friend's words over in his mind, but he still couldn't make the connection. "I still don't understand."

"Carlos, what happened when Isabel woke from her near-death sleep?"

Carlos's eyes flew open. His body tensed as memories flooded back. His eyes flew to Dominic's and he saw the truth. Isabel had gulped his blood greedily, his own lust blooming red hot as she drank. He remembered it holding him in a paralyzed thrall until he connected it with what Robert had done. It was only then he pushed her away.

Carlos paced, talking to himself in agitated whispers. "But Isabel was still human. I saw her with my own eyes just weeks ago. She dies in my arms." His head hung to his chest, fear stilling his already quiet heart for what his ignorance might have caused.

"Isabel *was* human, Carlos, as was Jeffrey. However, the amount of blood each had taken—Jeffrey from Robert, then Isabel from you—the two were lucky it didn't force a conversion. What it did was prolong their life much longer than it normally would have if they had only taken a small amount. They were literally but a bite away from turning." Dominic drained his glass. "Because of their saturated blood, Isabel and Jeffrey had quite a difficult time. The smell of their blood was an aphrodisiac, and it drew vampires everywhere. Even I was drawn to them, but because of my beliefs, I befriended them instead. I gave them my mark, layering it with yours to protect them."

Carlos slumped down in the chair next to Dominic. Leaning back against the cushions, he ran his hand through his hair. "Again, why didn't you tell me? I could have protected them as well."

Dominic picked up the bottle, pouring them each more wine. "And what would you have done? Been a permanent fixture in their parlor every weekend? Become the proverbial third wheel? Isabel and Jeffrey were married. How do you suppose you would have fit into that equation? Would you have been able to move on? Would they? The answer is no, my friend. Jealousy and resentment would have eventually eaten at you. If you take a moment and think about it, you'll admit I'm right."

Carlos had no answer. He sipped his wine and stared out into the black sky. "Did you know their family? Their children?"

Dominic spoke carefully; aware what he had to say would be painful for Carlos to hear. "No, not at first. They had already been together for twenty years, and by then were no strangers to tragedy and loss. I was there for the family that came afterward. I was there when their children were born, and there when they buried them. It wasn't easy for them living with their legacy, especially for the children. But one daughter...her name was Lisette…became enamored with the glamorous illusion.

"It was 1901. England was enjoying an occult revival, and the publication of Bram Stoker's *Dracula* a few years earlier captured Lisette's imagination. She held the fantastic notion that the vampiric world was somehow her birthright. It didn't take long for her to find out she was wrong. She died horribly, and poor Isabel almost didn't recover from it. It was because of what happened that Isabel's other children ended up denying their parents…why Alastrine's mother and grandmother kept themselves away."

Carlos's head jerked up. "Alastrine? You mean Trina? You know about Trina?"

"I've known Trina since she was a little girl and first came to live with Isabel. Such a beautiful, bright child, and so unafraid. I'm sad to say I haven't seen her in years."

"Then you know about us…her and me?"

Dominic nodded. "Julian called me before you even got on the plane to come here."

Carlos didn't know whether to laugh or kill something. "Trina doesn't know anything about this. There's no entry about it in any of the diaries. *Why*?"

"Isabel couldn't bring herself to write about it. It was just too painful for her, sweet woman that she was."

Looking at the floor, the little muscle in Carlos's jaw worked as he turned things over in his mind. Before she died, Isabel told him she had tasted both joy and sorrow during her life, yet when he kissed her goodbye, he had only tasted the joy. She had forgiven him. Had she also forgiven the vampire that took her daughter's life? "Dominic, did you or anyone else ever find who it was that killed Lisette?"

The older vampire hesitated. "Yes…"

Carlos's head snapped up. "Who?"

Dominic just looked at his old friend, the sadness in his eyes palpable. "Sandro."

Carlos sat up slowly. Red fury coursed through his veins. "Sandro Mendoza? He and I knew each other back then. He had to have realized the connection. Isabel's blood was saturated, you said so yourself, so her children inherited the same through her. *Son of a bitch!*"

"Sandro's always been a bad egg, completely self-indulgent. Why should that surprise you? He's always been of a jealous nature, especially towards you. Didn't you have an altercation with him on your territory not too long ago? Julian mentioned something…"

Carlos's mind reeled. "Trina! *Oh, God, no!* I introduced her to Sandro at the art exhibition at the Met. He made some kind of a veiled threat about returning my hospitality, and in my stupidity I thought it was about the club and his two young bloods…*shit!*" Pulling his phone out of his pocket, he pressed the touch screen to call Julian, but the phone buzzed. It was a voice mail from Margot.

"Carlos! It's imperative you call home as soon as you get this. Sandro sent a note inviting you to his estate. He said the entertainment would be well worth the trip and enclosed a picture of Trina. He has her, Carlos. Come home. We need you."

He pressed save, and turned to Dominic. "You heard?"

"Yes," he said, getting to his feet. "I hope you realize it's a trap."

"I know, but the alternative is unthinkable. I have to go."

Picking up the paring knife, Dominic turned it over in his hand. "I knew that's what you'd say." Jabbing the sharp tip into his wrist, he held it over Carlos's empty wine glass, filling it with his own blood. "Drink this. I know you're strong in your own right, and that Robert's blood was strong when he made you, but mine is even older and stronger. Trust me; you're going to need it."

Carlos drained the cup. "Where's the closest airport?"

"I'm not from here, remember? Nevertheless, I do know it's about a four-hour drive from Valencia to Barcelona or Madrid, respectively. Either airport will do. I'll arrange your ticket from here and have it waiting for you at check-in. I'll have someone take care of your hotel in Valencia and collect your things in the morning. Go, don't wait. However, when this is all over I expect you in Rome...with your questions and your young lady. *Entiendes?"*

"*Entiendo*. We'll be there."

Chapter 15

A scanner almost invisible to the naked eye sat camouflaged next to a nondescript door at the far end of the hallway. Maurizio slid his card through the slot and the door clicked open. A dizzying sense of *déjà vu* washed over Trina as she remembered the same kind of door leading down to the kid's quarters at Carlos's house. Was that why she was brought here? To be Sandro's new pet?

Maurizio led the way down and Trina's stomach fell even more. At the bottom of the stairs, there was no great room, no bedrooms or video game paraphernalia. It was empty and it was cold. A circular marble floor inlaid with zodiac symbols and surrounded by Greek columns graced the lower level.

In the center was a single plush, red velvet chaise, like a stage set for a monologue or a one-person play. Matching velvet curtains hung to either side, in effect the exit and entrance, and a single wooden chair was placed on the floor directly in front.

"*Ahh,* Ms. Markham, how good of you to join me tonight," a softly accented, and slightly familiar baritone called from one of the corners. The sound reverberated off the columns, echoing in the emptiness. "Please, take a seat."

With it clear in her mind exactly who and what Sandro Mendoza was, there was no way she would lay on that chaise like a hot buffet. The only other choice was the wooden chair, so she walked over and sat down. Maurizio was immediately behind her. She felt his hands slide onto her shoulders and his thumbs press into her back on either side of her spine. Was he planning on giving her a massage, or was he merely tenderizing dinner? Closing her eyes, she swallowed against the hysterical laughter bubbling up in her throat, shifting instead in her seat against his tight grip.

Maurizio's lips brushed the back of her ear and she stiffened, her fingers gripping the arms of the chair. Inhaling sharply, she could taste the clean, soft scent of his cologne.

"Really, Ms. Markham, I thought you'd appreciate my attempt at alleviating some of your tension. But perhaps my skills would be better employed elsewhere on your body," Maurizio murmured, nipping her earlobe.

Jerking her shoulder up and back, she shrugged him off. "Who said I was tense? I haven't done anything to warrant anxiety. Mr. Mendoza barely knows me," she shot back, her voice shaking despite her false bravado.

She had taken Cox's advice and dressed for the occasion. The clothes fit like a glove. No surprise there. It was no surprise either to find makeup and accessories waiting for her when she returned to her room. She knew she looked good, and under any other circumstances, she'd revel in feeling this beautiful. As it stood, she just felt like dessert. Maurizio's voice was low and rough, and she didn't need vampiric senses to guess his desire. A horny vampire licking his chops at her was the last thing she needed.

Maurizio chuckled behind her as if he could read her thoughts. Perhaps he could and was laughing at her, thinking she looked good enough to eat. *Bad analogy, Trina,* she thought, and heard him chuckle even louder.

But Maurizio quieted immediately, clearing his throat. It was no wonder, as Sandro stepped through the curtain to the left. He appeared just as handsome and just as cold as the night Trina had first met him.

Dressed in a silk smoking jacket and black trousers, he wore a pleasant but insincere smile. With the way he moved and his sycophantic, over-solicitous manner, he could be a candidate for office—even with the vindictive light in his eyes.

Trina's heart skipped a beat. What would make him look at her like that? They had barely it made through the initial small talk that night at the Met. All at once, it dawned on her. She wasn't a player in Sandro's game—neither the cat nor the mouse—*she* was the cheese! Something unspoken had happened the night of the art exhibition that set this whole thing in motion. Her nightmare had come true. Sandro's cruel face was the one she saw in her last dream. She had sent Carlos away, and now karma was the ultimate bitch, using her to lure him back into a trap.

"I see by your intuitive shock that you've finally figured things out. *Brava,* Ms. Markham. I'm impressed, but then again, Carlos's tastes always did run toward the clever. At least this time his choice is as appealing on the outside as well." Walking across the floor, he gestured appreciatively, stopping directly in front of her. "You look lovely, if I do say so myself. The effect is perfect."

Trina steeled herself and met Sandro's gaze head on. "I think you should know Carlos and I are no longer together. I broke it off nearly three weeks ago. I know for a fact he's out of the country and didn't say when he'd be returning."

Sandro seemed uninterested. "You're not telling me something I don't already know. Do I appear to you to be some kind of tenderfoot? Carlos and I have been playing this game of wit and parry for nearly a century and a half. He'll come, if only to save face. However, something tells me this time the stakes are much higher. Your presence will make things quiet interesting. So now, we wait, but in the meantime, I've arranged for a little entertainment, a demonstration, if you will, of what it truly means to be vampire. An experience you are sorely lacking…am I right, Maurizio?"

"Indeed, sir," Maurizio laughed, snapping his teeth together for effect.

Sandro turned on his heel. With a clap of his hands, the blonde who had accompanied him to the art exhibition walked through the curtain to the right. She stood, striking a pose in the entrance, and Trina wondered what else was hidden behind curtain number two.

The blonde seemed to glide across the marble floor. Her sheer robe barely skimmed the surface of her body, its translucent fabric creating the illusion of shimmering skin beneath its folds.

"Ah, Elsa. Good." Turning back toward Trina, he proceeded with the mock introductions. "Ms. Markham, I'm sure you remember Elsa from our delightful time together at the Met. Unfortunately, Elsa's memory isn't as keen as yours, but I assure you she has many other talents, as you will soon see."

The blonde with the vacant eyes sat on the edge of the chaise, her hands resting at her sides and her eyes staring blankly ahead at nothing. Sandro flashed a smile dripping with mendacity and malicious intent. "*Boys!*"

The two young vampires Trina had seen raping and draining that young girl in the back stairwell at the club walked through the same curtain as Sandro. Her body immediately tensed, and she had to cross her ankles, squeezing her calves together to stop her legs from shaking.

Sandro's eyes glowed. "Ms. Markham, I'm sure by now you've grasped the concept that a vampire is born to a legacy of blood. However, it is much more than that. It is power and strength. Carlos has shown you the barest glimpse into our nature. He is nothing more than a prime example of what happens when a vampire cannot sever its human bonds. The vampire becomes limited, weak, and sentimental. Now it's time for you to witness the vampire in all its preternatural glory. Behold our true form!"

The boy's faces contorted. Gone was the veneer of graceful elegance, their beauty and glamour replaced by hideous features. Their jaws seemed to unhinge, growing to accommodate fangs and rows of sharpened teeth. Their necks thickened with bulging veins, and their hands bent and clawed.

Trina's mind flew back to her bedroom and the way Carlos's face had looked when they were making love. He had turned from her, trying to hide his face as it changed. But she had seen it clearly, and his face looked nothing like this. He had fangs and his features had contorted some, but he still looked human. His hands and his neck hadn't become gargoyle-like in the process. Could Sandro be right? Was Carlos weaker because of his lingering humanity? What if

Sandro was correct in his presumption and Carlos came to save her, was the battle lost before it had the chance to begin?

The boys circled Elsa, licking their lips. A low hissing, like the sound of a snake getting ready to strike, emanated from their throats. Elsa lay down on the chaise with her robe open, its shimmering fabric draping to the floor in an ethereal cascade.

One of the boys ran a single clawed finger from her clavicle to just above her pubic bone. Rivulets of blood dripped in vertical rows down her torso and around the soft, fleshy mounds of her breasts. Kneeling on either side, the boys licked at the trickles, their hands shoved into their pants as they worked themselves into a hardened frenzy.

"Tommy and Dan are my latest protégés, and such naturals. Aren't they beautiful?" Sandro's voice was thick through obvious lust, but his pride was apparent. His eyes fixed on the two boys like an alpha lion watching his cubs make their first kill. Problem was lions sometimes ate their young.

His head swiveled back to Trina's horrified face. "They may be my newest additions, Ms. Markham, but Maurizio is my firstborn. My heir apparent, so to speak." Turning toward Maurizio, who stood behind Trina's chair, Sandro smiled. "Isn't that right, my son?"

"Whatever you say, sir," Maurizio answered, his voice clipped with bloodlust.

"Oh, dear. Forgive my bad manners, Maurizio. You may join the boys if you like, but I'd hurry if I were you. They do tend to be a little sloppy about things."

Maurizio's voice was still rough, but composed. "I'll wait for the prime choice that was promised me," he replied from above Trina's head, his hands sliding down from her shoulders to cup her breasts. She tried to struggle against him, but couldn't move. With one swift pass, the creamy silk shredded in his hands, its jeweled beading falling to the ground like so many pebbles. Plink, plink, plink.

"Careful now, *mijo*. We don't want to spoil things for Carlos when he gets here."

Maurizio growled in response. He held her immobilized and no matter what she did she couldn't lift her arms to protect herself. Grazing her nipples through the thin fabric of her bra, he slipped his thumbs beneath the appliqué and shoved the lace cups down. The full weight of her breasts fell into his hands. "You will taste as good as you feel when I sink my teeth into your flesh."

Trina screamed. Tears ran hot and fast down her cheeks, dripping onto her exposed breasts.

"It's useless to struggle, my dear." Sandro laughed, spreading his arms in a conciliatory gesture. "You are quite powerless." He walked around to the front of the wooden chair, his back to the sound of his other sons feeding. With his hands on Trina's knees, he leaned in as Maurizio continued his play. His face was so close she could smell his blood-scented breath.

"The reason why is rather an interesting story. Years ago, I came upon a girl very much like you. She made some absurd claim that she belonged with us, that her bloodline made her special. She was young and beautiful, and she was willing. I had to have her, so I did. Her blood was so potent, so out of the ordinary that I drained her, her heart stuttering to a halt beneath my hand. Yet, before I could retract my fangs, her blood sizzled through my veins like liquid fire. It held a power unlike any I had ever tasted, and somehow my body absorbed it.

"So great was this new ability that it unnerved me. It's taken me a century to master it, and the last decade to pass it on to my progeny. We simply call it *the voice,* and with it we can hold our victims helpless. We can manipulate their senses, make them feel things, do things they would never do. It's much more than a simple glamour or thrall. Maurizio is using it on you now. It's amazing, isn't it? And it even works on our kind. So far I've only tried it on young bloods, but tonight we'll get to see if it works on a much older and stronger vampire."

At that moment, Elsa screamed. The boys were bickering, arguing, and swiping at each other with razor-sharp claws while the pathetic blonde writhed on the blood-soaked chaise, covered in bites and blood.

The sound was so abject that even Maurizio and Sandro stopped to look. Slowly Sandro stood, turning toward the boys like a parent ready to admonish a pair of petulant toddlers. "Haven't I warned you both about this before? Look at the mess you've made…and poor Elsa. Is the way you treat my gift? I thought you both ready for this, but I guessed wrong. Rival or not, it's no wonder Carlos was moved to teach you a lesson. Strip that wet mess of a robe from her and let Papa show you how it's done."

Sandro put his hand out, whispering softly in Swedish. Immediately Elsa was calmed. She pushed herself up on the chaise, and as he continued to speak, she sat up, arching her back. Her eyes were half closed, and she nearly purred with need. Pushing her high, firm breasts forward, she slid her fingers over her jutting nipples, her body slick with blood. Sandro's face contorted, his fangs descending, and Elsa moaned in anticipation, leaning back against the curved edge of the chaise. Spreading her legs, she let her head fall back in an explicit invitation to both her sex and her throat.

With a hiss, he stripped, climbing between her thighs. He took her slowly, his hips grinding, building her till the room was saturated with the scent of sex and blood. Pulling her neck to the side, he plunged his fangs into her throat as he rode her, his eyes watching Trina the entire time.

In disgust, she watched Sandro feed from the blonde. Her belly coiled, ready to divest itself of whatever was left in her stomach. Chuckling, Maurizio leaned forward, his hands traveling over her chest again. "What's the matter, Ms. Markham? Not enjoying your crash course in Vampire 101? I'd bet my fangs you begged Carlos for it—and he gave it to you all right. I can smell him on you. He may be a lot of things, but he's still a vamp, and every one of us knows how to make a victim beg."

"Fuck you and everyone like you, Maurizio. I wasn't Carlos's victim. He'd never make me beg for something against my will. If I begged it was because he's twice the man and twice the vampire you'll ever be."

Maurizio snarled behind her ear, his voice thick and a little slurry through his fangs. "We'll see about that won't we?" Inhaling, he pressed his lips to her throat. "Your scent...*mmm*. It's really too bad you can't smell what I do," he murmured against her pulse. "When a human is aroused the blood races, and the taste of endorphins is hard for us to resist."

In a language that sounded older than sin, Maurizio whispered to her, making her emotions smolder and turn inward. Her anger turned hot, its flames licking at her lower belly. Trina's mind knew what was happening but she couldn't stop it. Maurizio was turning her anger to lust, fanning the fire but using it against her.

Sandro's eyes glowed as he watched. "Slowly, *mijo,*" he whispered. "I want her on her knees when Carlos gets here. I want him watching while we take her—me at her throat and you between her legs. " Closing his eyes, he thrust himself into Elsa; his obvious climax fed by Trina's coerced arousal. With a guttural snarl he ripped open Elsa's throat, draining the last of her life as his body jerked its climax in time with her death spasms.

***

Carlos hadn't slept in almost thirty-six hours. The flight into JFK International Airport was smooth and uneventful, but his mind was a dark tumult the entire time. Images of Trina haunted his thoughts, making the journey seem endless. He had brought nothing but danger and confusion to her life from the moment they met. This time things would be different. She was not going to suffer because of him. He owed it to her—owed it to Isabel.

A dark limousine waited for him at the arrivals gate, its windows tinted black against the afternoon sun. With nothing to declare and no time to waste, he simply spelled the customs agent into letting him pass. Everyone was waiting at home, and he knew not one of them was going to be happy about his decision to go it alone.

It was almost five p.m. when he walked into the house. They were all waiting for him in the kitchen like they hadn't moved an inch since the night he left for Spain.

Julian met him at the door, always the first in line with something to say. "I hope you realize Sandro is setting you up. He knows you too well, Carlos, and probably betting you'll do whatever it takes to save Trina."

Carlos ignored his comments, walking straight into the kitchen to face the rest of the firing squad. Everyone's eyes spoke volumes, yet no one said a word. As usual, they were waiting for him.

Margot looked the most shaken, so he bent to take her hand. "I know you all understand what's happened. The first thing I want to say is thank you for tracking me down as quickly as you did. Hopefully I bought us some time; geography isn't exactly one of Sandro's strong suits."

"This isn't a joke, Carlos. Sandro means to hurt you this time, and not just physically. He means to make you a laughingstock. He's threatened to bring the entire community down on us—accepting some of the kids we let go into his blood coven, and you know what that means." Her voice broke and Trevor tightened his arm around her shoulders.

Straightening, Carlos regarded her sadly. "I'm sorry for them, *mija,* but what would you have me do? We made it perfectly clear what could happen if they left before they were ready. I offered them every opportunity if they chose to stay, but you and I both know some of them wanted me to change them. Perhaps that's what they went looking for when they found Sandro. He's a master at manipulating the facts to his advantage, and everyone knows it. Right now Trina is my main concern. The kids that left did so of their own free will. She was taken."

"So we're just going to leave them to that sadist and his lies?" Julian asked. "Thank God most of them were either smart enough or scared enough to stay put. This changes everything. If going up against Sandro for Trina's sake wasn't enough, then this has to be. You have to let us go with you."

"No. The kids will be fine for now. They aren't Sandro's concern. Trina is the bait."

"And what do you expect us to do? Stand around while he tears you to shreds inside and out?" Julian demanded.

"He's right, *hermano,*" Miguel added. "None of us is letting you go it alone. We know you won't have a problem getting in—it's what Sandro expects. It's getting you out that worries us most. We could wait for daylight. He won't be expecting that. Then we'll only have to deal with is his human security."

"And what about the sun, Miguel? At that time of morning, it's not a concern for me, but what about you? None of you, not even Eric, has age enough to withstand it. I appreciate the thought, but you and your brothers would end up being a liability," Carlos answered tiredly.

Julian got up to pace. "At least let Eric go with you," he said, flinging his arm out toward the vampire scowling at the other end of the table. "He's got so much pent-up rage at Sandro he won't even feel the sun."

Carlos shook his head, not wanting to argue any longer. "No, and that's final. I'm positive Sandro has at least five vampires patrolling the grounds. Maurizio is bound to be there as well. *Christ,* he practically has that one on a leash. I'll not have my entire family slaughtered for a decision I made. Going alone I only risk myself. What's the worst that can happen?"

***

Pulling his motorcycle to the side of the road, Carlos cut the engine. He had been home for just a few hours, waiting for the sun to sink low enough for him to head out. From his rear saddlebag, he pulled out a flask. It was one of Dominic's, a thermal container the elder vampire used when he traveled. Carlos had found it in his carry-on in Barcelona. It had passed undetected through security, only for him to find it while looking for his iPod.

Unscrewing the top, he took a sip. Still warm. But the taste on his tongue wasn't animal blood, it was Dominic's. His old friend must have filled it knowing Carlos wouldn't think to feed again. Foresight was definitely one of Dominic's more appealing attributes. Thinking it amusing to sneak questionable items into a friend's carry-on before boarding an international flight, not so much. But that was Dominic's sense of humor.

Lifting the flask in silent salute, Carlos drained its contents. He tucked it back into the saddlebag for safekeeping and kick-started his Harley. The bike's Twin Cam 96 engine roared to life beneath him, its sheer power juxtaposed with his own. The sun had set. He was only a few miles from Sandro's estate, one of the last remaining along the majestic cliffs of the Palisades.

Carlos followed the road south. The twilight sky glowed purple off to the west, and New York's skyline on the other side twinkled, its lights snapping on like so many waking eyes. Sandro and his entourage would be in full throttle when he arrived.

The gates opened as soon as he pulled up to the entrance. Like Miguel said, he was expected. There was no one around and the front door was wide open, but Carlos knew he was watched. Sandro was no fool.

Inside, the vampire's private guard entered from various points. *Five vampires. How predictable,* Carlos thought dryly. His guess had been correct, and as expected, he was outnumbered. Their scent and the telltale sheen off their skin told him they were young bloods. *Surprise, surprise!*

Obviously chosen for their body size and strength, Carlos would have laughed at the banality of the situation if things had been different. Young bloods were strong, but they tended to be clumsy and stupid in a fight. Leave it to Sandro to choose his guards based on looks rather than skill.

A wry smile tugged at the corners of Carlos's mouth. Julian, Eric, and Miguel would enjoy themselves with this. He knew they were following close behind, regardless of his orders. Trevor, he also knew, would stay behind. He'd never leave Margot, especially not with Sandro's threats hanging in the air.

"*El Señor* is waiting for you downstairs," one of the guards announced. Then, pointing in the general direction, he stepped aside, allowing Carlos to pass.

Flashing them a bit of fang, Carlos smirked, "Storm's coming, boys. Better get out while the getting's good." They snarled in response, but he knew they wouldn't attack. It would ruin Sandro's plans, and the narcissistic bastard would never permit that.

Carlos didn't need much of a clue as to where he headed. The smell of blood and the thick scent of sexual arousal filled the air. His fangs tingled, but at his age, cravings were no longer controlled by pure instinct.

Frowning, he glanced back over his shoulder. *Instinct*. There was no question the guards were all young bloods, yet despite the titillating scents in the air their features remained human. Young bloods typically had no control over their vampiric nature, their faces contorting at the slightest provocation much in the same way teenage boys get hard-ons every time the wind blows. Something wasn't right. It was almost as if their senses had been purposefully dulled.

A door at the end of the corridor was open, and the scent grew more pungent the closer he got. Inhaling, his mind raced to separate the scents. Was one of them Trina's?

Her scent was burned into his memory and there was no mistaking it. She was definitely here, and she was bleeding. But there was something more. She was aroused. It was her sex he smelled, and a moment of confusion and anger boiled up inside him. Was this some kind of sick joke? Grim faced, he pressed his lips together, rejecting the thought. There was no way Trina was here of her own volition.

The air turned acrid in his nose as he went down the stairs. More attuned, he inhaled again. The scent was still hers, but it was off. The taste on the back of his tongue was tinny, metallic, like the taste of fear in the blood. Trina's blood may have been laced with arousal, but it was also laced with dread. Something was making her react, forcing her to respond. Carlos's body tensed. He knew exactly what it was:

the same thing that forced his own body to respond to Robert's almost three centuries ago.

Stepping down onto the marble floor of Sandro's lair, his nostrils flared, assailed by the overwhelming smell of debauchery and death. He spotted Trina immediately. She was in the center of the room, tied to a chaise. The upholstery was saturated with blood, heavy and dripping from its edges into a puddle of red. Her arms were above her head, tied with a blood-smeared piece of fabric, and her legs were spread-eagled, anchored to either side of the chaise. Between her thighs, her sex was red, swollen, and covered in bite marks, leading from her femoral artery and back again. They had been feeding from her, and worse.

Standing directly over her were the same young bloods Carlos had thrashed and thrown out of Avalon two months prior. Sandro stood at the far end of the chaise behind Trina's head, his fingers playing with her hair. Maurizio stationed himself at his side, ready for anything.

Rage, hot and deadly, flooded Carlos's body. Without thinking he blurred forward, ready to rip Sandro's heart from his chest without a care for whom or what got in his way.

Simply raising his hand, Sandro stopped him with one word in mid-assault. Hitting an invisible wall, Carlos's breath rushed from his body in loud huff. *"Stupid, hotheaded fool,"* his own thoughts admonished. Sandro was calculating, and the only way he'd beat him at his own game was to stay calm.

An evil smile broadened across Sandro's face. "Ah, Carlos. Just in time for the festivities. We've been waiting for you to begin. As you can see, we've prepped the young lady beautifully, and now she's ripe for the taking. I usually allow my guests to partake first, but since you made it perfectly clear you find this type of diversion distasteful, I'll do the honors myself."

Sandro's words were like a sucker punch to the solar plexus. Power emanated from his voice in waves, sending electric shocks through Carlos's limbs rendering them immobile.

"Quite a shock," Sandro said. "Even I'm amazed. The ability to render victims utterly powerless is rare among our kind. However documented, even I wasn't certain it would work on an immortal of your age and strength. But just look at you!" He clapped his hands together. "At first I couldn't believe it either. It's a power I acquired a little more than a century ago from a pretty little thing named Lisette. I lived in England at the time. It's ironic that hers is the only name I can remember from all my victims. But I suppose it's a matter of good form, considering."

Sandro's eyes glowed as the other vampires surrounded Carlos. He stayed put but Maurizio flanked Carlos, watching him, his eyes narrowing with distrust.

The boys circled, their faces burning with contempt and eager revenge. "Come on, boss, let us do him. Or better yet, let us pull his fangs out and then do him, just like he said he'd to do to us!"

Carlos growled low in his throat, and both boys flinched, taking a step back.

Maurizio snorted, folding his arms across his chest. "What a couple of pussies! He's completely powerless, yet you still piss your pants."

Tommy's eyes jerked to the side. "Fuck you, Maurizio! Sandro tells you to shit, and you ask what color." He raked his claws across Carlos's cheek in anger.

Blood streaked red from temple to chin on Carlos's face. He snarled in fury and frustration, his eyes like daggers, yet he still couldn't move. As his mind worked, possibilities were formed and rejected like lightning. Sandro's power lay in his voice, the same as Robert. Yet, Sandro's powers worked on vampires as well as humans. Did Robert have this same level of power? If he did, perhaps he wasn't aware of it. If Lisette's blood carried this power, then it was something she inherited from him through Isabel. The questions whirled. Did he carry it too? Did Trina?

Closing his eyes, he searched his memories, centering his focus much in the same way he had when he fought for the strength to defeat Robert. He dove deep into his own mind, and found that same profound place inside. He let his senses envelope him, warm him, and only when they were once again all that encompassed him, he went even deeper, further into his vampiric consciousness.

At the base of his psyche he found something he never knew existed. It was a dark pool, its waters so dark and rich with heart's blood it made his mouth water. Dipping his fingers into the source, he brought the viscous fluid to his lips. The moment he tasted the thick coppery liquid, he knew the power was his, inborn, not something corrupted or stolen from another. His, pure and true.

Carlos's eyes flew open. The cold reality of what he was about to do washed over him, and for the first time in centuries he had no compunction about life or death. No false faith in right or wrong. Blood meant life and blood meant death. In that moment all his questions were answered. It was all about balance—good and evil, light and dark. One didn't exist without the other.

Love was the only mitigating factor. It was the great equalizer—not death, not power. Death came to all living things, but a life lived without love was a living death. There was no single purpose under heaven, only choices, and the free will to either seek and find, or forever remain blind.

Power coursed through his body. It sizzled in his veins, lighting every nerve ending like the sun itself. He heard the whispered voices, tempting him to use his power to be the master of all that surrounded him. Theirs was a siren's song, and he saw perfectly how both Sandro and Robert had been seduced. He clamped down on their murmuring, instead filling their empty words with the love he felt for his family, for Trina, for Isabel, and for Dominic. Suddenly, the voices were silent. Still, the power remained, fluid and pure, in his veins.

Turning his gaze toward Sandro, he uttered one word. *"Liberación."* Immediately his body released from Sandro's hold.

The vampire's eyes widened, even as he took an involuntary step backward. "Kill him! Rip him to shreds!" The others turned at Sandro's command, hissing and spitting blood. Maurizio flew at Carlos, his claws raking his chest and throat.

Hunching over, Carlos's arm shot up to block another swipe, countering with a backhand and sending Maurizio skidding across the floor. Sandro's laughter echoed behind him.

Carlos was stunned at the lust and malice he saw in the vampires' eyes. Power gathered at the back of his throat. For years they had brought cruelty to so many through violence and blood. Now he'd let them die by it as well.

The words swelled from his mouth *"Mueran por sus propias manos!"*

The three vampires turned mutinously on one another, Sandro's orders forgotten. Fangs dripping, Tommy lunged at Maurizio. "I'm gonna kill you, you motherfucker!" Dan darted out between them, his eyes blazing and full of hate. Grabbing Tommy by the throat, he threw him into the marble columns. "You asshole! You always have to be fucking first! This time the bastard's mine!" he growled, turning on Maurizio.

Sandro vented a stream of expletives ordering them to stop, but Maurizio just turned and hissed his mouth bloody from the gaping hole he tore in Dan's chest.

"It's over, Sandro. Can't you see that?" Carlos said. "Your boys are killing each other, dying by their own hands. But you…you can't even recognize that you've lost. The laws of our kind may forbid me from killing you, but the laws of the universe say otherwise."

Tommy fell to the ground at Sandro's feet, his throat ripped out and his breath gurgling through torn cartilage as he tried to speak. With a disgusted look, Sandro kicked him, rolling him over to muffle the sound. "Talk, talk, talk…that's all you're good for, Carlos. So you acquired some power along the way. I'm not impressed. You're still more wet nurse than warrior, as far as I can see. We were meant to be gods. But instead, you've become as pathetic as the blood whore you love so much," he said, yanking Trina's hair.

Carlos kept his face impassive, but his fingers twitched, wanting to rip the smug look from Sandro's face. He couldn't afford to act rashly. There was too much at stake, and Margot's warnings hadn't gone unheeded. Sandro was an elder, and vampire politics held no quarter when it came to manslaughter— or vamp-slaughter—and there were no extenuating circumstances. He might have escaped censure for Robert's death, but he wouldn't be so lucky this time. *Unless…*

"The choices I make and the choices I give are what grant me my power. But that's beyond your comprehension, Sandro, it always has been," Carlos said. "All you see is what you can take. But hear me now. Human or not, Trina is my chosen mate. I don't think I need to explain how that changes things. I'm offering you a choice. You can either let her go and live, or die where you stand."

"Ha! I'll take what you love with me to hell first!" Fisting Trina's hair, he wrenched her head and neck over the back edge of the chaise. In seconds, his mouth was tearing at her flesh. He severed her jugular, and blood spurted everywhere from the open artery.

Trina was bleeding out, dying in front of Carlos. Every muscle and nerve-ending in his body surged with force. With only minutes to spare, he flew at Sandro, pulling every ounce of strength he could find from within himself. Leaping over the chaise, his hand shot around Sandro's throat. Heart's blood, crackling with power filled him completely, suffusing his body with heat. His fingers blazed with raw energy, blistering Sandro's flesh. The vampire struggled, his eyes bulging and blood running from his nose and mouth as Carlos crushed his throat.

With a single twist, he separated Sandro's head from his body, letting the rest of him crumple to the floor. Kicking the head aside, he grabbed the twitching headless form and punched a hole through its chest, removing the heart. It turned to ash in his hand, the rest flaking off, covering the blood-smeared floor like so much soot.

Wiping his hands on his pants, Carlos rushed to Trina's side. Her head lolled at her shoulder, her wounds gaping and stark against her pale skin. Immediately he bit down on his wrist. Blood pooled up, and squeezing his fist, he allowed it to gush from the puncture marks onto her throat.

Carlos held his breath, not sure if he was too late, but the rip in her artery mended and slowly the gashes in her skin knit together. At least she was no longer hemorrhaging. Her other bite marks had stopped bleeding, and he silently prayed it was due to Trina's own natural coagulation and not because there wasn't enough blood left in her to bleed.

Leaning forward, he slid his arm beneath her neck, propping her up. "Trina. *Mi vita,* I know you can hear me. Open your eyes." He could hear her heart stuttering weakly, and knew there wasn't much time. Biting down on his wrist again, he held it over her mouth, letting it drip gently onto her lips.

Trina's eyes fluttered open. Her face was drawn and covered in blood, but relief washed over him when he saw she was cognizant. "Thank God! Drink," he urged, holding his wrist over her mouth. "It's the only way, *querida,* please. I won't lose you again."

Barely conscious and scarcely able to move, Trina shook her head weakly. Her eyes held his for split second, and she whispered one word. "Wait."

Her eyes rolled back and she lost consciousness completely, her head falling to the side again. "No!" Carlos yelled his voice harsh and breaking with grief. She wasn't dead, but if she didn't take his blood, she'd soon be.

Leaning her head back, he put his fingers in her mouth, prying it open. He'd force feed her if he had to. "Trina, please."

A hand clamped over his wrist like steel, yanking it backward. "Carlos! No!"

Whipping his head around, he saw Eric holding his arm up by his wrist. "Let go of me, Eric! Where the hell did you come from? Trina's dying. Let go!"

Eric shook his head. "Carlos, stop. It's not what Trina wants. Think! If you change her now, you condemn her. What would her last emotions be? Terror? Pain? Is this what you want for her—to chain her to an endless existence of feeling nothing but malice and bloodlust? Do you really want her to have to struggle with that, like you did? Like I'm still struggling?"

Miguel and Julian came to stand beside Eric, their faces saying the same thing. The three were disheveled and covered in blood, and

Carlos knew then the young bloods upstairs were no longer a problem.

Carlos's chin fell to his chest. It was like being caught in some cruel circle where history repeats itself: first Isabel, now Trina. This time he knew better than to make the same ignorant mistake. Exhaling, he looked up into their faces and shook his head. "Of course not. That's not who I am, not what we do."

Eric nodded. "Good. Then give her enough blood to stabilize her so we can get the hell out of here. In the meantime, we'll go round up what's left of Sandro's human staff. There are only about six, including that butler. We'll send them over to Rosa. She's certainly the one to straighten them out. I can only imagine what Sandro did to them, but they were certainly quick to help us out."

Julian and Miguel cracked up. Eric said more in the last few minutes than he had in months. "Come on. They're probably upstairs waiting for us with stakes and holy water!" Julian laughed quietly, clapping Eric on the shoulder.

Giving Carlos some privacy, the three headed toward the stairs, stepping over splotches of blood and cracked marble. Eric stopped, looking back at Carlos over his shoulder. "Just remember, she said *wait*. She didn't say *no*." With a wink, he turned to catch up with the others.

Carlos smiled tiredly. Wait.

Well, what else did an immortal have, if not time?

Chapter 16

The curtains were drawn back, and the lights of the city below shined with an ethereal light. There was no other way to describe Rome at night. It glowed. From the lights reflecting off the bridges crossing the Tiber, to the lights illuminating St. Peter's Square and the Vatican, the entire city seemed bathed in gold.

Trina stood at the window, a glass of wine in her hand. Pushing the French doors open, she walked out onto the terrace overlooking the gardens below. A soft summer breeze fluttered the bottom of her silk dress. She took a deep breath and sighed dreamily, leaning on the curved wrought-iron railing. The air smelled delicious and her mouth watered. So many scents—food and wine, the tang of lemons and pomegranates, and the pleasant woodsy smell of Italian cypress wafting down from the hills surrounding this glorious city.

She had been in Rome for forty-eight hours and already she was in love. These days, she could have been in a mosquito-infested swamp and still have the same silly grin on her face.

Eight weeks ago, she thought her life was over. And even afterward, she never thought she could be happy, feel whole again. Thanks to Carlos's blood, her body healed quickly, but nightmares and terror gripped her for weeks and weeks on end. She woke up screaming every night, huddled into a corner in her room. Carlos refused to leave her side, slowly bringing her back from the edge—minute by minute, day by day.

"A gold doubloon for your thoughts," Carlos said, coming up behind her. Sweeping her hair to the side, he kissed her bare shoulder, sliding his hands up and down her arms.

"Your extreme age is showing again. They're called euros, now…remember?" She chuckled leaning back against his chest.

Hmph. "The gold standard is still the gold standard. Speaking of which, I have something for you," he said, kissing the top of her head." Taking a step back, he reached into his pocket and pulled out long velvet box, handing it to her.

Trina took it and opened the lid. Inside was her great-grandmother's locket. It was beautiful, cleaned and restored to its former brilliance. Running her fingers over the filigreed edge, she smiled, thinking how Isabel would have loved to see it like this.

Looking at him over her shoulder, she blinked back tears. "Thank you, Carlos. I don't know what to say. This means the world to me."

"There's more. Open it."

Trina took the locket from its velvet bed, its gold flickering in the light as it dangled from her fingers. Laying it in her palm, she clicked the release. Inside, Isabel's miniature was still there, as was Carlos's, but now a third portrait graced the inside. Hers. Carlos had a third compartment designed to hold not only her miniature, but the key to her great-grandmother's diaries.

Spinning in his arms, she threw her own around his neck. "You've given me my life back, Carlos. Not just in body, but in mind and heart. Without you, I would have sunk so far into my own darkness that I would have never recovered. You gave me back the ability to hope…the capacity to love."

Tracing the edges of her jaw, Carlos's fingers brushed the scarred tissue scoring the side of her throat. Reaching up, Trina pulled his fingers away.

"I try not to look at it," she said with a shrug, her voice catching a bit as looked away.

Taking the locket from her hand, he undid the clasp and fastened it around her neck. His fingers brushed the edges of her scars again, but this time he covered her hand with his when she tried to push him away.

"I know a way we can fix that," he said, placing a finger under her chin and raising it so she had to look at him.

"I can't," she said, her voice full of regret. Seeing his jaw tighten she quickly added, "But not for the reasons you think. I'm not afraid and I harbor no prejudice."

Carlos looked at her, his eyes searching. "Why, then?" He took both her hands in his, not letting her walk away. She was going to look him in the eye and tell him her reasons.

"Please, Carlos…this is hard enough as it is. I owe you everything, and I love you more than anything in this world. All I want is to be with you, but I won't ask you to do this. I can't. I won't be the reason you change who you are, what you believe. You've never changed anyone unless they had no other choice. I had my chance and I said no. Besides, I don't deserve it."

His face was incredulous. "You don't deserve it?"

"After everything I said to you and your family, and the trouble I caused, how can you sound so surprised? I've been a condescending fool. Self-righteous and pontificating. I looked down my nose at your way of life without pause, letting my own opinions blind me from seeing all your kindness. I sent you away with my holier-than-thou judgments, telling myself it was for the best. I even convinced myself I was doing you a favor in not forcing you to choose. And look what ended up happening."

"What happened with Sandro had nothing to do with you. You were just a pawn. If it wasn't you, it would have been one of the kids or possibly even Margot."

"Yet, you still came after me. After all the trouble I caused."

"And I'd do it again. But you're wrong about something else."

"What?"

"You didn't say no," he said, running his fingers along the edge of her cheek. "You said wait."

Trina smiled, tilting her head to the side. "I did?"

"*Si, señorita*, you did, and I've been waiting, and will continue to wait until you send me away. Maybe even after that. I've lived my life for centuries being all about choice, but now I choose to live it being all about love. In the end it's the only choice that matters, whether you're human or vampire."

Trina brought Carlos's fingers to her lips. "Then I choose you. Forever."

A brilliant smile spread across Carlos's face. "Then we'd better let Dominic know we'll be otherwise occupied tonight," he said, nipping her bottom lip, drawing a little blood.

"Ouch! Exactly how much is this going to hurt?"

Swinging his arm around her shoulders, he led her back into the bedroom. Closing the doors behind him, he pulled her into his arms. "As much as you'd like it to," he answered, smiling against her mouth as he kissed her.

Acknowledgements

When an author publishes a book, whether it's their first or their five hundredth, it's nothing less than a defining moment in their life. Since I began this writer's journey, I've run the gamut in terms of emotion…from 'no excuses do the work' to 'what was I thinking?' to 'be careful what you ask for cause you just might get it!'.

This is my second book, and I still have to pinch myself. So many people have helped and encouraged me, even when the writing dragon had me spewing fire and belching smoke at every turn.

My unbelievably patient husband, Bill, for putting up with the insanity and verbal barrages that accompany being glued to my laptop for hours. Our three kids for knowing enough to leave Mommy alone when she's writing, despite laundry piling up and pasta for dinner, yet again.

I would be remiss not to thank my father and mother and my wonderful mother-in-law for their guidance and their help, and my siblings for their support.

To all my hometown friends, especially Karen Marsh, Ginger Hardman and Ginny Ryan. My wonderful beta readers, Gloria Lakritz and Penny Nichols, for giving it to me straight—good or bad. My author friends, Tracy Mitchell, Karen Fuller, and Kelly Abell for putting up with my incessant questions. And to author Amy Lane and the Amazon Paranormal Romance Forum where we met and started our 'word of the day' thread. The words grew into snippets of stories, and from there my snippet of a story grew into this novel.

I have to thank, Jen Safrey for reading, editing and holding my hand through the publishing process.

And last but certainly not least, I want to thank God for all his blessings. The longer I live, the more I learn to appreciate what could very easily be taken for granted. God bless. I hope you enjoy the book.

About the Author

Marianne Morea was born and raised in New York. Inspired by the dichotomies that define 'the city that never sleeps', she began her career after college as a budding journalist. Later, earning a MFA, from The School of Visual Arts in Manhattan, she moved on to the graphic arts. But it was her lifelong love affair with words, and the fantasies and 'what ifs' they stir, that finally brought her back to writing.

Visit her website: http://www.mariannemorea.com

If you enjoyed Blood Legacy, please feel free to email me. Reviews are always welcome on any of the major book sites, such as Amazon, Goodreads or Barnes&Noble!

If you enjoyed *Blood Legacy,* check out these other books by *Marianne Morea!*

The Cursed by Blood Saga

Also! Look For These Upcoming 2013 Titles!

Shadowed Soul, by Marianne Morea

Secrets of the Moon, book one in ***The Guardians Series,*** by Marianne Morea

Where Demons Dare to Tread, by Marianne Morea

Hollow's End, by Marianne Morea

Praise for the Legacy Series....

"*...Blood Legacy* is simply the best vampire romance I've read in ages, and I really hope we'll get to see the super cast of supporting characters in future books. They all deserve a voice as eloquent as *Blood Legacy* is for Carlos and Trina. Bring them on, Ms. Morea! I'll be first in line to review them..."

~ Merrylee Lanehart, TwoLips Reviews LLC.

"I first read Marianne's book "Hunter's Blood" and loved the fast-paced style and how the novel kept me intrigued, so when I heard that she had released another book. I knew I just had to read it and I enjoyed it! Five Stars for *Blood Legacy*!

~ Paula Phillips. The Phantom Paragrapher @ Blogspot.com. (New Zealand)

"You heard it here at the Paranormal Romance Guild! In August 2010, Marianne Morea submitted her first piece to us for review called Hunters Blood. I had the pleasure of reading and reviewing it, her first novella. From my review on this site [Amazon], I mentioned, *'Ms. Morea has separated herself from the crowd, and has executed an enchanting story of the paranormal.'* This year she has come out of the gate with a breathtaking, well written, well researched novel about love lost and redemption called Blood Legacy."

~ Gloria Lakritz, Senior Reviewer, Paranormal Romance Guild

CPSIA information can be obtained at www.ICGtesting.com
Printed in the USA
LVOW10s1924200813

348821LV00021B/1112/P